It was unmistakably the voice of her friend Ruth Winthrop, who stood outside the office, her hand on her hips, her head tipped to one side. It wasn't completely dark yet but a harsh high-wattage bulb in the ceiling fixture lighted the corridor.

"How nice, they gave you a cell of your own." Ruth leaned into the tiny room where Helma had been working. "I thought this place would be a little more lively."

At that instant, shouts rang out from behind the Promise Mission, not the shouts of a quarrel or a disturbance, but of surprise.

Helma was already on her way toward the mission's back door. "Call 911," she ordered the man at the security desk who'd risen from his chair, a doughnut halfway to his mouth.

"911?" Ruth asked, close on Helma's heels. "You don't even know what it is yet."

"We can't waste time. Grown men are in shock."

"Well, that's reason enough to declare an emergency," Ruth grumbled.

❦   ❦

"Capable, cool headed, and above all scrupulous, Helma Zukas is someone to reckon with . . . Serving up an abundance of distinctive dialogue, rich character development, and above all the dignified Miss Zukas, Dereske has created the ultimate in this genre."

The Bellingham Herald

Other Miss Zukas Mysteries by
Jo Dereske
from Avon Twilight

Avon Books are available at special quantity discounts for bulk purchases for sales promotions, premiums, fund raising or educational use. Special books, or book excerpts, can also be created to fit specific needs.

For details write or telephone the office of the Director of Special Markets, Avon Books, Inc., Dept. FP, 1350 Avenue of the Americas, New York, New York 10019, 1-800-238-0658.

JO DERESKE

MISS ZUKAS IN DEATH'S SHADOW

AVON
TWILIGHT

This is a work of fiction. Names, characters, places, and incidents either are the product of the author's imagination or are used fictitiously. Any resemblance to actual events, locales, organizations, or persons, living or dead, is entirely coincidental and beyond the intent of either the author or the publisher.

AVON BOOKS, INC.
1350 Avenue of the Americas
New York, New York 10019

Copyright © 1999 by Jo Dereske
Inside cover author photo by Teresa Salgado Photography
Published by arrangement with the author
Library of Congress Catalog Card Number: 99-94467
ISBN: 0-380-80472-7
www.avonbooks.com/twilight

All rights reserved, which includes the right to reproduce this book or portions thereof in any form whatsoever except as provided by the U.S. Copyright Law. For information address Avon Books, Inc.

First Avon Twilight Printing: December 1999

AVON TWILIGHT TRADEMARK REG. U.S. PAT. OFF. AND IN OTHER COUNTRIES, MARCA REGISTRADA, HECHO EN U.S.A.

Printed in the U.S.A.

WCD 10 9 8 7 6 5 4 3 2 1

If you purchased this book without a cover, you should be aware that this book is stolen property. It was reported as "unsold and destroyed" to the publisher, and neither the author nor the publisher has received any payment for this "stripped book."

For K., always

ACKNOWLEDGMENTS

I am grateful to Al Archer for generously sharing his time and experiences in operating a mission and for patiently answering my many questions. Special thanks to Ruth Archer and the dedicated staff at the Lighthouse Mission in Bellingham, Washington, especially L. Ruit, Carol, and David.

CONTENTS

ix

🌿 chapter one 🌿

SETTLING IN

On Monday night, one hour into the first evening of her sentence, Miss Helma Zukas had encountered one fistfight, a man who tried to hide his green beans by shoving them into his pants pocket, and one severe case of head lice. Although the experience might not be what she'd envisioned, none of the challenges was totally unexpected—or went unmet.

The heat didn't help. Eighty-two degrees at 6:30 p.m. was rare for the northwest corner of Washington state, even in August. Helma picked up a lone fork from a table and set it on her tray, making a mental note to check the newspaper in the morning to see if the day's temperatures had set any records.

It was the fourth day of unpredicted heat and sunshine. Each morning the *Bellehaven Daily News* continued optimistically to predict cooler temperatures and partly cloudy skies. No clouds except a few white puffs that enhanced each evening's sunset had been spotted since the previous Thursday.

Not that Helma could actually *see* the sky from the windowless dining room of the Promise Mission for Homeless Men. Except for the heat that was doubly oppressive inside the cement block building, the sky might as well be bursting with rain; she wouldn't have known.

"They've got a flophouse in Phoenix that's air-conditioned," a bearded man whose remaining hair grew in

1

a tonsure said in a loud voice as Helma passed, her tray laden with odds and ends of dinner detritus she'd removed from the tables. The man sat at the end of a long table, the last person remaining in the dining room, his elbows and fore-arms forming a fortress around his coffee mug and a white crockery plate so clean that Helma suspected he'd licked it. The sleeves were torn off his worn denim shirt and its collar was gone. "Yup, that's right," he said. "Air-conditioning."

The tone in his husky voice was too accusatory to ignore. "The average August temperature in Phoenix, Arizona, is approximately twenty-five degrees warmer than Belle-haven's," Helma told him. "Air-conditioning here in the Northwest is hardly worth the investment." She reached for the salt and pepper shakers on his table and he darted out one gnarled hand and swept them inside the space around his plate, hunkering over them like treasures. His eyes gleamed, challenging her.

"May I have those, please?" Helma asked. She set her tray on the table and stood firm in front of him, one hand out-stretched toward the glass and metal shakers. "Unless you'd rather put them away yourself before you leave the dining room. I'm nearly finished here."

He didn't budge but Helma saw the tiniest shift in his eyes. "I can take your plate at the same time," she offered, even though a sign hung on the peach-colored cement block wall blaring letters as large as a traffic sign's: PUT AWAY YOUR OWN DISHES.

"You one of them do-gooders?" he asked, narrowing his eyes, not budging his arms.

"Could you define the term, 'do-gooder'?" she asked, step-ping closer to the salt and pepper shakers.

He guffawed. He wasn't as old as he looked, only beaten, weathered, and used up. His eyes and skin, even his clothes, were faded to gray. He was the kind of man who'd gone invisible, the kind of man Miss Helma Zukas normally only spoke to in warning tones.

He unclasped one hand and pointed a finger at her. The fingertip was missing and the partial fingernail blackened and swollen. "Gotcha. You're that librarian who was sentenced to work here, right?"

"I *am* a librarian," Helma conceded. "Yes."

His laugh resembled a throaty snort usually accompanied by a handkerchief. "They let you out of jail to work here, right?"

"I have never seen the inside of a jail," Helma informed him.

"Well hell, I've never seen the inside of a library," he said. His laughter boomed and he slapped his hand flat on the table. Helma leaned over and snatched the salt and pepper shakers and headed toward the kitchen, her back straight, followed by the man's laughter, which was punctuated by wheezing words that sounded like, "brarian," then more fleshy slaps on the table top.

"Charlie bothering you?" Portnoy the cook asked as he slid the first of three wire racks of dirty dishes into the commercial dishwasher and pulled down the articulated metal door as if it were a garage door. The machine rattled and hummed, gearing up. A fan sitting on a metal chair beside the stove stirred the steamy air, bringing no relief.

The Promise Mission for Homeless Men was not an institution Miss Helma Zukas was likely to enter by choice, but now that she was here she fully intended to make the best of it. The mission was one of those "invisible" places common to cities of any size, passed a hundred times without real recognition, a vague place that conjured up sorrowful images like those associated with places no one entered voluntarily: "Poor house," "old people's home," and "debtors' prison." Helma had never met anyone who lived or worked at Promise Mission, or anyone who knew anyone who had.

The mission occupied a three-story concrete building built into the side of a steep hill on the lower end of Bellehaven. The area had once been industrial and derelict, overlooking the train yards. Behind the mission, a steep empty lot was tangled with weeds, overgrown bushes, and wild blackberry plants heavy with fruit ripening in the August heat.

But to stand on the front steps of the mission and raise

one's eyes above the train yard was to gaze out into Washington Bay. Not across the bay to the opposite strip of land as Helma did from the balcony of her apartment in the Bayside Arms, but the long view toward the distant mouth of the bay where by sailing through the humpy islands and around the Olympic Peninsula, one would eventually sail into the open sea and the wider world. On exceptionally clear days the Olympic Mountains on the peninsula a hundred miles away emerged like craggy ghosts, shimmery and insubstantial.

When Helma had arrived at the mission that evening to begin her sentence, Brother Danny the director had been in the midst of a meeting and had sent her down to the dining room. "Dinner's about to be served," he'd told Helma, hastily apologizing for his preoccupation and pointing to the nearby stairwell. "Ask the cook how you can help. I'll be down as soon as I'm finished here."

Helma had followed the taped and spotted "Dining Room" signs down a flight of concrete stairs, careful not to touch the block walls, their pale green paint worn to gray at shoulder and hand heights. At the bottom of the steps, solid steel doors held open by triangles of wood led into a square dining room. It was empty of diners but packed with various sizes of tables and mismatched chairs. A kitchen and serving area occupied the end opposite the doors. The room was austere: peach walls, bare linoleum floors, a few framed prints lost on the long stark walls. In the hot room, four men were setting out food at the serving counter. They'd stopped, gazing at Helma without welcome. Finally the biggest man had come forward and said, "We heard you were coming. Grab an apron."

"Thank you but I brought my own," Helma had told the man, removing a fresh apron and a pair of new orange rubber gloves from her bag, rubber gloves she intended to wear the entire evening.

And so she began her first evening, serving food from metal pans, cleaning off tables, moving too fast to think, assuming her place in this alien confusion of wayward men.

"Do you know Charlie?" Helma asked Portnoy now. He was the only staff remaining in the kitchen. She removed the salt and pepper shakers from her tray and set them on a shelf that held even more, realigning them all so that the rows were balanced: salt, pepper, salt, pepper . . .

"Charlie's a regular, a little bit . . ." Portnoy rolled his eyes upward, "but that's not unusual around here. He's okay, as they go, seeing as where we are and all."

A cockney accent would have fit Portnoy perfectly. He was more than a big man; he was an enormous man—with bare forearms as thick as thighs and as pink as a baby's flesh. His skin was hairless, unlined and shiny tight. His pale hair, so fine that Helma could see his scalp through it, stuck to his skin in the damp heat. He wore an arrangement of white aprons that covered his clothing so well he might not have been wearing anything else. "Call me Porky," he'd told Helma when they met. "Everybody does." But Helma couldn't and wouldn't. Portnoy he remained.

"Are there many regulars?" Helma asked as she placed her tray in the next rack of dirty dishes destined for the dishwasher.

Portnoy frowned at a dial on the dishwasher, then tapped it with his thick index finger. "More than you'd think. The men come and they go, but they don't go too far. They don't always stay here—too many rules—but they like the eats."

Helma removed her can of disinfectant spray from her bag. She checked the folded rags beneath the sink and chose the cleanest one, which appeared to be the remains of a t-shirt, and began cleaning the counters, spraying first, then wiping, and finally repeating the process. "Do you come in to cook every meal?" she asked.

Portnoy turned and looked at her, then laughed a high-pitched *har har har* that set his chins wobbling. "I don't come in, I *am* in."

"I beg your pardon?"

"I live here, right now anyway. I can cook." He patted his huge belly. "Big surprise, huh? So that's what I do."

"You're a resident here?" Helma asked, pausing, her can

of disinfectant cleaner pointed at a particularly stubborn brown ring on the counter.

"Yeah," he said with a touch of wariness. He adjusted his aprons. "That change anything?"

"Of course not," she said, although she admitted to herself that the prudent sense of caution she'd felt on entering the mission couldn't be intensified very much more.

"Being here's okay," Portnoy went on. "I've seen worse places. We got a little crime here right now but we'll take care of it. Always something in this world, eh?"

Helma had no intention of becoming involved, none at all. She'd been sentenced to fifty hours of service at the mission in lieu of paying an undeserved traffic ticket, that was all. It wasn't any of her business. But, only to be polite, she asked, "What kind of crime?"

Portnoy set aside the pitcher he'd been inspecting as if to determine whether it was worth washing and leaned toward Helma, narrowing his pale eyes. "Thievery. It's gotta be a resident. The same modus operwhatever, always pilfering from somebody's stuff when his back is turned. Started a week or so ago. You expect some of that, you know. Brother Danny doesn't ask for backgrounds, but if a man's here, there's a reason and a lot of reasons you're better off not looking into."

"It isn't me," a voice interjected. Charlie stood in the doorway, holding his plate and a fork. "I'm no thief."

"Then where's your cup?" Portnoy asked him.

"I've only got two hands," he complained, pulling a cracked mug from his pants pocket. "I was just carrying it the easiest way I knew how; I wasn't stealing it." He thumped the cup on the counter and said, "Brother Danny ought to call the cops—catch that sucker." He frowned at Helma. "He doesn't trust government stiffs—not any of them. Not even the mailman, and not . . ." He jabbed his finger first toward Helma, then more weakly toward Portnoy and left the kitchen, already unbuttoning the shirt he was required to wear inside the building.

"Charlie's always on a rip," Portnoy said mildly. "Even

when he's so mucked up he doesn't know whether he's on foot or horseback he gets excited about something." He shrugged. "Hot night like this, a lot of them'll go outside. Sleep in the bushes so they don't have to pray with Brother Danny. Curfew's at eight."

Helma glanced up at the wall clock: only forty-eight and a half hours to go on her sentence. She'd elected to serve her time three hours a night, five nights a week for three weeks and two days. Not that her fine had been too exorbitant to pay. She'd been wrongly accused of making a right turn on a red light, of "sailing through" the intersection. It was the principle of the accusation Helma was protesting. Helma Zukas was an innocent and wronged woman.

"Everything going okay?" Brother Danny entered the dining room, still looking distracted. He was tall, young appearing, with brown hair turning to gray, a man who'd arrived in town less than ten years ago and single-handedly founded the Promise Mission, paying cash for the land and building, actual cash in rubber-banded stacks pulled from a duffle bag. And then, the widely circulated story went, he'd brushed his hands together and said cheerfully, "That's it. I'm plumb cleaned out." Where that money came from he'd never said, but since then he'd cajoled more cash, furnishings and food donations, even volunteers, from skeptical Bellehavenites.

"Feel like a brief tour?" he asked Helma. Brother Danny's background was his private business but he spoke with a southern accent and when asked, said he came "straight up from the lowest levels of the deepest south," which made him an exotic in northwest Washington. He wiped his brow with the back of his hand and looked at Helma over the top of glasses that slid downward on his glistening nose.

"I'd like a tour, yes," Helma said as she removed her gloves.

"You've seen the kitchen firsthand," he said, waving behind Helma. He spoke rapid-fire, at odds with the drawl of his words. "We serve three meals a day: to residents or any man, woman, or child who's hungry, no matter what their story is; we don't ask and we don't care. All the food is donated so sometimes we eat high on the hog and sometimes we eat low as a dog, isn't that the truth, Porky?"

Portnoy gave him a thumbs-up sign and mopped at his shiny face with a dish towel. "Let's go up," Brother Danny told Helma. He led the way back up the stairs, taking them two at a time, to the main floor where three men waited by the front counter to sign in. Brother Danny said "Hey" to the men and leaned down to pick up a crumpled gum wrapper. "Inspection committee's coming at eight-thirty, don't forget," he told the man at the desk who nodded without glancing up. Then he led Helma down another green, concrete-walled hallway where they skirted three faded backpacks leaning against one another. "We've applied for a grant for some foundation repair and a new roof and the committee's coming in to look us over."

"Isn't eight-thirty at night an unusual time for a grant committee inspection?" Helma asked.

Brother Danny nodded and a lock of graying hair fell forward. He had a habit of smoothing his upper lip with his forefinger as if he wore an invisible moustache. "You're right, but I hoped it would be cooler in the evening, put folks in a happier mood. Everybody on the committee's local so I could have postponed the inspection but we're so desperate for this grant I'd climb Bayview Street on my hands for it."

He ushered Helma into a large room painted the same peach as the dining room where a six-foot cross hung behind a lectern at one end and a basketball hoop hung at the other, with blackboards on portable walls in between. A long, battered wooden table was set up in the middle. "This is our chapel, gym, classroom, overflow sleeping area, and tonight, our boardroom," he told Helma. He straightened the mismatched chairs around the table, casting a critical eye around the room. "Now if I attended a meeting in a place like this, I'd sure as sunrise start handing out money, wouldn't you?"

"I'd seriously consider it," Helma agreed.

He laughed. "Men who stay longer than three days have to sign up for basic classes," he went on, pointing toward the blackboards, "what you all might call etiquette, job skills, basic budgeting, things like that. We've got a few used computers in there." He waved toward a door off the gym end of the room. "Always looking for more." Helma could see the corner of a computer monitor, its blue screen filled with lines of text although the chair in front of the computer was vacant.

"Portnoy mentioned you've had a series of thefts," Helma said.

"Portnoy?" Brother Danny bounced on the balls of his feet like a boxer warming up. "Oh, Porky. Yeah, a little thievery's a given around here. You've got to be grateful for what *isn't* stolen. But I'd sure rather they stole from us than each other. *I* expect to lose an item here and there, but to some of these men, their belongings—no matter how poor—are sacred. I've seen fistfights over a book of matches."

"You haven't called the police?"

He sighed. "I'm loathe to. We don't need that kind of publicity. People in town already . . ." His voice trailed off and he waved his hand to encompass the area outside the mission. "This end of town's going upscale. Ten years ago this was the skids. If I'd stopped to think about it—nice view and all—sure it's going to become hot—maybe I wouldn't have found a place so close to the water. You've got to either be rich or homeless to live here. Prime property right now." He considered Helma and she could see his thoughts shifting. "To be a librarian, you have to be a top-notch organizer, isn't that right?"

"It does help," Helma acknowledged.

"I've got a job you might give me a hand with. Our donors . . ."

They were interrupted by a voice shouting down the hall, "Phone, Bro."

"Excuse me," Brother Danny said to Helma, reaching for a phone that hung on the wall. "It'll just be a second."

"I'll wait outside," Helma told him.

As she stepped into the hallway that led back to the main entrance, Helma was just in time to see a young man rifling through one of the backpacks that had been left in the hallway. In triumph, a satisfied smirk on his face, he pulled out a pair of dark socks, then glanced around to see if anyone had witnessed his crime and peered directly into the observant eyes of Miss Helma Zukas.

❦ chapter two ❧

UNRAVELING

In her surprise at witnessing a crime in progress, Helma forgot the advice she'd been given by Brother Danny never to confront a "guest" of the mission, that it was more prudent to inform him or the manager on duty. "Do those socks belong to you?" she asked the man kneeling beside the backpacks.

The thief rose and slipped the rolled socks into the pocket of his baggy shorts. "They do now," he said, gazing straight at her yet not meeting her eyes. He spoke without guilt or shame or even embarrassment at being caught. She guessed that he was in his late twenties or maybe early thirties; his face bore a hardness that made it impossible to tell. His brown hair, which was overlong and looked as if it had last been self-cut with blunt scissors and no mirror, was slicked back off his forehead, the sides and back hanging below his ears. He wore baggy shorts that might have been blue once and an equally baggy and faded black t-shirt.

"I think not," Helma said in her silver-dime voice, a voice developed through seventeen years of apprehending magazine vandalizers, book thieves, rude patrons, and out-of-control children.

The man froze, as did most people who experienced that voice, his hand still in his pocket. The voices outside the open window paused, too, and a moment later Brother Danny stood in the hallway beside Helma.

"Anything interesting going on here?" he asked pleasantly,

his tenseness betrayed only by a twitch beside his left eye.

Helma continued to contemplate the man, saying nothing. His expression didn't change but he swallowed, his hand still on the bulge of socks in his pocket. Then he took his gaze from Helma and gave Brother Danny a wide smile that didn't reach his eyes. He wasn't dirty; in fact he looked quite clean, but there was a darkness about him that reminded Helma of grime and dead of night. Helma knew without a doubt that he was about to lie.

But before he could utter a word, even as the smile cooled and his lips parted, another voice sounded from farther down the hallway. "Skitz was just stealing a pair of socks, that's all." The voice was deep but childish, the words clumsy as if the speaker had recently learned to talk.

Fifteen feet behind the thief, another man sat on the floor leaning against the wall, a huddled shape Helma hadn't noticed. He wasn't heavy but he was rounded, compact, wide-eyed and, Helma perceived in an instant, simple. He might have been younger; he was definitely softer. One earpiece of his glasses was held together with a wad of dirty white tape. His fair hair was cut short in a style that required little care, probably not even combing.

The thief, whom he'd called "Skitz," cursed quietly without glancing behind at the smaller man, then said, "Thanks a million, Tony."

"You're welcome, Skitz." Tony smiled and nodded his head.

"If you need socks, young man," Brother Danny offered, "we've got a storeroom full of clothing. You're welcome to take whatever you lack."

Skitz lifted his foot to expose battered high-top sneakers and white socks with red swoops on the cuffs. "I don't need any socks."

"Perhaps your friend does," Helma suggested, nodding toward Tony's bare feet in scuffed brown loafers that appeared too big for him.

Skitz shrugged. "Not my problem."

Brother Danny crossed his arms and smiled benignly at

Skitz and Tony. He rocked a little on his feet, then hummed deep in his throat, his mouth closed. He looked like a man waiting for a bus he knew would be a long time coming and he was in no hurry for it to arrive.

Skitz stared at him, his face flushing. He lightly kicked one of the backpacks and glanced at Brother Danny who continued to hum what Helma now recognized as a song about a bobbin' robin. Finally, Skitz pulled the socks from his pocket and thrust them deep into the proper backpack, his lips tight.

Brother Danny stopped rocking and humming. "Have you fellows eaten tonight?" he asked.

"Sure," Skitz said. He shoved his hands back in his pockets, slouching, waiting to be dismissed.

"Unh-uh," Tony disagreed. "We ate yesterday. Skitz stole us two corn dogs." He heaved a deep breath. "He forgot the mustard, though."

"Shut up, Tony," Skitz said.

Tony bobbed his head. "Okay, Skitz."

"You're too late for dinner," Brother Danny told the men, "but Porky's still in the kitchen. He'll make up some sandwiches for you."

"Yeah," Skitz mumbled. He turned and slouched toward the doorway, roughly nudging Tony with his foot as he walked past him. "Come on, Big Mouth. Time to eat."

"Okay, Skitz," the smaller man said, rising eagerly but awkwardly to his feet, pressing his hands against the floor, on his knees and then flat against the wall.

When the two men disappeared around the corner, Brother Danny turned to Helma. "Are you ready to take on this project I mentioned?"

"Is that the only action you plan to take?" Helma asked. "You caught a man stealing and now you've offered to feed him?"

He shrugged with as much indifference as if he were going to begin humming another tune. "It happens. He knows I've got my eye on him. Now how about that project?"

"I need to go back to the kitchen for my apron and gloves

first," Helma told him, thinking that if this were the library, Skitz and his friend would, at the very least, be banned from the premises for six weeks.

Brother Danny frowned. "Would you mind asking Porky to fix Skitz and Tony food they could take out of the building?"

"May I ask why?"

Brother Danny looked pained. He rubbed his forefinger across his upper lip. "Skitz aggressively panhandled one of the committee members a couple days ago and I sure as heck don't want to remind him of it. I'd just as soon the committee member didn't see either of those two."

"Can you be sure it was them?"

"One of the other men—Charlie—lives mostly on the street and he saw it happen. Down by the drugstore. Know where I mean?"

Helma nodded. It was a popular spot for panhandlers: a long windowless wall off Bellehaven's main street. She'd passed as many as six panhandlers sitting or leaning against the drugstore's wall. Mostly younger people but occasionally older, more permanently lost looking men and women. Whenever she passed by the wall, Helma's policy was never to respond to their requests, never even to make eye contact.

"Charlie said the committee member told Skitz to get a job," Brother Danny told her, "and the exchange went downhill from there."

"I met Charlie." Helma hesitated, then said. "He might be exaggerating." She wasn't actually judging Charlie, only making a suggestion based on observation.

Brother Danny sadly shook his head. "That's what I'd hoped, but another witness with a cell phone called the police. By the time they arrived, Skitz and Tony had scrammed but the descriptions fit them to a T; lock, stock, and barrel, the whole enchilada."

"Oh."

A train whistle blew in the switching yards below the mission and Brother Danny nodded as if answering it. "This particular committee member already has doubts about the mission, and I don't want to refresh his memory, especially not tonight. The men we serve here are people we want to help get back on their feet, not," he paused and then spoke as if he were quoting someone, "lock up and drop the key down the sewer."

"Are Skitz and Tony two of your 'regulars'?" Helma asked.

"Not yet. They've spent the night here twice in the past week or so. Probably for showers and laundry. That and bad weather brings them inside." He grinned. "I don't guess my preaching's an irresistible draw. Otherwise it's a sleeping bag or blanket in the bushes, maybe down by the creek." He shook his head, his eyes still on the hallway where Skitz and Tony had disappeared. "They eat a lot of meals here, though. A curious duo," he said, more to himself than to Helma.

"Do you suspect Skitz is the person who's been stealing from the residents?" Helma asked.

Brother Danny shrugged. "Maybe. He looks like he's got a bad spark to him, doesn't he?"

Helma wasn't certain what "having a bad spark" meant but she agreed with the way it sounded. Skitz had the look of the thief they'd caught in the library that spring walking boldly out of the staff lounge wearing George Melville's leather jacket with three stolen wallets stuffed in the pockets.

"We see all kinds," he continued. He gazed off as if he could see through the cement block walls. "Sounds crazy but the toughest ones—for me, anyway—are the men who follow every rule to the letter without question, just grateful for a bed and meal. The really lost ones. No spark, good or bad."

He turned back to Helma. "This is a pretty menial task, but our donor records have been thrown together helter-skelter. We try to keep up but it just buries us. We're short-handed in the office, always have been. We've got a couple of paid employees but everybody else is a resident employee and they come and go. Not a lot of continuity around here. Would you be willing to put the records in some kind of order?"

"I could do that," Helma assured him.

"Great, I'll go find the files and you can meet me in my office."

Helma followed him through the main lobby, which was now empty except for a dazed-looking woman standing at the desk. Three bulging plastic grocery bags lay at her feet. "Why not?" she was asking the swarthy man behind the counter. "I've got a right."

"We're a *men's* shelter," the man told her.

"Do you need a place to sleep tonight?" Brother Danny asked her.

"Got to go somewhere," she said. She turned toward Brother Danny but averted her eyes from his.

"We've got a place," he told her. To the man behind the desk, he said, "Call Richard to drive her over to the women's center."

Helma returned to the kitchen and picked up her apron and gloves. Her disinfectant cleaning spray had disappeared. She glanced briefly around the kitchen and let it go. Five more cans were lined up beneath her kitchen sink in her apartment. She passed on to Portnoy Brother Danny's request to keep Skitz and Tony as low profile as possible.

"Those two?" Portnoy asked. He was pulling leftover meat loaf and half of a commercial apple pie from the cooler. Bread and mustard sat on the counter. "No prob. I'll send them on a picnic with enough food to keep them stuffing themselves until midnight. Then they'll go to sleep like a couple of babies, guaranteed."

Skitz and Tony sat at a table near the dining room door, waiting for their food. Skitz leaned back in a chair, eyes closed, his legs splayed while Tony sat opposite and talked nonstop in a singsong voice.

As Helma passed, Skitz's eyes shot open. He didn't move but he intently peered at Helma. She felt a shiver along her arms at his cold appraisal.

"What were you in for?" he asked. Tony closed his mouth, scratched his head, and stared at Helma just as fiercely. He slouched in his chair, mimicking Skitz.

"I beg your pardon?" Helma asked.

Skitz's eyes half-closed. Tony glanced over at him and did the same. "White-collar crime, am I right?" Skitz asked. "You don't look tough enough to be any Ma Barker. You light-fingered in the cash drawer? Do a dance with the numbers in the computer? That's the kind of bad stuff a woman mostly does. 'Nice' crimes."

"I am *not* a criminal," Helma Zukas avowed for the second time that evening.

"Aw, come on. Don't hide your light, as they say. Some of the best people get caught." He jerked his thumb behind him toward the kitchen. "Porky spilled your story. Can't keep much of a secret in a place like this. So what did you do?"

Helma was not in the habit of explaining herself to anyone, certainly not a stranger, and least of all a man who was a potential thief and derelict, and who knew what other nefarious deeds he'd already accomplished in his life.

"Excuse me," she said. As she walked away Tony said in fervent sincerity, "That's right, the best people get caught. I always get caught."

The mission offices were off a short corridor that led from the main lobby. A steel door with a double lock separated them from the public area and now the door stood open and Helma heard humming from the second office.

"Come on in," Brother Danny invited. His office occupied a corner with a view of Washington Bay. Helma glanced out the window at the lowering sun and sparkling water. Two kites, one of them a complicated affair in the shape of a dragon, fluttered in the view. The Olympic Mountains weren't visible but a hazy cloudbank marked their presence. Helma knew that if she were able to see in the opposite direction, behind the mission, Mount Baker would be "out," its white cap hanging almost eleven thousand feet above Bellehaven's waterfront.

"I'm almost embarrassed to show you this mess," Brother Danny said. He held a cardboard box that read "French Cut Green Beans" along one side. It was crammed to overflowing with forms, formal letters, scraps of paper, and scrawled notes.

"Do you have any of these on computer?" Helma asked, taking the box and glancing at the top piece of paper: a note penciled on lined paper that read, "Here's $5.00. Make sure it goes to good use for those bums or God will get you."

Brother Danny's eyes brightened. "No, but we've got computers. And all the standard software—I think. Is that something you know how to do?"

"Yes. I could develop a simple database for you."

"Excellent. There's a computer in the room next to my office. It's for my use but . . ." He shrugged. "No time to learn. Let me know if you need extra disks or . . . anything." He showed her to the office next to his, which barely had room for the folding table that held the computer, and an armless office chair. Hooks lined the windowless walls at Helma's chin level. "Old closet," Brother Danny apologized. "Not much air circulation." He glanced at his watch. "I'd better get going. I want to double check that everything's in order for this inspection. Thanks for doing this."

Before Helma could enter the mission's donor records on a computer program, she was compelled to put them in some kind of logical order, which naturally, because of her calling in life as a librarian, was alphabetical.

She sat next to the dark computer and, across the top of the table, organized the donors' letters by last name, discreetly ignoring the amounts donated but noting how many donors were also loyal patrons of the Bellehaven Public Library.

Alphabetization resembled assembly-line work, or walking, or what Helma had heard meditation was supposed to be like: mindless, comfortable, nearly a fugue state. She was unaware of anyone coming or going and worked in a state of silence, only noting occasionally a bead of sweat trickling between her breasts. She barely heard the clank and rumble of the train engines switching cars in the train yard a few blocks below the mission, even though the clatter was loud enough to be right outside the building. Her hands flew, paper rustled. To those who lived by the alphabet, there was something as soothing as a lullaby in the dependability of its order.

She was startled from her reverie, accidentally placing "Drake" between "Bonner" and "Byer," when she heard her name called.

"So okay, Helma Zukas, where the hell are you?"

It was unmistakably the voice of her friend, Ruth Winthrop. Before she rose from her chair, Helma moved "Drake" to its correct place between "Dodd" and "Duchovny."

Ruth stood outside Brother Danny's office, her hands on her hips, her head tipped to one side. The office door was open but the lights inside were switched off. It wasn't completely dark yet but a harsh high-wattage bulb in the ceiling fixture lighted the corridor.

"Don't you have a clock around here?" Ruth asked.

Helma glanced at her watch. "Eight-fifty-six," she said aloud, shocked.

"That's right," Ruth said. "I thought you were set free from this place at eight o'clock sharp."

Ruth wore shorts, which made her six-foot body appear to be eighty percent legs. Her bushy hair was tied back off her neck in a rough ponytail and her skin was tan from the summer's intermittent sun. The man who'd been staffing the front desk earlier stood at the end of the hallway, watching her.

"I lost track of time," Helma explained. She glanced again at Brother Danny's empty office. He was probably at his eight-thirty meeting with the grant committee.

Ruth leaned into the tiny room where Helma had been working. "How nice, they gave you a cell of your own."

"What are you doing here, Ruth?" Helma asked. Her nose twitched at the smell of Ruth's perfume.

"Curious, that's all. Is my makeup intact?"

"Considerably," Helma told her, glancing at Ruth's purple eyeshadow and thick mascara. Her lipstick formed a blood-red bow.

"Good. It's new stuff, guaranteed to hold up in the heat of the desert. Cost me a fortune."

"You probably won't have much opportunity to wear it in this climate."

"A girl has to be prepared. I thought this place would be a little more lively." She waved at the man at the end of the hall and he disappeared.

"Most of the men are outside because of the heat. Plus, there's a grant committee meeting going on and Brother Danny's trying to . . ."

"Keep the kingdom peaceable," Ruth finished. "Money's such a great motivator for good behavior."

"You usually say guilt is the great motivator," Helma reminded her.

Ruth shrugged and smoothed each arched eyebrow with her finger. "Scratch one and you usually find the other. Can I have a ride home?"

"You walked down here?" Helma asked, glancing out the window into the dusky night. With the train switching yards and vacant buildings left from bygone boom times, the street wasn't considered a safe place for a woman to walk alone. The area's gentrification was still spotty: certainty more than fact. Helma knew Brother Danny was right: it was only a matter of time.

"Sure. It's safe. I just pretend I have a ray gun in my pocket." She slipped her right hand into her shorts pocket to illustrate. "Bad guys understand that walk. Can you leave now?"

Two things happened so close together that in thinking about them afterward, it really wasn't surprising that they were fatally connected. Brother Danny hurried in through the front door and glanced down the corridor toward his office, then strode toward Helma and Ruth. His forehead glistened with perspiration, his expression so distraught that Helma peered at his hands to see if he was wringing them. But no, he only held a box of sugar cubes. "I had to go buy these. Is he here yet?" he asked.

"Whom?" Helma asked. She handed Brother Danny a clean tissue from her left pocket and he mopped his face with it.

"Quentin Boyd, the chairman of the grant committee."

"Quentin Boyd," Helma repeated. "Quentin Vernon Boyd is the chairman of the grant committee?"

"Yes. Have you see him?" Brother Danny wiped the tissue across his neck and looked over Helma's shoulder as if the chairman might be in the tiny computer room.

Ruth frowned at Helma. "Hey, isn't Quentin Vernon Boyd that guy you . . ."

At that instant, shouts rang out from behind the Promise Mission, not the shouts of a quarrel or a disturbance, but of surprise, perhaps even mingling with a single masculine scream.

"Dear Lord," Brother Danny said. He dropped the box of sugar cubes which broke open, scattering snowy cubes across the dark tile floor.

Ruth raised her head, adding, "Oh shi . . . Sorry."

But Helma was already on her way toward the mission's back door. "Call nine-one-one," she ordered the man at the front desk who'd risen from his chair, a donut halfway to his mouth.

"Nine-one-one?" Ruth asked, close on Helma's heels. "You don't even know what it is yet."

"We can't waste time. Grown men are in shock."

"Well, that's reason enough to declare an emergency as far as I'm concerned," Ruth grumbled.

Helma stepped out into the evening twilight, at first disoriented. The mission sat on a sloping street and the back door exited onto ground level. She faced the rough hill that rose up behind the mission, covered with worn grass, merging into the wild shrubs and blackberry bushes of a vacant lot.

"What is it?" Ruth asked, stopping beside Helma. Brother Danny halted beside Ruth, breathing heavily.

On the slope, near a patch of tall grass, a group of men stood looking down at the ground, silent now. There was no indication that anyone had shouted, and definitely not that any of them had succumbed to a scream. The approaching darkness gathered around the still men, oppressive. Brother

Danny hesitated a moment as he surveyed the scene, then slowed his breathing, squared his shoulders, and said in a resigned voice, "Excuse me, gentlemen."

Two men parted to let him step between them into their circle, and Helma quickly stepped in behind him.

"Is somebody dead?" Ruth asked, staying behind. "Tell me now." She spoke in a loud voice that broke the shocked mood of the scene. Feet shifted; breaths were exhaled; someone coughed.

"If he ain't, he's a living miracle," one of the men replied.

In the center of the men, a man lay on his back in the weeds. It was too shadowed to make out his features but the earth around his head was darkly blotched. Brother Danny mumbled the fast staccato of a memorized prayer as he knelt beside the man and felt first his chest and then his neck.

"The police have been called," Helma announced to the group of men. "Assistance will arrive in a few moments."

"Better get here quick, hot as it is," a voice replied.

"If you men on that side," Helma said, nodding to four men on the uphill side of the slope, "will move, there will be enough light from the street lamp to determine his condition."

"Anybody got a shovel?" a soft voice asked and someone else tittered. The majority of these men, Helma realized, were not seeing their first lifeless body. But then, she realized sadly, neither was she.

The men stepped aside but not so far as to lose their view, and light shone on the body in the trampled grass.

Quentin Vernon Boyd, chairman of the grant committee that was inspecting the Promise Mission for Homeless Men, well-known real estate developer, and also the newest member of the Bellehaven Public Library Board of Directors, lay dead at their feet.

"Oh, Faulkner," Helma said quietly.

❧ chapter three ❧

FIRST IMPRESSIONS

As usual, Bellehaven police cars were on the scene within moments and just as quickly but far more quietly, the men surrounding the body of Quentin Vernon Boyd disappeared into the evening. By the time the front doors of the first police cruiser opened, only Helma, Ruth, and Brother Danny still stood vigil beside the dead man. And Brother Danny looked like he'd rather be anywhere else. He fidgeted, stroking his upper lip, his Adam's apple bobbing as he convulsively swallowed. Ruth had removed a comb from her pocket and was busy rebanding her hair, determinedly facing away from the body.

Helma alone calmly studied the frozen face of Quentin Vernon Boyd. The last time she'd seen him, that calm face had been distorted by rage as he claimed that "smut" was being harbored in the Bellehaven Public Library and disseminated to the unsuspecting public. The scene had occurred at his first library board meeting following his appointment.

"Smut, I said!" he'd shouted, his mouth twisting and eyes bulging, an overlong strand of silver hair falling onto his forehead. The other four board members had leaned away from him, their faces pained and embarrassed. Ms. Moon, the library director, had fingered the crystal that hung on a long gold chain around her neck and then rolled it rapidly between her palms, her head bent downward.

Helma alone had risen to face Quentin Vernon Boyd. "There is no smut in this library," she'd told him in her

23

silver-dime voice. "There is human experience and discourse, reflecting varied beliefs and persuasions, but not smut."

"Have you read every book in this library?" he'd demanded, rising from his own chair and pointing his index finger at her.

"Have you read *any* book in this library?" she'd asked in turn, ignoring Ms. Moon's gasp. It was a much-discussed fact among the staff that they'd never spotted Quentin Vernon Boyd in the library—not once—and that he'd only applied for a borrower's card two weeks earlier, the day before the mayor had appointed him to the library board, a position that required the member be an active library card holder. "And please refrain from rudely pointing at me."

The exchange had escalated, although Helma felt that she at least had retained her composure. And now here he lay in the weeds on a darkening summer night, dead at her feet. Unbidden came the thought, "So that's that."

The first two policemen approached, holding large flashlights in the gloom the way only policemen did: upraised like daggers in a classic opera. Beams moved jerkily across the ground and then flashed over the scene, briefly touching Helma's face and passing on before she had time to blink. The policemen kept their free hands poised over unsnapped holsters.

Four men stepped out the back door of the mission building, walking in a tight group toward the scene. They wore casual clothing, and might have been residents of the Promise Mission for Homeless Men, but the fact that they weren't was evident in the way they carried themselves: the squared shoulders and raised chins, the certainty of their positions in life confirmed by every confident step. Here were men who moved as if they'd swiftly and competently take charge if the policemen hadn't already arrived. When Helma recognized the owner of a Bellehaven insurance company, she realized she was seeing the remaining members of Quentin Boyd's grant committee.

"What the hell?" the insurance man asked. His voice rose above the policemen's muted conversation, demanding answers. "We heard your sirens. I'm Dietrich Morgan. What's going on here?"

"Keep back, Mr. Morgan," advised one of the policemen. His flashlight beam swept across the dead man and the four members of the committee froze.

"Jesus H.," breathed one of the men, raising his hand to his heart. "Is he . . ."

"Totally," Ruth told him, her voice mechanical. "Totally and completely."

"How?" another of the men, who Helma recognized as an instructor from the local college, asked. The four men regrouped, gathering closer together, shoulders nearly touching, all of them gazing at Quentin Boyd's body.

No one answered. The accumulating law officers began their investigation, concentrating on the crime scene and evidence, momentarily oblivious to the people watching. As Helma observed the meshing of procedures, she wondered if to them, the investigation was as natural and automatic as alphabetizing was to her. No, she chastised herself: a *life* was involved here. She shook her head to banish the thought.

"What's wrong?" Ruth asked. "I mean, besides the obvious."

"I was just thinking."

A young voice called from the street, "Was it a fight? Who got slashed?"

The speaker stood in the shadows and Helma couldn't see him despite the way the murder scene was brightened by police lights. The evening was soft and warm and fragrant, smelling of the sea and ripening blackberries, not a night for murder. But then, was any night?

"Maybe we should get out of here before our cop buddies show up," Ruth told Helma, glancing around at the gathering crowd. She hugged herself and rubbed her arms as if the warm temperature had suddenly dropped. "We're like the perennial witnesses, the harbingers of death. If there are sirens and we're around, bingo, you can bet there's a body stuffed in the bushes. Remember that story about the newspaper photographer who realizes that the same people are in the crowd at every death scene he shoots? Bradbury, wasn't it? I mean, you ought to know."

"Ruth, a man is *dead*."

Ruth turned her head away but waved her hand toward the body. "Yeah, and this is the guy you said you'd do anything to keep off the library board, right?"

"Not to this extreme. I wouldn't wish this on the worst of enemies."

Ruth grunted. "I think this is exactly what we're supposed to wish on the worst of enemies. It's what makes us human: imagining all kinds of disgusting things for the pals we hate. How else do we get to justify war and mayhem and ripping each other to shreds except by our humanity?" Ruth's voice rose. She waved her arms and Helma saw one of the policemen turn to regard them. The four members of the committee looked at Ruth curiously. Ruth was warming up.

"You're absolutely right," Helma hastily told her.

"What do you mean?" Ruth asked suspiciously, dropping her arms to her sides. A red light flashed, making Ruth's eyes gleam.

"That we should stay out of the way so the police can investigate."

"Yeah, the police chief of your dreams isn't here anyway. Let's scram."

"Wait a minute," a voice said, warning in every syllable.

Helma turned to face Detective Carter Houston. Ruth groaned. Helma hadn't noticed his arrival on the scene. The rotund detective was known for his doggedness, his tidiness, and his lack of humor, especially in all matters concerning himself. It was this lack that roused some primeval urge in Ruth to bait Carter Houston unmercifully. He'd been a member of the Bellehaven police for three years and whenever his patience was sorely tried, a faint Texas drawl crept into his precise English. Helma had never seen him in casual clothes, only in neatly pressed plain dark suits, white shirts, and forgettable ties.

"Carter," Ruth said now, leaning down as if she were

about to pat his head, "I heard you'd been transferred to traffic investigation."

"Have you determined how this man died?" Helma asked him.

"How long have you two been here?" he asked, ignoring both their questions, touching the tip of his finger to his tongue and flipping to a clean page in his notebook. He smoothed the page and held his pen poised, gazing from Ruth to Helma to Ruth again, waiting for answers.

"We two responded to shouts from the men who found the body," Ruth told him.

"Where are those men now?" he asked, glancing around the crowd, which was conspicuously devoid of any residents of the mission.

"Maybe they went home," Ruth suggested.

"They're probably inside the mission," Helma told him. "I believe the majority were guests for the night. Curfew is at eight o'clock."

"But they're not locked in at eight," Carter said, his voice accusatory as if Helma were telling him lies. He stood with his feet close together, his arms tight to his body.

"Of course not," Helma told him. "The mission isn't a prison."

He grunted and asked, "Would you recognize any of them?"

"It was already too dark," Helma told him.

"They all look alike to me," Ruth said.

Carter ordered one of the policemen to go inside and find the men who'd discovered the body, then he excused himself and with notebook in hand returned to the crime scene. Ruth eyed his retreating back speculatively. "Bellehaven's finest," she murmured. Helma saw one of the policemen hand Carter Houston a wallet. He flipped it open and counted bills, then dropped it in a plastic bag.

In the flashing lights from several vehicles parked around the scene, the committee members still stood in close rank a few feet from Helma and Ruth, watching the police. The red and blue beams eerily shifted facial features. "A bulldozer is more appropriate for this place than a grant," one of the committee men said. Louder than necessary, Helma thought.

"Do you believe one of the men staying in the mission killed Mr. Boyd?" she asked him.

"Who else?" He snorted and his head reared back. In the shadows, Helma didn't recognize him but she thought his voice sounded familiar. "Quent swore this place needed to be moved out of here, not improved. Who can argue with him now?"

"I wouldn't even try," Ruth said, "but you're jumping the gun, don't you think, I mean so to speak? His body's not even cold."

"He was right all along," the man said stubbornly.

"Your grant meeting was scheduled for eight-thirty?" Helma asked.

"That's right," the insurance man, Dietrich Morgan, told her. "I told Brother Danny that was a ridiculous time to schedule an inspection, but that's when he wanted it." His silver hair was swept back off his forehead. He was taller than Ruth and stood with shoulders squared, like ex–military.

"Did Quentin mention he'd be late?"

"He didn't. He was always on time, punctual to the minute. I knew something was wrong when he didn't show up. The longer we waited, the more serious I knew it was."

"Hindsight," Ruth murmured beside Helma, but she took a step closer to the taller man, speculative interest apparent on her face. Men taller than Ruth, no matter their age, always sparked her interest, even when a body lay in their midst.

Standing fifteen feet away on the slope of the hillside, Brother Danny spoke with two officers and Helma watched with dread as all three men turned when Brother Danny pointed toward Helma and Ruth.

Over the policemen's shoulders, as they walked toward the two women, Helma caught a glint of movement as the street lamp shone on a shiny object. At the top of the hill overlooking the scene, where the slope's vegetation shifted from grass to tangled wild blackberry bushes, a figure rose as if it had been sitting in the cover of the bushes. It was a short stocky figure—a man—and there was nothing furtive about his movements, it wasn't as if he were trying to hide, only to get a better view. Tony, Helma thought. She looked for the taller, more slender figure of Skitz but didn't see anyone else. The light reflected off Tony's glasses, making his eyes pinpoints of light. By the time the two policemen reached Helma and Ruth, Tony was gone.

"Would you like the chief of police to be here, Miss Zukas?" one of the policemen asked.

"Why?" Helma asked, ignoring Ruth's nudge against her arm.

"Because he . . . you and he . . . I can call him," he stammered.

"I don't think that'll be necessary," Helma told him.

"He's out of town anyway, isn't he?" Ruth asked.

Helma turned to Ruth. "How did you know that?"

"You told me. Some meeting in Seattle, right?"

She was right; Wayne Gallant *was* in Seattle, but Helma didn't recall telling Ruth.

Helma explained again how they'd heard the men shout and then had run outside to discover the body. Detective Carter Houston, standing on the periphery, listened, then leaned forward and asked Helma, "Did you know the deceased?"

Helma hesitated just long enough that Carter Houston stiffened. His eyebrows rose and he leaned forward, his nostrils actually flaring.

"I didn't know him personally," Helma explained, "although he was recently appointed to the library board of directors, the library's governing body. I'm only familiar with him in that context. He was not a library user."

Carter Houston wrote furiously in his notebook, looking up quizzically at Helma's last statement. It was completely dark now, the clear night churned by the lights on top of the police cars. The air was sultry, unmoving, for a moment reminding Helma of summer nights before she left Michigan. The policeman who Carter had sent into the mission re-

turned, alone. "Nobody will admit they saw a thing," he told
Carter.

"We'll talk to them one by one," Carter told him. "Don't
let anybody leave."

"Carter," Ruth said, "do you think these are the kinds of
men who sit around and wait for a cop to question them?
They've scattered to the underpasses by now. The only ones
left will be those who missed the whole show."

"We'll follow standard procedure," Carter said, then
snapped his mouth closed as if he'd given away police secrets.

Another policeman approached Carter and Helma stepped
close enough to hear the officer quietly tell him, "We found
something."

Ruth and Helma followed to see the object the policeman
had highlighted with his flashlight. On the ground lay a package of Nutter Butter cookies, unopened but one end crushed
as if it had been dropped or stepped on. It lay no more than
five feet from the body.

Now, with the extra lights and a lessening of shock, Helma
had a better view of what might have happened. Quentin
Vernon Boyd lay on his back, his feet toward the mission.
Drops of blood glistened black in the sparse grass between
the body and the street. "He was shot in the head?" Helma
asked, noting the dark stain on the ground beneath the dead
man's upper body.

Carter Houston didn't answer but the policeman standing
next to him unconsciously touched his neck. So he'd been
shot in the neck and had tried to reach the mission, stumbling
toward the back door before he fell. But why the cookies?

"Maybe the killer dropped the Nutter Butters," Ruth offered. "The bullet didn't stop Quentin so the killer hit him a
good one over the head with the cookies and then fled in
terror. I mean, nobody around this place would accidentally
drop *cookies*."

"We heard the men shouting," Helma pondered aloud,
"but why didn't we hear the gunshot? It would have been
louder, more startling."

"A silencer?" Ruth suggested.

"Maybe. Is Mr. Boyd's car here?" Helma asked. The mission's small parking lot was against the building to their right, surrounded by a chain-link fence.

"I don't see it," one of the committee members said, craning his neck to see the cars parked in the lot, most of them older models in various condition, generally not good.

"So it might have been a carjacking," Ruth suggested. "One of those spur-of-the-moment things criminals are fond of doing. What kind of a car did he drive? A big one, I bet."

"A Lexus," the committee member told her and Ruth nodded in satisfaction.

"Everyone step back," Carter ordered. He motioned behind them toward the mission, using his whole hand, his fingers straight.

"Yeah, yeah," Ruth said, taking one small step. "Keep your shirt on."

"Why are you here at the mission, Miss Winthrop?" Carter Houston asked her.

"Well, Mr. Houston," Ruth drawled. "I came down here to meet my friend here, Miss Zukas. She's been sentenced to . . ."

"I know about that," he cut her off. "Did you drive here?"

"Walked."

More scribbling in his notebook. Then he flipped it shut and said, "You may as well go home now. I know where to find you both." His eyes were hidden as light reflected off the lenses of his glasses and Helma was again reminded of Tony. She glanced up at the bushes but didn't see anyone sitting or standing there. There was no movement in the thick brush.

"Aren't you going to tell us what you've got so far?" Ruth asked Carter.

"Do you need a ride home, Miss Winthrop?" he asked, drawling out the words "ride" and the first syllable of "Winthrop."

"From you?"

"One of the men."

"In that case, no thanks," Ruth said, managing to sound regretful. "Helma here has me covered."

The last image Helma had of the sad tableau was of Brother Danny standing in the shadows and this time he *was* wringing his hands.

"Too bad your chief wasn't there," Ruth said as Helma maneuvered her Buick past a barricade and between two police cars blocking the street to the mission. A small crowd of people stood on the corner across the street. A TV van from the new local television station was parked half on the sidewalk, its side door slid open. As she waited for traffic to clear so she could make a left turn, Helma rolled down her window and advised a woman holding the hand of a five- or six-year-old girl, "A crime scene isn't the proper place for children." The woman made a rude gesture that Helma ignored. Then she pulled into the street and answered Ruth, "The chief isn't 'mine.' "

"He could be, if you weren't such a chicken."

"Friendship is the cornerstone of any relationship," Helma explained. She and chief of police Wayne Gallant had become friends, definitely. That much was true.

"Cornerstone? We're not talking building construction here. We're talking about something a lot juicier."

"I'm not, you are."

Ruth rolled down her window and rested her elbow on the frame. "Your loss."

Romance was an abiding interest of Ruth's. Her own complicated love life was beyond Helma's understanding even though Ruth shared most every detail Helma would listen to. Her longest, and most unlikely relationship with Paul from Minnesota was back on what Ruth called "long-distance hold" and she was uncharacteristically silent about its prospects.

Ruth stretched and asked, "Who do you think killed Quentin Vernon Boyd? Catch those initials: QVB, isn't that a TV channel?"

"You're thinking of QVC," Helma told her. She tapped

the brake as a van pulled away from the curb in front of her without signaling. "Quentin was a powerful figure. His real estate business is reportedly very successful, he was a philanthropist of sorts, but . . ."

"But what?" Ruth asked.

"He had strong opinions. It's understandable that he may have had enemies."

"I see his name and his wife's all the time, connected with every charity in the book; somebody had to love him, if only for the money he brought in."

"That's probably true," Helma conceded.

"But not at the library, am I right?" Ruth turned on her seat to face Helma, her face expectant, the way she looked when she anticipated a good story. "Come on, just the facts."

"His ideas of access to information were contrary to those of the American Library Association," Helma explained, ignoring Ruth's "Hah!" Actually, George Melville the cataloger had called Quentin "a rabid anti-reading anti–gray-matter zealot."

"He was a very contentious member of the library board, even during the short time he served."

"Conveniently short. I bet you weren't the only one who hated him."

"I didn't hate him," Helma clarified. "But I do believe everyone at the library was right to be concerned over his views."

"Yeah, yeah," Ruth said with an impatient wave of her hand. "Freedom to read and all that. So where were you about the time he bought it?"

Helma stopped at a red light next to a low-slung car filled with teenage girls and pounding music. "I was organizing donor names for Brother Danny."

"In that little room where I found you? Any witnesses?"

"I don't recall seeing anyone else," Helma admitted. A police car stopped on the cross street as the light changed and the car full of teenagers sedately drove away, their music suddenly switched off. "But I doubt my whereabouts will become an issue."

"Don't forget our bloodhound buddy Carter Houston is all hot and heavy on the trail. He'll turn everyone into a suspect—including me, I bet. I'd better come up with an alibi."

"You don't need an alibi," Helma assured her as she stopped her Buick in the alley that fronted Ruth's house, a converted carriage house in the older, more genteel section of Bellehaven. The light over Ruth's front door had burned out years ago and never been replaced. The single street lamp at the end of the alley barely illuminated her sidewalk. "There's no reason for the police to question you."

"Oh yes there is. I love Nutter Butter cookies. They were better before they 'improved' the recipe, but I did eat a package for dinner last night."

❧ chapter four ❧

NOT ENOUGH CATS

Helma climbed the outside stairs of the Bayside Arms to the third floor, pausing once to brush a sandy footprint off a tread. Her apartment, where she'd lived the past seventeen years, sat at the far end of the landing. An elevator would have also lifted her to the third floor, but Helma only chose elevators when there was absolutely no other alternative. From one of the second-floor apartments, an air-conditioner droned and hummed, this week probably being the only period of time during the year it would be used. At the third floor, she paused on the top step and looked up into the clear sky. The lights of Bellehaven blocked all but the brightest stars. Now that she was away from the air-conditioner, she also heard the voices of walkers enjoying the summery night, their figures hidden by darkness. Following the evening's events, the disembodied voices were disturbing, vaguely ominous.

After the combination of a long day at the library and her first evening at the mission, Helma was too exhausted to keep the images of the dead man at a safe distance. Any loss of life was a tragedy but even Helma had to admit that some losses weren't quite as wrenching as others. Quentin Vernon Boyd had been a difficult man. She wondered briefly about his wife and partner in philanthropy, Lily. Did Lily know yet? Was she mourning the loss of her husband or did she feel the tiniest twinge of relief? Helma shook her head to banish the thought. Marriages were a mystery to her; she shouldn't be guessing at their intricacies. But still . . .

Apartment 3E next to Helma's own was dark. Two weeks ago, Mrs. Whitney and Aunt Em had moved into the same senior apartment complex where Helma's mother lived, and Mrs. Whitney's old apartment now stood vacant. August was a high vacancy month in Bellehaven; it was between quarters at the local college and the students wouldn't return for another month. The Bayside Arms was an adults-only complex, the age of adulthood beginning at a debatable twenty-one.

Mrs. Whitney had been Helma's neighbor almost as long as she'd lived in the Bayside Arms and she felt a twinge of regret at the blank window where Mrs. Whitney had frequently sat knitting and crocheting bright yarns to make crafts she eagerly bestowed on anyone who'd been kind, from her own grown daughters to the meter reader. Helma had learned to subtly avoid being inundated by Mrs. Whitney's generosity, although she had never turned down the gifts of baked goods from the older woman, who always baked more than she could possibly eat.

The light over Mrs. Whitney's apartment door had either burned out or been turned off. It was too dim to see the floor of the landing and Helma touched the railing as she passed. Beneath her the parking lot was quiet, condensation already forming on the roofs of cars parked in the open. Helma Zukas always removed her keys from her purse well before she reached any lock she intended to open and as she inserted her key into the deadbolt on her apartment door, she heard a sound beneath her, near the Dumpster. She froze. It had sounded like the heavy metal lid being dropped. She removed her key from the lock, stepped away from her door, and stood near the railing, studying the area around the big green Dumpster. No tenant walked away after having deposited his garbage, no cat or dog slunk into the shadows. The night was still; not even a car passed along the street.

Helma released her held breath and returned to her door, thinking the murder had made her apprehensive. She longed for the comfort of a hot bath. Inside, her apartment felt close and stale even though she'd left a screened window open on the bay side of the building. The faint rotting-seaweed odor of low tide seeped into the warm apartment. After a quick glance to assure her furnishings were in the same state as she'd left them, Helma opened her glass and cup cupboard, where taped to the inside of the door was a sheet of paper neatly divided into fifty squares, one for each hour of her sentence. Using a felt pen and a ruler she kept beside her telephone, she Xed out squares fifty, forty-nine, and forty-eight, stopping herself from drawing half an X over square forty-seven. She supposed the extra time she'd accidentally spent at the mission that night didn't actually comprise a portion of her sentence.

That completed, she opened the sliding glass doors and stepped out onto her balcony. Boy Cat Zukas leapt down from the balcony railing, circled her legs without touching her, and slunk inside. It was as close to greeting one another as Helma and the once-stray black cat ever came. They avoided touching each other, although whenever Helma sat in her living room or worked in her kitchen, Boy Cat Zukas was usually nearby, pointedly ignoring her. He wasn't allowed beyond the living room except once when a large moth had flown through the apartment and she'd let him chase it until he'd emerged from Helma's bedroom carrying it in his mouth. She hadn't wanted to see what he intended to do with the moth, although she did acknowledge, "Good cat," as she opened the balcony door for him and his prey.

The night air was soft, liquidy warm. Stars hung over the far side of the bay, away from the city lights, turning the sky gauzy. A silent airplane blinked overhead, mixing with the stars. Quiet laughter and the clinking of dishes sounded from the balcony beneath Helma's. Across the dark curve of Washington Bay, where she knew the mission sat two blocks from the water, she glimpsed the glow of flashing red and blue lights. It would be hours before every vestige of the night's tragedy was erased.

Quentin Vernon Boyd: his was a well-known name in Bellehaven. Why would . . . Helma closed her eyes and counted to five, removing the image of his inert body from her mind.

Evenings like this were rare in Bellehaven and Helma settled into one of the wicker chairs on her balcony, not even wearing a sweater, breathing slowly and deeply, thinking about the living, not the dead.

She was interrupted by lights flicking on in Mrs. Whitney's apartment. Voices, one of which she recognized as Walter David's, the manager, filtered through the walls. Then the sliding glass doors opened and two people stepped onto the balcony. Helma remained still, hoping she wouldn't be noticed.

"Well, I just don't know if it's private enough," a throaty woman's voice said. "I like to sunbathe au naturel. It's the *only* way to get a decent tan."

"We don't worry about tans much around here," Walter David said. He rubbed his wide jaw and stepped aside as if that would give the woman a clearer view of the dark bay.

The woman laughed, her voice booming in the quiet evening. "Oh, don't be silly. You can't expect me to believe all that ridiculous talk about rain, can you? It's a ruse you naughty residents have devised to keep people from moving here. I've been visiting for three days and it's been absolutely *glorious*, day and night. Just like home."

Walter David caught sight of Helma and waved. "Hi Helma, I'm just showing the apartment. Sorry it's so late."

"Oh my, does everyone go to bed so early in this part of the country?" The woman squinted over at Helma. She appeared middle-aged, thin, wearing white shorts and a pastel top. Bracelets and jewelry jangled. In her arms she carried a white longhaired dog she continuously stroked. "Now, I hope you don't have a cat," she said to Helma, her voice overloud between balconies. "Wiley *despises* cats. He just goes *wild*." She kissed the top of her dog's head. "Don't you, sweetie?" She looked back at Helma. "Wiley barks his little throat raw when he sees a bad old kitty cat. Nothing can make him stop. It's such a nuisance."

"I'm sure it is," Helma agreed. "There are several cats in this complex. They like to sun themselves on the balcony railings. Frequently they even leap between balconies and peer into the apartments, sometimes in the middle of the night."

That laugh again. "Wiley would put an end to *that*, I can assure you."

Walter David glanced out over the bay. "Looks like something's going on over there," he said, pointing toward the distant flashing lights.

Helma's phone rang and she excused herself, hearing as she entered her apartment the woman say, "Helma? What kind of name is that?" but unable to hear Walter's answer.

"Wayne Gallant here," he said in his professional voice. "I just talked to Carter Houston and he said you and Ruth were at the scene. I wanted to make sure you got home all right."

"We did," Helma assured him. "Thank you." She pulled a chair away from her table and sat down, smoothing her hair and unbuttoning the top button of her blouse. The chief of police's voice sounded hollow, as if he were speaking on his cell phone from inside his car. She pictured him behind the wheel, the greenish dash lights softening his strong features. "Have any arrests been made?" she asked.

"Not as of five minutes ago."

"It's only been an hour and a half," she conceded. "I suppose it's too soon."

"Not if it were an open-and-shut case, but this one looks a little more complicated." The phone line hissed and then cleared.

"There's no weapon and he was shot in the neck," Helma said, twisting the phone cord around her finger and remembering the way the policeman had touched his own throat. "Plus," she tried, guessing, wishing she could see the chief's face, "he was shot from behind."

"And if you count all the men in the vicinity of the mission," the chief said, "we've got a whole raft of suspects." Helma released the phone cord and reached for pencil and paper, jotting down those three confirmed facts.

"You suspect one of the residents at the mission shot him? Couldn't his place of death be coincidental?'

"Sure it could be, but we'll have to check out the obvious: the men staying there. It won't be easy. Some of them are miles away by now." He hesitated. "Are you going back there tomorrow night?"

"I still have forty-seven hours to serve on my sentence," Helma reminded him, absently glancing up at her cupboard door where her chart of hours hung.

"You could postpone it for a couple of weeks," the chief urged her, "or even transfer to another community service, maybe the senior center. The judge would understand. I could talk to . . ."

"No thank you," Helma told him, straightening in her chair. "These are the situations that arise. We can't always protect ourselves from the realities of life—or death."

There was silence from the other end of the phone. Helma waited. "I guess not," Wayne Gallant finally said.

"Has Quentin Boyd's wife been notified yet?" she asked.

"Not yet. She's at a meeting and they're trying to locate her now."

Helma knew that contacting surviving family members was the responsibility he dreaded most about his position. "Is she a suspect, too?" she asked.

But instead of answering, he told her, "I'll call you tomorrow night, if that's all right."

"Certainly," Helma said. "I'm always pleased to hear from you."

Like most of the dwindling number of newspapers in the country, the *Bellehaven Daily News* had recently become a morning newspaper instead of evening, and the delivery girl still hadn't perfected her early morning schedule, so Helma heard the belated thump of her paper on the balcony, just as she was putting on her sweater, prepared for another long day: first at the library, then the mission. She picked up the paper and unbanded it as she hurried down the steps to the parking lot. *Prominent Philanthropist Murdered*, the headline read over a stock photo of the mission stretched across four columns of the newspaper. A ten-year-old portrait of

Quentin Vernon Boyd filled the two right-hand columns, closest to the edge of the paper, more hair, more benign than the face Helma recalled. She paused on the steps and skimmed the story, which didn't tell her anything she didn't already know. The mission was mentioned a few too many times for journalistic good taste. The more notable properties Quentin had developed, followed by a long list of organizations, charities, and foundations that had benefited from Quentin and Lily Boyd's attention was included in the article on Quentin. Police were "questioning" possible witnesses and a statement would be made later that day.

"It looks like it's going to be another hot one." Walter David stood at the bottom of the steps, wearing thong sandals, shorts, and a t-shirt, holding Moggy, his white Persian cat. He glanced up at the hazy sky.

"As soon as this burns off," Helma agreed. She'd awakened to the sound of the fog horn, unable to see the other side of the bay, but the morning had already cleared and now the sun was a sullen light behind the haze, but not for long. Within an hour the sun would burn away every last particle of mist.

"I'm sorry if I bothered you last night, showing Mrs. Whitney's apartment," Walter David apologized.

"It *was* a little late," Helma told him, refolding the paper and slipping it in her blue bag to read more closely at the library.

"I know. That was the only time Ms. Duval could look at it."

"Is she interested in signing a lease?" Helma asked.

He shrugged. "She'll let me know later this morning. She didn't like the idea of so many cats in the building."

"I see."

Walter David shifted uncomfortably. He boosted Moggy to his shoulder where the white cat lay like a limp sack and gazed at Helma without blinking, its round blue eyes dominating its flat face. "Maybe you didn't know, Helma, but you and I have the only cats in the building now."

"Doesn't Mr. Bellows in 2C have a tabby cat?"

"Not anymore. It gorged itself on David Mennard's fish fertilizer, remember? And Mrs. Trenton's Siamese died last Christmas. I'm surprised you forgot how she tacked that death announcement on the bulletin board by the elevator."

"Did you explain to Ms. Duval that I was incorrect?" Helma asked him.

"No." He shifted from foot to foot again. "But I just wanted to tell you, you know, for future reference."

"Thank you Walter."

"You're welcome."

It was a ten-minute drive to the Bellehaven Public Library and when Helma entered the workroom through the library's service entrance, curly-haired Eve, the fiction librarian, was standing beside her cubicle, her eyes wide and her hands to her mouth. She wore a yellow sundress and matching earrings shaped like sunflowers. "Oh, Helma, did you hear the horrible thing that's happened?" she asked.

"Yes, it was a tragedy to lose a board member," Helma agreed.

Eve frowned. "A board member? Oh, at the mission. Were you there? Did you see it?"

"I was there when the body was discovered, but I didn't see very much."

Eve nodded but Helma could see her attention wasn't totally on the death of Quentin Vernon Boyd. Her eyes shifted beyond Helma, unfocused. She absently tugged on a sunflower earring.

"Has something happened here at the library?" Helma asked Eve.

"No. I mean not yet, but it's going to. Ms. Moon plans to announce it at an emergency meeting." Eve took a breath and lowered her voice. "The state is going to audit the library."

"Our financial records?" Helma asked.

Eve nodded vigorously. "That's what George said. Do you think we're in trouble?"

"I don't see how we could be," Helma told her. "There

are very strict procedures for handling money in a city department and I'm sure an audit every few years is standard practice." She tucked her purse and blue bag in the bottom drawer of her desk and rose to see George Melville, the bearded cataloger, deep in conversation with Harley Woodworth, the morose social sciences librarian who George frequently referred to as "Hardly Worthit." They stood beside Harley's cubicle, which was separated from Helma's by a bookshelf that could have been taller. The two men rarely spoke so energetically.

George looked up and grinned at Helma. "You know that thing they say about death and taxes? Maybe there's another saying about murder and audits?"

"What do you mean?" Helma asked.

"It's like a hand from the grave," Harley Woodworth said gloomily and sat on the edge of his desk, folding his hands together. His narrow shoulders slumped. "He knew we didn't want him on the board."

"Not from the grave, Harley," George corrected. "He's still above ground. Maybe from the casket."

"Can you please explain what you're talking about?" Helma asked. She glanced toward Ms. Moon's door. The director's office was empty. Ms. Moon had recently hung green velvet curtains over her office windows to "contain the spirit of my work," and her office was beginning to resemble the underside of a tree too thick for sunlight to penetrate. Light from her desk lamp reflected softly off the velvet.

"It's not official," George warned her. His eyes twinkled. "But it's more than gossip. Are you sure you want to hear?"

"Please," Helma said with a touch of impatience that widened George's grin.

"Ron, my bowling buddy on the Easy Rollers, works in the mayor's office. It seems that Quentin Vernon Boyd, who so desperately lobbied to join our jolly library board, pulled some strings through his connections and implied that the library didn't always follow generally accepted accounting principles. So, he recommended an audit. In fact, according to Ron, he scared the mayor by saying that he was so suspicious that he wouldn't *think* of sitting on the board until there'd been an audit. So here we are: QVB is dead and we get the audit." He winked. "Whoever did the dirty deed didn't get to it soon enough, I guess."

"That's horrible," Eve told George. "He had a dog: I saw him out walking it once."

George frowned. "And?" he asked Eve.

"People who walk their dogs can't be *really* evil," Eve said with certainty. "Especially if they raise them from puppies."

George gazed at Eve. "That's a striking piece of logic, Eve."

Her chin raised. "Well, it's true."

"I wonder what old QVB had against us," George mused. "Why did he want to put us through the torture of an audit?"

"It wasn't us personally," Helma told him. "He disagreed with the public library's mission to serve the total populace."

George stroked his beard like a villain. "And you tried to set him straight at his very first board meeting."

"Ooh," Eve said, turning to Helma, her blue eyes wide. "Maybe it was *you* he had something against."

"If he requested an audit *before* he became a board member," Helma pointed out, "I doubt if he knew who any of us were."

"We'll probably all lose our jobs," Harley Woodworth said. He twisted a rubber band around his index finger, turning his fingertip purple.

"Why? What have you done?" George asked him.

"It's the association," Harley, who was attracted to the gloomiest side of life, asserted. He stood and hiked his pants even higher. "This place will be crawling with auditors, maybe even detectives. You can't hide an investigation like that from the public; people will refuse to pay their library fines because they won't trust the money's going to good use. Library use will fall off and the library will lose its relevance. Books first and then us. Like eight-track tapes and AMC Pacers. Poof." His voice trailed off and he opened his jaws while keeping his lips closed, considering the library's imminent collapse.

"Not with a bang but a whimper," George said in a funereal voice.

Sally, one of the newer pages, entered the workroom and stepped up to Helma. She was flustered, her cheeks pink. "Two men are out front," she said in a whispery, uncertain voice. "They're demanding to see you. I didn't know . . ."

"They're here already," Harley said, looking at Helma with an expression close to awe. "And you're first."

Helma glanced at her watch. The library didn't open to the public for another hour. "Are they book salesmen?"

"These men are . . . well, they might be 'behaviorally unpredictable,' " she said, using Ms. Moon's term for the disruptive, the unbalanced, and the unsavory who found their way to the library. "I know the library's not open but they're making a scene outside the front doors. Should I call the police?"

That was the proper procedure, the standard by which Helma had always operated. Being in the public eye had its disadvantages and dangers. She firmly believed in avoiding complicated dealings with the "behaviorally unpredictable."

"Of course," she said, and then a sudden thought crossed her mind. "No, wait. I'll at least see who it is." Once, the library had responded to patrons' complaints by asking a disheveled man who appeared to be holding a conversation with his book to leave the library, only to discover that he was a highly respected professor at the local college.

Helma walked through the shadowy and quiet library, savoring the order and silence, thinking it was a little like taking a walk through Boardwalk Park in the early morning, before the world became too busy and too public.

Dutch, the ex-army sergeant who'd taken command of the circulation desk after Mrs. Carmon retired, grimly watched Helma approach. "This is highly irregular," he said, squaring his shoulders and nodding his thumb-shaped head toward the front doors.

Helma felt the unusual urge to salute Dutch and tell him

"at ease." Instead, she ignored him and walked toward the glass front doors of the library. There, side by side with a garbage bag and backpack at their feet, stood Skitz the sock stealer and Tony, his companion. Both men wore the same clothes they'd worn the night before. Skitz's hair was uncombed and beneath the boredom, his face was drawn, as if he'd spent a sleepless night. Tony was grinning widely, his face pressed against the glass, his hand waving at Helma like a windshield wiper.

❧ chapter five ❧

UNPREDICTABLE VISITORS

For a long moment Helma stood in front of the glass doors, contemplating the two men who in turn studied her. Skitz stood a step behind Tony, staring, although the stare was aimed somewhere above Helma's head. He needed a shave. Now she could see that the faded printing on his black t-shirt read, "Wherever you go, there you are." Earrings lined up on the outside of his right ear glinted in the sunlight that was already breaking through the morning's haze. Again she noticed the hardness around his eyes and thought of Brother Danny's assessment: "a bad spark."

Tony's plaid shirt was buttoned askew, his jeans held up by a belt that gathered in at his own thick waist. Since the hems of his pant legs didn't meet his anklebones, Helma could see he wore black socks, and she wondered if the two men had taken advantage of Brother Danny's storeroom after all.

Once she saw that her visitors were Skitz and Tony, the fact that she *didn't* have to deal with them, that she *could* return to the workroom, didn't cross Helma's mind. She pivoted on her navy pumps, turning back to the circulation desk where Dutch stood at the counter busily checking in books that had been slipped into the drop box overnight. His lips were pursed in disapproval. He didn't look up when Helma stopped on the opposite side of the desk. "Excuse me," she told him. "My key's in my purse, may I borrow yours?"

"To go out there?" he asked. Books continued to methodically pass through his hands without faltering, one after the other, his rhythm as confident as a seasoned assembly line employee's. Helma admitted with some admiration that Dutch *was* efficient.

"To come back *inside*," she said. Dutch's efficiency faltered. He set the scanner on top of a barcode and ran one hand across his buzz cut.

"Or I could bring *them* inside," Helma suggested, nodding toward the two men outside the door: Skitz as glowering and resentful as an arrestee on a TV police show; Tony with his cheek squashed against the glass, smiling.

Dutch harumphed and unhooked his library key from the chain of keys hanging on his belt. "What if they attack you and steal my key?"

"I'm sure Ms. Moon would issue you another one," Helma said as she took Dutch's key, noting how the dragon tattoo on Dutch's arm gleamed as if it had been polished.

"She'd have to change all the locks," Dutch warned.

Helma pushed the bar on the rightmost door and stepped out onto the concrete steps. Mount Baker was just emerging from the haze, white against the clear blue sky. This day would be just as fine and as hot as the day before.

"Hi, hi, hi," Tony greeted her before she'd swung the door completely open, eagerly grabbing the outside handle and pulling the door wide. "Is this where you work?"

"It is, but the library doesn't open to the public until nine-thirty," Helma told the two men. "Is this an emergency?"

"A reading emergency?" Skitz asked. One side of his mouth raised in a sneer.

"There *are* times when information is crucial, when a question needs to be answered immediately," Helma explained. "Not only does the library provide reading material but it dispenses vital knowledge to the public."

"The Internet's going to put you out of business," Skitz declared, raising his voice. "Hope you know how to do something else. Got a trade of some kind? Like can you type or short-order cook?"

"What is it you need this morning?" Helma asked. She wasn't about to stand on the library's front steps and discuss the future of librarianship with a homeless man who stole clothing.

"I like the Internet," Tony said. "Skitz can find the va-va-voom websites." He made fists and jerked them backward to his side while he thrust his pelvis forward.

Skitz shrugged. "That was something last night, wasn't it? The dead guy?"

"You weren't there when the police were questioning the residents," Helma said.

"I had things to do."

"You left before curfew."

"Skitz had things to do," Tony repeated, his inflections identical to Skitz's. "He went away and left me sitting in the bushes, didn't you, Skitz? I ate blackberries."

"Shut up, Tony."

"Okay, Skitz."

A city truck passed the library and the driver slowed to look at Helma and the two men. Helma turned to Tony and held his glance. He blinked rapidly, shifting from foot to foot but he didn't look away. "Did you see the man get killed, Tony?" she asked.

"I fell asleep," he told her and broke eye contact, looking down at his worn loafers.

"Neither of you saw anything suspicious when Mr. Boyd was killed?" Helma asked. She crossed her arms and gazed between the two men.

"Nothing," Skitz said. "Missed the whole show. Was that the dead guy's name: Boyd?"

His question sounded false but there was no point in pressing the two men. "If there's nothing I can do to help you," Helma told them, "I'll return to work."

"Go ahead," Skitz's eyes never left her face but still he didn't meet her gaze, shifting his sight from her nose to her forehead to her chin. "We just wanted to see if what they said was true, that you were a librarian down here. You might have been lying."

"I'd never lie about anything so vital," Helma assured him.

"Yeah, well congratulations and hip-hip hooray," Skitz deadpanned. "Maybe we'll come back sometime and get on the Internet."

"Va-va-voom," Tony said as he picked up the black garbage bag. Skitz hoisted the backpack over one shoulder and the men ambled toward the street: two drab figures walking in the manner of men without a destination.

When Helma unlocked the library door and stepped back inside, it was to come face to face with Harley, George, and Eve, who stood in the foyer where they had an excellent view of the library's front steps.

"New friends?" George asked, nodding toward Skitz and Tony.

"They're just men I met at the mission last night," Helma told him.

"That skinny one doesn't look very healthy," Harley said, taking a step back from Helma. "Did you touch him?"

"No, Harley," Helma told him. "I did not."

"You don't have to touch them sometimes," Harley said, easing back another step and making motions with his hands like jumping insects.

"Do you think they're the guys who murdered Quentin Vernon Boyd?" Eve asked. She gazed after the departing men, twisting one of her sunflower earrings.

"I think if they had, they'd have tried to leave town by now," Helma said.

"My aunt says the mission is filled to the gills with murderers, thieves, and rapists," Eve said, "and that they all hide out there with our blessings. 'It's a den of antiquity,' she says."

"Iniquity, too," George said.

"But what's it *really* like inside the mission?" Eve asked Helma. "Are there bars?"

"Did you see the murder victim?" Harley asked, leaning

back toward Helma. "Could you describe his injuries? Were there open wounds?"

"There are no bars," Helma said, "and it was too dark to see the victim clearly."

George cracked his knuckles and Helma winced. "Sorry," he said, shaking out his hands. "Sorry you were there when it happened, too. The paper said QVB was on his way to a meeting at the mission. Weird time for a meeting. Did Brother Danny feel more fondly toward him than we did?"

"It was an inspection tour of the mission, the final procedure of a grant application. I do know the grant was important to the mission, but no one mentioned Mr. Boyd on a personal level."

"And QVB had the power to grant or deny?"

"He was the chairman of the committee," Helma said.

"He had his fingers knee deep in a lot of pies," George commented, "whipping up resentment everywhere he went, probably. They should investigate people on every committee he's been involved with, just as much as those guys at the mission. Including us. Anybody who's cried over QVB's death, please raise your hand."

Nobody did and George nodded. "And he only attended one board meeting. Just think what he was capable of when he got up a head of steam."

"I read about people like him in my *True Paranoia* magazine," Harley said. "They act benevolent but what they really want to do is take control of places. People, too. He wanted power over the library and the mission."

"Like an alien," Eve said dreamily, "when they take over your body and make you do things you'd never imagine doing otherwise."

George looked speculatively at Eve. "Yeah?" he asked. "Like what?"

"Our experience with Mr. Boyd was difficult but maybe that was an exception," Helma interrupted. "Given time, his more extreme views might have been moderated."

"Like removing every book from the library that has a four-letter word in it?" George asked.

"Or assigning a librarian to stand behind each person who uses the Internet?" Harley added.

"And don't forget the audit," Eve reminded them. "He might as well have said we were a bunch of embezzlers. His wife Lily is sweet. I wish she'd been the one the mayor appointed to the board."

"Maybe she iced him to get his spot," George said, then held up his hands in surrender at Eve's gasp. "Just joking."

"That's mean," Eve told him.

"She *was* definitely the library user of the two," George conceded. "But she was just laying the groundwork for QVB. Everybody knows that's the way they operated. The Mrs. buttered up the committees, foundations, or whatever, and the mister cracked the whip."

"Since they worked as a team," Helma suggested, "she might have had some influence over him as his term progressed."

George grunted. "That's not the way I heard it."

Ms. Moon entered the public area and Helma saw the director pause beside the circulation desk and say, "Thank you, Dutch," before she walked over to the four librarians. Her drapey peach-colored dress billowed and rippled. A faint chiming tinkle accompanied every step although Helma saw no sign of a bell. Ms. Moon had recently had all her blond waves cut off—"so she'll get better reception," George had suggested—and now she wore her hair in a style only an inch longer than Dutch's buzz cut. With her round face and round body, he'd also observed that she resembled a classically constructed snowman. Although Helma had told George he was being unkind, she did admit to herself that the description was apt.

Ms. Moon peered beyond the group and out the library doors. George glanced over at Dutch and murmured, "Tattle tale."

"Has anything unusual happened this morning?" she asked, smiling and opening her arms to the librarians.

"Not a thing," George told her. He pointed toward the oak and naugahyde chairs. "I was wondering if we should replace the furniture in the foyer. What do you think?"

For an instant, a flash of heat sparked in Ms. Moon's eyes, then the smile reappeared, dimpling her cheeks. "That's an excellent idea, George. Would you head a task force to investigate the subject?"

Eve snickered which she tried to cover by blowing her nose. "Excuse me," she said. "I have to finish a purchase order."

"Cataloging calls," George added.

As the group hurriedly dispersed, Ms. Moon said, "Helma, may I have a word with you?"

Helma stopped and Ms. Moon said with a pained expression on her face, "Regarding the transforming experience of Quentin Vernon Boyd last night."

"Are you referring to his murder?" Helma asked.

Ms. Moon blanched and glanced around the public area as if Helma had blasphemed before small children. "It was an unfortunate incident. Because you were present at the time, some people may see a connection between the library and the mission." She ran her tongue across her lips. "Perhaps you can refrain from mentioning the association."

"You're asking me to lie?"

Ms. Moon made soothing motions in the air around Helma. She'd long ago banned any form of touching in the library. "Of course not. I encourage you to cooperate fully with the police but should reporters question you, perhaps there will be a way to downplay the connection. I mean, your brush with the law last month, your sentence to work at the mission, being on the premises during the ultimate crime against a member of the library board, *and*," Ms. Moon waved her hand toward the library's front doors, "the recent attention that the behaviorally unpredictable seem to be bestowing on you."

Helma felt her eyes widen and her mouth momentarily drop open. *She*, Miss Wilhelmina Cecelia Zukas, professional librarian for seventeen years, was a potential *embarrassment* to the Bellehaven Public Library? She opened her mouth to speak, then closed it again in futility, so astonished that no adequate words of rebuttal came to mind.

"Thank you," Ms. Moon told her, smiling. "I knew you'd understand." And she turned and walked toward the workroom, accompanied by the faint chiming, her pace as smooth as if she strode two inches above the floor.

"Phone, Miss Zukas," Dutch said impatiently, as if he were calling her name a second or third time.

"I'll answer it at the reference desk," Helma told him.

Dutch harumphed meaningfully, holding out his hand.

"Thank you," Helma told him, dropping the borrowed key into his palm. "I know how much this key means to you."

Before she picked up the telephone, Helma realigned the pencil holder and stapler with the edge of the desk pad.

"You simply can't go back to that place," Helma's mother said without preamble. "It isn't safe, not with murderers sleeping there."

"We don't know that, Mother."

"Then who else could have done it? Tell me that. Quentin Vernon Boyd! Of all people. Nobody's safe. Poor Lily. It's a shock to everybody here, I assure you, just a shock." She paused. "Did you see it, dear?"

"I was working inside at the time."

"Oh, that's too bad. I mean, it's too bad there wasn't a witness. What does the chief think?" she asked, caution in every syllable.

"He was out of town at the time, so I don't know."

"Oh," said her mother, brightening. "Then he'll want to discuss every detail with you. When do you expect to see him? Soon, I imagine."

"I'm not sure. Have Aunt Em and Mrs. Whitney found the curtains they wanted?"

Distracted from Helma's personal life, her mother set off on a tale of how "ridiculously fussy those two old women are, wanting curtains guaranteed not to fade for twenty years; they'll both be lucky to live that long." Helma listened without comment while she made notes for the new day.

"Oh my, did I leave my blue scarf at your apartment on Saturday? The one with that Greek god on it?"

"Do you mean Michelangelo's *David*?" Helma asked.

"That's the man. I want to wear it with my pink pants suit to our Big Band Night. It's on Friday and everybody's going, just everybody. Do you think you could bring it over before then?"

"Of course," Helma told her. "Either tomorrow night or Thursday."

"Now you talk to somebody about having your sentence changed," her mother advised before she hung up. "There aren't any men in that place who'd be of interest to you, anyway."

On her lunch hour, Helma drove back to the Bayside Arms to retrieve a can of spray disinfectant cleaner from beneath her kitchen sink to replace the can that had disappeared at the mission the night before.

A tall slender woman stood on the third floor landing in front of Mrs. Whitney's empty apartment. Her long brown hair hung straight down her back and bangs brushed her eyebrows. A red dog sat at her feet. She gazed at Helma expectantly, as if she'd been waiting for her.

"May I help you?" Helma asked.

"Are you the manager?" The red dog's ears perked up and it squirmed but it remained politely seated, its eyes as expectantly watching Helma as its owner's.

"No, I'm sorry. The manager's name is Walter David. He lives in 1A, on the ground floor."

Behind her bangs, the woman frowned. "The man said he'd get the manager for me. From the way he spoke I thought it was a woman."

"What man?" Helma asked.

"I think he was an employee." Her face flushed. "He didn't look like he lived here." She shrugged. "I'm sorry. That wasn't fair. He was just 'rougher' than I expected."

Helma thought of the men who lived in the Bayside Arms and couldn't picture a single one who looked out of place, who she'd describe as "rough." She glanced down at the grounds; Walter David usually cared for the plants and lawn himself.

The woman held out her hand. "My name's Sara Hill. I'm looking for an apartment and I saw the sign out front."

Sara Hill's hand was long-fingered and thin, her handshake light. She spoke in a quiet voice and Helma suspected she moved quietly as well and probably didn't play loud music or have loud boyfriends.

"I'll phone the manager for you," she offered. "Maybe he doesn't realize you're waiting."

"Thank you. The man assured me he'd tell him but . . ." She shrugged.

Sara Hill and her red dog waited on the landing while Helma called Walter David. He answered on the first ring and Helma explained that the woman was waiting to inspect Mrs. Whitney's old apartment. While she spoke she removed a new can of spray disinfectant from her cleaning supplies.

"That's weird," Walter told her. "I've been sitting here doing accounts for the past hour and no man came by to tell me about her. I'll be right up."

Helma told Sara Hill that Walter was on his way. "I hope you like the apartment."

"Me too."

Helma hurried down the stairs, wondering if the polite red dog barked at cats.

Back at the library after lunch, Eve ducked her head into Helma's cubicle and said breathlessly, "I just ate lunch with Susan, the judge's secretary, and she said they caught the guy who murdered QVB and it *was* somebody from the mission. Doesn't that give you the creeps? You'd better not go back there. I wouldn't." Eve shuddered.

"Who was it?" Helma asked. "Do you remember his name?"

Eve tore open a giant-size pack of Doublemint gum and shook out two sticks. "I don't know but she said he walked right up to a policeman who was giving a lady a traffic ticket and confessed. Right in the middle of the street. Tony somebody, I think."

❧ chapter six ❧

CONVERSATIONS WITH STRANGERS

An hour after Eve's announcement that a man named Tony had confessed to the murder of Quentin Vernon Boyd, Tony's companion Skitz appeared in the library—alone. Helma sat at her station at the reference desk, prepared to field questions from the public. The day was slow, not because there was a decrease in the hunger for knowledge and reading entertainment among Bellehavenites but because the library was, as Harley said, "damnably hot." Air-conditioning had never been an option or a consideration and unless the staff members brought their own to work, neither had fans. In the heat of the day only a few people braved the building, in shorts and sleeveless shirts, grabbing quick summer reads and heading back into the sunshine and blue skies before the weather changed, as it surely would.

Helma, feeling that sleeveless clothing lost its attractiveness after a woman reached a certain age, wore a pale green, short sleeved dress in a breathable natural fabric. It was the most summer-appropriate clothing she owned, except for her underwear, which she bought from a catalog that arrived in her mailbox in a tasteful brown wrapper. Her summer lingerie selections, which were limited because summer weather in Bellehaven was so fleeting, were the lightest and briefest she could purchase, in colors that were also as coolly invisible as possible. All chosen with library comfort in mind, of course.

Skitz didn't approach the reference desk. He slouched at a table facing Helma, his feet on his backpack beneath the table, a book in front of him, the pages of which he turned either too fast or too slow to be reading. He'd partially combed his hair and given himself a patchy shave since she'd seen him that morning. The sparse library patrons gave him a wide berth, glancing at him and quickly glancing away as if his condition were contagious.

Helma studied Skitz for a few moments, her finger holding her place in the latest issue of *Library Journal*. What was the difference, the subtle difference that made people hastily turn their heads away, that made Skitz a person to avoid while another young man sprawled on a chair just as casually, dressed just as slovenly, might cause someone to shake his or her head, wondering when he'd accomplish anything, or to even smile fondly?

Ms. Moon might call it an aura of danger. Helma Zukas was not prone to fancifulness but she sensed that surrounding Skitz was an air of . . . yes, she'd definitely have to say, danger. But *why* she couldn't say exactly: perhaps the way his eyes looked permanently narrowed, without any vestige of youthfulness, the shifting gaze that was both bold and wary, the way he occasionally stretched his shoulders as if weights sat on them. Maybe those were the weights her father meant when he used to say disparagingly of someone, "he's got a chip on his shoulder." Curious, Helma pulled the *Dictionary of Americanisms* off the shelf behind her and read that the phrase's first use in the United States was in *The Long Island Telegraph* in 1830, "when two churlish boys were determined to fight, a chip would be placed on the shoulder of one, and the other demanded to knock it off at his peril."

When she glanced up again, Skitz was staring at her. He slid his eyes away and then casually stood and stretched, leaving his book open and upside down and his chair in the aisle. He ambled over to the reference desk as if he had nothing better to do on a scorching Tuesday afternoon.

Despite his lazy walk, the looseness of his joints, there was a touch of menace to him and Helma stopped herself from instinctively leaning back, away from his approach.

"What's Zukas mean?" he asked, pointing to the name-plate in the slotted wooden holder on the reference desk.

"I'm not sure of the word's definition but it's of Lithuanian origin," Helma told him.

"I knew a Lugan once," he said, using the derogatory term that made Lithuanians stiffen unless they were using it themselves. "Big guy. Played basketball. Hands like this." He made motions with his hands to demonstrate a size twice his own.

"Did he belong to a team?" Helma inquired politely, wishing this were a normally busy day with lines of people impatiently waiting for attention.

"Yeah, a prison team. Beat the guards once." He grinned at Helma. "That's what he claimed anyway."

"Did you have a reference question I could help you answer?" Helma asked.

If Helma hadn't been looking directly at Skitz she might have missed the brief faltering of his grin. As it was, he cocked one shoulder and gazed down at the desktop, then idly picked a pencil from the pencil holder and threaded it between his fingers. "You saw Tony last night, right?"

"At the mission with you? Yes." Helma moved the pencil holder out of his reach.

"No. I mean later," he said, staring intently at the pencil laced through his fingers. "On that little hill behind the mission, when the police were futzing over the dead guy."

"I saw a figure. I thought it was your friend Tony, but I couldn't say for certain."

"I left him there while I went to score . . . for some provisions. He wouldn't have moved."

"I understand Tony confessed to Quentin Vernon Boyd's murder," Helma said.

Skitz didn't look up from the pencil. He kicked one foot lightly against the reference desk. "Yeah, but that doesn't mean a da . . . thing. Tony confessed to blowing up that Pan

Am flight. He claimed he was the Unabomber. Last month he confessed to a drive-by shooting and he can't even drive. He's just got a thing about confessing."

"A false confessor," Helma said. "That's the term for someone who confesses to crimes he or she didn't commit. Although I do feel the term can be misconstrued since the word 'confessor' also refers to a priest."

Skitz blew through his lips. "Yeah, well so what. Knowing the term doesn't change anything, does it?"

"I don't know how else I can help you." She smiled hopefully at a woman approaching the desk behind Skitz but who then veered toward the Internet computers.

He leaned closer and Helma smelled the odor of cigarettes and old clothing. "Tell the cops you saw him." He wasn't making a request; he was ordering her. Helma felt a familiar prickle at the back of her neck, typical on occasions when she was told she was wrong, or accused of an activity she didn't do, or given any type of command.

"I'm afraid not," Helma told him, her voice louder than she intended. A man at the newspaper rack raised his head and she spoke more softly. "I couldn't positively identify the figure I saw as your friend Tony. Besides, that puts him at the scene of the crime. Is that what you're hoping to do?"

"He told them he killed the guy and ran away. That he threw the gun in the bay. But you saw him sitting on the hill when the cops showed up. And he was still there when I came back."

"Then you should inform the police of that fact."

He gave Helma a withering look. She *did* lean back away from him then; she couldn't help it. "It doesn't matter what *I* say. But you're a librarian; they'll believe you."

"I won't attest to anything of which I'm not certain," Helma said.

The pencil threaded between Skitz's fingers snapped in two. His voice rose and from the corner of her eye, Helma saw Dutch leave the circulation desk and take two steps closer to the reference desk, puffing up to soldierly stature.

"Tony's never done anything wrong," Skitz said. "He's stupid, not a criminal."

"I can see you're upset," Helma said, "but if you'll keep your voice down we can discuss this problem so I can assist you."

Skitz leaned back and tipped his head. "You learn that song and dance in some workshop?" He made quotes in the air. " 'Affirm the whiner's frustrations.' I've heard it a hundred times. It's a bureaucratic cookie-cutter response to the pissed-off and the powerless. Get them out the door so you can forget they exist."

"Is this pencil-neck giving you trouble, Miss Zukas?" Dutch asked. He crossed his arms, the arm with the green and red dragon tattoo on top.

Every pretense of the easygoing, ambling man vanished. The expression on Skitz's red face as he looked at Dutch was deadly. Helma realized without a doubt that Skitz was dangerous, capable of causing damage and losing control, even in a library. She hurriedly said, "No, Dutch. We're discussing a mutually frustrating situation, thank you."

When Dutch, after making noises that sounded like snorts, returned to his post, Skitz stood with narrowed eyes, finally meeting her gaze. "Then you'll help Tony?"

"How is he related to you?"

"No relation. You know that *Mice and Men* book?"

"By Steinbeck?"

"Yeah. I read it a year ago, just before I met Tony. This guy was . . . well, Tony was in a tough spot and I was a soft touch, that's all." An expression close to a smile curved his lips. "So you'll help Tony?" he asked again.

Helma Zukas had dealt with the public long enough that she recognized when she was being had. Excuses why library fines should be forgiven, why one person's reference questions should be answered before anyone else's or why a rare book just *had* to be borrowed. The smile on Skitz's face didn't reach his eyes. The *Of Mice and Men* story was a clever ploy, guaranteed to appeal to any dedicated librarian. But still she sensed that no matter how it was couched,

Skitz wanted to help his friend and had turned to her because there was no one else. Loyalty in friendship was among the virtues Helma valued most highly. Something in their brief encounter the night before had convinced him he could trust her—or at least sway her.

"I'll mention it to the police," Helma told him. "But only that I *think* I saw Tony, that's all."

"Cool," he said, slipping back into sullen disregard. He set the broken pencil on the reference desk without apology and sauntered out of the library, pausing by the circulation desk to give Dutch another deadly glance, which Dutch returned with equal virulence.

"Your little buddy going to become one of our regulars?" George Melville asked.

Helma hadn't seen him step behind the reference desk and she started in surprise. "I doubt it," she told him.

"At least not until the weather changes," George said, picking up the latest issue of *What Every Librarian Should Know,* and heading back toward the workroom.

"I heard that a suspect confessed," Helma told Wayne Gallant when the chief of police phoned her an hour later. With so few people in the library, Helma took his call at the reference desk, speaking in a low voice.

"He did," he said with little enthusiasm.

"But you doubt the confession?" Helma asked.

"Sometimes you have to suspect the confessors as much as you do those who swear they're innocent."

"I might have seen the man who confessed—Tony—last night, watching the police investigate Quentin Vernon Boyd's death."

"Can you be sure?" he asked, his voice all business.

"No, he was in the shadows, but at the time that's who I thought it was. Does that mesh with his story?"

"Not exactly," he said, and Helma sensed immediately that he regretted even giving out that much information.

"Have you found the gun?" she asked. Dutch walked past her, straightened a newspaper at the end of the counter, then

walked slowly past her again, veering less than a foot from
her chair, stopping and bending to pick up something invisible from the floor.

"Not yet. Are you still going to the mission tonight?"

"I intend to serve my sentence as it was pronounced," she
assured him.

"I figured you might," he said. "I plan on dropping by
tonight so I'll talk to you in more detail then."

On such a hot day there were naturally more phone reference questions than face-to-face inquiries and Helma found
herself fielding two or three, and once, even four blinking
lights at a time on the reference desk telephone. During the
summer, the library closed early on Tuesdays and Thursdays,
and fifteen minutes before its five o'clock closure, there was
a flurry of blinking lights. By the time Helma answered the
last one she had a mild headache.

"I'll have to find the poem and call you back," she told
the quiet-voiced woman who'd just requested a copy of a
poem of which she could only remember the first line. "May
I have your name please?"

The woman hesitated and then said, "Lily Boyd," and gave
her phone number. "I'm only interested in the first stanza."

Privacy was paramount in the library; exchanges were
made in strictest confidence so Helma only politely assured
the woman she'd phone her within five minutes and said
nothing about Lily Boyd's loss of her husband Quentin the
night before.

As Helma looked up the poem's first line in *Granger's
Index* she was curious as to why Lily Boyd would be looking
for a poem in the midst of her grief. But when she located
the work in a poetry anthology she understood completely.
The poem was a long eulogy for a dead love. Lily Boyd
obviously wanted it for her husband's funeral service.

When Helma returned Lily Boyd's call and told her she'd
found the poem and that she could pick it up at the reference
desk in the morning, the woman said, "Oh, but I need to give

it to the minis . . . someone tonight. Do I have time to send a friend down to pick it up for me?"

"We close in five minutes," Helma told her. She knew where the Boyds lived. It was roughly between the library and the mission, a Victorian house that sat on a bluff overlooking the bay. Impulsively, Helma told her, "I can drop it off at your home in about twenty minutes."

"Oh, could you do that?" Lily Boyd asked, her voice catching. "I'd be so grateful. I mean, if it isn't too much trouble."

"No. I have to be on that side of town." Then she broke with protocol and said, "I'm sorry about your husband."

"Thank you," Lily told her. "That's so kind. Thank you."

Ms. Moon stopped Helma as she was preparing to leave the building. She was flustered, her normally benign face flushed. "The state is going to audit us, it's official," she said, her dulcet voice gone staccato and breathless. "The mayor just called me." Beneath her drapey clothing she rocked from side to side.

"I'm sure there's no reason to be concerned," Helma told her. "The library's always adhered to strict fiscal rules. Hasn't it?"

"Of course," Ms. Moon said. "Certainly." She raised her hand to her mouth as if she were about to chew her fingernails, then turned it into a fist and jerked it back to her side. In her agitated state she disclosed more information than usual. "And the rumors are true: Quentin Boyd *is* the person who requested the library audit. He asked for it."

It wasn't until Helma was pulling out of the library parking lot that she wondered what Ms. Moon had meant when she said Quentin Vernon Boyd had "asked for it." The audit? Or his death?

Helma drove four blocks out of her way to the row of homes perched above the bay. The view here was the long view to the south, higher and even more unencumbered than the mission's view. On clear days the viewer saw the entire bay to its mouth, which led to the passage through the San

Juan Islands and on even clearer days, the snowy peaks of the Olympic Mountains were visible on the distant Olympic peninsula.

The Boyds' house was a well-known landmark, a Victorian "painted lady" of six or seven different harmonizing colors: gingerbread and turrets, leaded glass and dark wicker furniture on the front porch. It was the kind of house that would look perfectly natural with a black funeral wreath hanging on the front door. Helma pulled into the driveway and parked her Buick behind a silver BMW. A maroon Lexus was visible through the open door of a detached garage. The green gingerbread on the eaves of the garage exactly matched the house's.

The yap of a small dog sounded from deep inside the house as Helma climbed up the wide front steps past a plot of blooming black-eyed susans. She paused, then pressed the doorbell, which was a softly glowing pearl button in the belly of a bronze frog. The doorbell chimed and a woman's voice hushed the dog but it continued barking, a persistent *yip yip yip* without inflection. Lily Boyd answered the door herself. She was a small woman in her early sixties, not more than five feet tall, with silver hair cut stylishly short. She wore a light pants suit and sandals. The bridge of her nose was red, as if she'd just removed a pair of reading glasses.

"I'm Helma Zukas from the library," Helma told her. "I've brought a photocopy of the poem you requested."

"Oh, I'm so grateful. Won't you come in?" She opened the door wider.

"Thank you but that's not necessary."

"No. Please do. It would be nice to talk to someone not connected with the . . . formalities." Lily Boyd fluttered her hand, beckoning Helma inside and then touched her heart as she closed the door. "I expect there will be so many people, don't you?"

They passed through a foyer of dark wood. Sconces of leaded glass hung on either side of a gilt-edged mirror. Two oil landscapes hung on the opposite wall. There was no sight or sound of the dog.

"Your husband was a well-known and influential man," Helma said, uncertain what Lily was asking. "I'm sure he had many friends."

"And enemies, don't forget. A man confessed, did you know that?" She led Helma into a cozy front room with a bay window facing the water and patterned carpets, and motioned Helma to a wingback chair. Lily sat on a matching settee across from Helma, her feet resting on one of the small footstools that sat beside three of the chairs, obviously for that very reason.

"Yes, I did hear that," Helma told her. The chair was too large, stiff-seated and smelling of furniture polish. She felt as if she were "perched." On the oak table beside the chair sat an open real estate magazine and a small yellow legal pad. No words were written on it, only a vertical column of five- and six-digit numbers.

"Then maybe it'll be over quickly. It was a homeless man, I understand. Why would he choose my husband?" She folded her hands tightly together, not really expecting an answer. "I never dreamed when I dropped him off last night that I'd never see him again."

"You dropped your husband off at the mission?" Helma asked.

Lily nodded. "We both had meetings to attend last night. Mine was with the Young Readers steering committee. I skipped the dinner and was just going to the meeting afterward. Quentin was going to ask Dietrich Morgan for a ride home. Dietrich was his closest friend. I know he'll be at the . . . funeral." Lily spoke rapidly, distractedly, her eyes shiny as if tears waited to spill.

"Did you see anyone along the sidewalk or near the mission when he got out of the car?"

"Why do you ask?"

"I just wondered," Helma said, remembering that Lily didn't know Helma had been present when her husband's body was found.

Lily shook her head. "I think I remember a man walking a dog, but I couldn't swear to it; but then I wasn't paying much attention. I was scheduled to speak to the group and I always suffer from a little stage fright beforehand. That's why I skipped the dinner; I knew I couldn't eat." She took a deep breath and said in a low voice, "Quentin would have hated the tawdriness of all this." In another room, a clock chimed quarter past the hour. Lily jerked her head as if the chime were unexpected. She turned her intent gaze back to Helma. "How are you coping at the library?"

"We're all sorry about your husband."

Lily Boyd surprised Helma by tipping back her head and giving a small laugh. "Now really, a few of you *must* be relieved that Quentin will no longer be on the library board. He told me he'd met with some resistance at the first board meeting he attended."

"That's true," Helma conceded. "He and I . . ."

Lily held up her hand. "You don't need to explain. I understand. Quentin was a clear thinker; he was the most intelligent men I've ever met, a man able to cut through Gordian knots." She shook her head in regret. "But he also had very strong ideas that put him at odds with people. He couldn't compromise. That was his greatest flaw." She smiled sadly at Helma. "And I'm aware he had controversial beliefs about what the public should be permitted to read. Beliefs I didn't agree with. Perhaps with time . . ." She trailed off.

"I won't deny it was a concern to us," Helma told her, "and frankly, several of us did wish you would have been appointed to the library board instead of your husband, but that doesn't change the fact that we *are* sorry."

"Thank you, dear. Your honesty is refreshing. So many people do, what's that term? They 'suck up' to us, hoping we'll champion their cause. I thought of lobbying for your board position but I'm better at groundwork than becoming engaged in the nitty gritty. That was Quentin's forte. That's why our marriage worked so well." She turned her head away and said, "But Quentin was able to do a great deal of good during his lifetime. Don't overlook that."

"I'm sure he'll be remembered for many years," Helma

said. She rose from the uncomfortable chair. "I must go now. Thank you for inviting me in."

"Thank you for delivering this poem. It means so much to me."

Lily Boyd walked Helma onto the porch and held her small hand out to Helma. "Have a pleasant evening."

Helma felt the older woman watching her as she descended the steps and got in her car.

Two blocks from the mission, Helma spotted Ms. Moon opening the trunk of her car in front of a small house. She'd known Ms. Moon lived on this side of town but hadn't known exactly where. Ms. Moon rarely mixed her private life with her library commitments. She pulled two plastic bags of groceries from her trunk, both emblazoned with the Hugie's grocery store logo. Helma was surprised that Ms. Moon drove to the south side of Bellehaven to shop when there were other grocery stores closer.

Ms. Moon raised her head and Helma pressed the gas pedal, passing her house without turning to look at her. In her rearview mirror, she saw Ms. Moon standing in her driveway holding her grocery bags, gazing after Helma's car.

❧ chapter seven ❧

SURPRISES

Helma parked her car in the mission's parking lot, careful that all her windows were securely rolled up and all four doors were locked. An eight-foot chain-link fence surrounded the small lot. On the side next to the mission building were three kennels for the dogs of guests and residents. "Sometimes a dog is all a man has," Brother Danny had told her, "so we accommodate it."

The newest car in the lot was at least seven years old. Except for its pristine condition, Helma's Buick, now twenty-two years old, fit right in. She stepped around a misparked Ford with a bashed-in door and taped window, glancing in at the jumble of belongings filling the backseat. A yellow cat sat in the shade beneath the car and Helma noticed that the front passenger window was open far enough for the cat to climb inside. Bowls of food and water sat atop a pile of newspapers on the front seat. She passed a blue Dodge Dart with a handmade wooden luggage rack painted with faded peace signs and then walked through the gate to the sidewalk, making sure her purse was securely closed, flap side tucked against her body.

"Hey, Helm."

"Helma," she corrected, stopping to stare at Ruth who sat on the stair wall beside the front door of the mission. "Ruth, what are you doing here?"

"Well, can't you figure it out from the clues? This is my Major Barbara outfit." Ruth lifted the long brown skirt to expose sensible brown shoes. Helma was surprised Ruth even owned sensible shoes. She wore a short-sleeve black blouse with only the top button undone. Her bushy hair was pulled back into a severe tail tied by a brown ribbon. The one incongruity was her usual dramatic makeup, which over-powered her drab apparel. "Hot, though," she said, lifting her arms away from her body.

"Why are you here?" Helma asked again.

"Don't they always say criminals return to the scene of the crime?" Ruth guffawed. "Just joking. Why do you think I'm here? I've come to keep you company during your time of imprisonment, share your burden, give succor to the downtrodden." She raised her eyebrows at a tall, heavy-shouldered man entering the mission. He stopped and stared at Ruth with as much surprise as Helma.

Before he could say a word, Helma stepped forward and told him, "You can register at the desk inside the door. Dinner will be served in a few minutes."

"I know the drill," he told Helma, barely glancing at her, and touched his forehead toward Ruth in a kind of salute before he stepped inside.

"Besides," Ruth told Helma, "I have a surprise for you."

"What is it?" Helma asked.

"It'll be here later. You're not thrilled to see me?"

"Ruth," Helma tried to explain. "These men are not like the men with whom you normally associate."

"You'd be surprised," Ruth told her. She fanned her long skirt. "How did women stand it back in the olden days? And I bet they even had to wear underwear."

"Some of these men are criminals," Helma went on. "Or mentally ill."

"Or just down on their luck. Not to worry. I'm only here as a companion volunteer, no nefarious motives. What are we supposed to do?"

There'd be no deterring Ruth now that she'd dressed for the part, Helma knew. All she could do was hope that Ruth grew bored with her role before she created any trouble.

"We'll help in the dining room and then do whatever Brother Danny needs, most likely office work."

"And we're finished by eight?" Ruth asked. "Not as late as you stayed last night?"

"That was a mistake. I lost track of time. We'll finish tonight by eight o'clock. That's curfew for the men."

"Lock down time," Ruth said. "So okay, lead on."

Dinner, and also breakfast and lunch, was served in shifts. First to the men who were staying at the mission and forty-five minutes later, to the public, which included anyone who needed a meal—men, women or children—no questions asked. "All we require is a signature on a list," Brother Danny had explained. His eyes had twinkled. "God has shared a meal with us—more than once. So have Abraham Lincoln and Marilyn Monroe."

Helma stood behind a windowed counter and passed out breadsticks, then ladled steamed broccoli onto the men's plates. A fan stirred the air but the heat in the kitchen was stifling. To her left a small baldheaded man dished up pizza or fried chicken, or both, as much as a person was willing to eat. He was stooped, his head seeming to rise directly out of his shoulders and when he turned to look at Helma, he had to turn his entire upper body.

"It's a good time of year for vegetables," the bald man said, pointing to the broccoli. "A trucking company brought in fifty pounds this morning. Refrigeration problem."

"I had it easy today," Portnoy added, stepping between them and sliding another tray of hot chicken into the slot in front of the bald man. "Pizza came in from the Pizzeria, chicken from the Chicken Hut, cakes from the grocery store. Life is good."

"And if these hadn't been donated?" Helma asked.

"Somebody," he rolled his eyes heavenward, "always provides."

"Or Brother Danny," Helma said, wanting to see credit given where it was due.

"He's somebody, isn't he?" the bald man asked, stepping

back to his position in front of the chicken. "I'm Frank. You the librarian?"

"I'm Miss Zukas."

"Miss Zukas," he repeated, frowning. "I had a piano teacher in Boise named Miss Lukas. Don't suppose it's any relation?"

"I don't believe so." She glanced at the stack of dishes and silverware on the counter and asked, "Where are the napkins?"

Frank snorted and plunked a roll of paper towels on the counter. "You're looking at 'em. We live by donations here. Money doesn't go for *napkins*."

"Were you here last night?" Helma asked him. "When Mr. Boyd's body was discovered?"

"I've been here every night the past thirteen and a half months," Frank told her. "This is home for now."

A pudgy man wearing a football helmet with a set of antennae duct-taped to the dome stopped in front of Helma and held his plate close to his chest. A TV remote control covered with Chiquita banana stickers was visible in his shirt pocket. He regarded Helma defiantly. "George Bush was the president, you know and he hated broccoli you know and you know he didn't have to eat it."

"And neither do you," Helma told him.

His face fell and his shoulders slumped. He turned and walked away, swaying with each step like a cartoon sailor.

"Petey likes a little argument," Frank said to her, disapproval on his face. "You could have jollied him along a little."

"I beg your pardon?"

"Bet you don't jolly anybody along, do you? And nobody tries much to jolly you, either, am I right?"

When Helma stood looking at him uncertainly, he said almost gently, "Never mind, kid. Yeah, I was here last night. Why?"

"What did you see? Broccoli?" she asked the man who stood in front of her. He stood unsteadily, red-eyed and slightly vague.

"Double scoop," he said and Helma obliged.

"A dead man is what I saw," Frank continued. "That kid Tony said he popped him."

"Do you believe him?" Helma asked.

"I've seen crazier things."

"What's crazy about Tony having killed a man?"

Frank snorted. "Too soft. He's a talker, but then you never know. I believed O.J. for a long time."

"Did you see Tony after Quentin Boyd was killed?" Helma asked, remembering the pudgy figure rising from the black-berry bushes. She absently scooped broccoli onto the plate of a young man who looked like he should be in high school.

"Nope, but I saw him with the cookies."

"Cookies? Do you mean the Nutter Butters?"

Frank nodded. "Tony had a package when he and Skitz walked in. I was bagging garbage and saw it under his arm."

"Are you sure it was a package of Nutter Butters?"

He nodded. "Same as the cops found near the dead guy."

"Did you tell the police?"

"Hell, no." He scratched his nose with the handle end of the serving tongs. "Well, not until after Tony turned himself in, anyway. They were snooping around here this afternoon, looking for perps and proof, I guess."

"Hang up the yammer and serve the chow," a huge man wearing a too-small t-shirt grumbled.

"You got it," Frank told him and piled both chicken and pizza on a plate for him. The man turned down the broccoli but asked for five breadsticks. During the next lull in line, Frank turned again to Helma and said, "But I'll tell you what I *didn't* see: I didn't see any gun on Tony."

"He wouldn't have been carrying it in the open," Helma pointed out.

"Yeah, but you can tell. A guy moves different when he's got a weapon, like he's got one of those 'make my day' signs hanging around his neck. You watch sometime; you'll see what I mean."

Helma glanced over at Ruth, whose job was to wipe off the tables and keep the dessert table in order. "A friend of mine claims that, too," she said as Ruth sternly shook her finger at a man who'd obviously said something crude. Ruth didn't crack a smile; she was deep in her role.

"That your friend?" Frank asked, nodding toward Ruth. Then he went on as if Helma had answered in the affirmative. "I'll bet she *is* a pistol."

"Hey, look who's still here." Charlie stood in front of Helma, holding his plate in one hand and pointing his shortened finger at her. "It's the criminal librarian." He cackled, his mouth wide, displaying a rotting canine tooth.

"Move on, you old fart," Frank told him.

"Don't give this place a bad name, hear?" Charlie told Helma before he left the line, cackling to himself.

Forty-five minutes were up and the dining room was emptying of mission men, ready to refill with a long line of community members: street people, a few elderly men and women, a younger woman who spoke in a loud voice to no one, and several couples plus two single women with children.

Just as it had the night before, the tension in the dining room increased when the public entered. Many of the men lived by methods Helma didn't care to investigate. They might have been rivals or enemies on the street and now they had to sit peaceably together in the kingdom of the dining room, or leave. Helma recognized a few men who spent rainy days in the library, some reading, some pretending to.

Ruth stood in the center of the dining room, pivoting on her brown shoes and staring at the people lined up to eat. Her mouth opened, then closed to a thin line of red lipstick. A young mother looked at her and then looked down at the floor. Ruth threw her dishrag on the nearest table and stalked to the kitchen. "Who's in charge here?" she demanded.

"The guy upstairs," Frank told her.

"Cute," Ruth snarled, towering over him. "I'm speaking in the temporal sense."

"He's still upstairs," Frank told her. "Brother Danny; he'll be in his office."

"Kids," Ruth spat out, waving her arms, her face red, filling the kitchen. The man washing the dishes stopped and stared, open-mouthed. "There are *kids* out there. What the hell are kids doing here? This is a mission for derelict *men:* bums and addicts, drunks and dead beats. People like you guys. Who's taking care of the kids? They shouldn't be here." She stomped her foot. "This is Bellehaven, paradise nation, land of seafood and double latte fru fru mocha drinks. Not this."

"So go complain," Frank told her. "We'll turn the little buggers out."

"That's not what I mean, you hairless shrunken cretin, and you know it," and she slammed out of the kitchen.

"A pistol, all right," Frank said calmly, watching Ruth leave. "Won't do her any good."

The line had paused during Ruth's ruckus and now Frank motioned it forward. Helma, who'd already spent one night on the line and knew about the children, stepped to the freezer and pulled out the half gallon of chocolate ice cream she'd held back from the men.

"Can I have two scoops?" a boy of eight or nine asked as Helma dished out ice cream for him. He was slender and solemn with a leather patch over one eye.

"Barry," his mother admonished. She was young, in her mid-twenties, with long hair and restless hands. "High strung," Helma's mother would have called her. "Barry," she said again.

"He may have two scoops if it's all right with you," Helma told her.

"Yeah, okay. Go ahead then," she said, one hand combing and pulling at her hair, one foot pivoting back and forth as if she were practicing a dance step.

"Thanks lady," Barry told Helma as she added a second scoop of chocolate ice cream to his bowl.

"You're welcome. You may call me Miss Zukas."

"Zoo?" he asked as he reached for the bowl.

"Zukas," Helma repeated. "Two syllables."

The boy frowned and walked away while beside her,

Frank chuckled and said, "Two syllables? The kid probably thinks that's a rock group."

Ruth returned when only an elderly couple was left in the dining room, slowly and carefully finishing their meals, paper towels spread tidily across their laps. Cleanup had begun. Ruth's face was grimly determined. "Something has got to be done about this," she said. She glanced around the kitchen as if she could find the answer behind pans of leftovers or oversized containers of condiments.

"Ruth," Helma pointed out, "something *is* being done. At least the children are being fed here, even if it is a men's mission. It's one more option for them."

"It isn't right. Now give me that disgusting pot of glop."

Helma did and Ruth banged it on the counter before she covered it with plastic wrap. As she helped clean up the meal's remains, she banged and slammed at every opportunity. Ruth's life was one of equality: equal extremes. The intensity of her passions matched the intensity of her hatreds. Her joys equaled her rages, her causes her disinterests. The one thing that all these traits had in common was their lack of longevity. After a friendship that spanned two decades and two sides of the nation, Helma knew not to argue or join but to remain neutral.

"You're right. Something should be done," Helma said to Ruth who stalked past, carrying empty cans to the recycle bins and grumbling to herself.

Ruth turned and glared at her. "But *I* mean it. I really do."

Ruth's surprise, which Helma had forgotten, arrived before Chief of Police Wayne Gallant's promised visit. And it was delivered by Skitz. Ruth and Helma were working on the new donor database and the men of the mission were at prayer services with Brother Danny. Since it was another warm night, many of the men had disappeared after dinner, preferring to sleep outside rather than attend religious services.

Helma typed data into the computer while Ruth read names and amounts to her, adding comments wherever inappropriate. "I didn't think he'd be *this* cheap," or "Whew, must be a guilty conscience at work on this one."

"This is private information, Ruth," Helma reminded her.

Ruth looked around the small room. "So who's listening?" She made zipping motions across her lips. "My lips are sealed."

They were a quarter way through the green bean box. A shoebox filled with even more receipts had appeared on top of the green bean box and Helma envisioned forty-four more hours of good clean office work to get her through her sentence.

"Do you know Lily and Quentin Boyd were planning a trip to Venice next month?" Ruth asked after she read off, "Sherwood: twenty-five dollars."

"No, I didn't," Helma said, as she clicked her cursor to another column on the computer screen. "How did you know?"

"A friend who works at the Lucky Traveler. It was supposed to be a thirty-fifth anniversary trip or honeymoon or something kinky like that. She said it was first class all the way, top of the line, money-not-an-issue. You can make major bucks in real estate. Maybe the killer thought dear old Quentin was carrying a wad of cash."

Ruth was repeating gossip so Helma didn't answer except to acknowledge that the real estate business *was* more lucrative than other careers, "such as librarianship." "But he wasn't robbed," she added. "I saw a policeman with Mr. Boyd's wallet; there was still cash in it."

"It could have been an interrupted robbery," Ruth said. "Venice," she repeated, her voice softening and her eyes going distant. A form dropped from her fingers. "Imagine it. Canals and gondolas and guys in cummerbunds poling you through the city, singing drop-dead romantic arias, maybe. Wouldn't you love it?"

Helma rarely traveled to unknown places, feeling when she did that she'd turned invisible, ghostly even, slipping through other people's lives and landscapes, unlikely to see a person and certainly not a sight she recognized. She admitted she preferred the substantiveness of the familiar.

"Aha!" Ruth suddenly said, rising, her face broadened by her big smile that showed the majority of her teeth.

Two men stood in the doorway. One was Skitz and for a moment, Helma didn't recognize the slender, graying man with him. He was well dressed, distinguished, and successful looking. "Hello, Helma," he said, holding out his hand.

The years fell away as if a mask had been removed. The longish face with the cleft chin, dark eyes no longer distorted by glasses, the diffident tip of the head. "Forrest?" she asked as she stood. "Forrest Stevens?"

"That's right," he said, shaking Helma's hand in both his own, smiling at her, the handshake ending but still holding her hand.

"This is a surprise. I haven't heard from you since the reunion." Behind her, Ruth began to hum the Scoop River High School fight song.

Forrest couldn't seem to stop smiling, even as Helma gently removed her hand from his and took a small step backwards, feeling her back press against the computer.

"I know. I decided not to write because I had a lot to think about. I was ashamed of . . . everything. I'm here to make it up to you."

Helma's head swam. Images from the Scoop River High School's twentieth reunion flashed through her mind. Saturday Island, Forrest who'd portrayed himself as a doctor until he was cruelly unmasked as having a far less professional career, and his unexpected confession about his feelings toward her during high school.

"There's nothing to make up," Helma assured him. "Not a thing. How could there be? We discussed everything at the reunion; it's in the past, forgotten." She took two deep breaths and touched the stubborn curl on the left side of her head. "What brings you to Bellehaven?"

"I . . ."

At that moment, Ruth nudged her and intoned, "Da da da *dum*." Helma turned to see Wayne Gallant step through the doorway of the crowded office. He was still in shirt and tie, his hair neatly combed to cover his widow's peak. He was a big man and in the tiny office, Helma felt she hardly had room to breathe. They were all crammed so close together that each could have touched any other person in the room. She stood straight, trying to put the moment in perspective, trying to calmly inhale the stifling air and to make proper introductions.

"Forrest," she said, pausing to swallow the squeak in her voice, "this is chief of police Wayne Gallant. And this is Forrest Stevens, an old classmate from Scoop River, Michigan."

"Nice meeting you." Forrest stepped forward and shook the chief's hand, still smiling and finally answering Helma's question. "I'm here to convince Helma to marry me."

🌿 chapter eight 🌿

DEEPENING NIGHT

The five people in the little office stood as if a bright light had flashed in their midst and they were desperately trying to blink away its nimbus so they could see again. Pressure built in Helma's ears like a too-high, too-fast jet plane ride, the kind that required a yawn or scream to break.

Ruth shattered the silence by croaking "Marriage?" as if it were an alien word.

"Subtle move, guy," Skitz said with a disdainful curl of his lip.

"I mean it," Forrest said. He smiled the smile of a man who's seen the light. "Life's changed. I'm different now."

Wayne Gallant said nothing. He crossed his arms and studied Forrest, then Helma, his face unreadable. In the train yard below the mission, steel brakes screeched and train cars rumbled and slammed together.

Helma felt all those eyes turn to her, waiting for her response. She weighed the recent events and their consequences and heard herself say, "But we've just had a murder here."

"Well done," Ruth murmured beside her. "That clears up everything."

"That's what Ruth told me," Forrest said, still smiling. "Can I help?"

"*This* is your surprise?" Helma asked, turning to Ruth who

leaned against the wall, grinning as if she couldn't stop. "Forrest? Why didn't you tell me?"

Ruth shrugged. "Then it wouldn't have been very surprising, would it? Besides, it's really Forrest's surprise, not mine."

"I didn't call or write because I was afraid you'd turn me down before we could talk in person," Forrest explained. "Now, instead of just hearing it on the phone you'll realize how much I've changed—and how serious I am."

"I can't . . . I'm not . . ." Helma tried to say.

Skitz slouched against the wall beside the door. "Can we do this later?" He tipped his head toward Wayne Gallant and asked Helma, "Did you tell him about Tony or not?"

"I did," Helma said. She looked at Wayne Gallant, her thoughts some distance from the subject. "Didn't I?"

Skitz made motions between them. "Okay, so we've got a cop here. Discuss."

Wayne Gallant, who still hadn't said a word, now uncrossed his arms and looked at Forrest. "I have police business to discuss with these people. If you could . . ."

"Oh sure, come back later, you mean?" Forrest answered without looking away from Helma. "Or see Helma later, anyway. I mean, that's why I'm here. I still have your phone number so I'll phone you, Helma. I'll be here until Sunday. Unless you'd rather I called you at the library. Which is better?"

"Home," she told him. "After eight o'clock. I'm not home before then."

"She's committed to her work here at the mission," Ruth said in a solemn, almost holy, voice.

Forrest took Helma's hand again and looked into her eyes. He stood so close to Helma she could feel his breath against her cheek. "This is so like you, helping the unfortunate. I owe so much to you." He squeezed her hand once more and left the room, glancing back over his shoulder at Helma and giving a brief wave.

When Forrest had disappeared, Ruth said, "Twenty years erased as if they were nothing." She slapped her hands together with a sharp crack. "This could be a chance meeting in the high school cafeteria."

"This is not humorous, Ruth," Helma told her.

"Oh, come on. Give the poor guy a break. It'll be fun."

The chief of police was all business. He hadn't so much as glanced at Forrest's retreating figure. But he did frown at the spot where Skitz had been standing. Skitz too was gone. "Who was that?" the chief asked, nodding toward Skitz's vacant place.

"His name is Skitz," Helma told him. "He's a friend of . . ."

But Wayne Gallant had stepped into the hall, looking both ways and Helma thought she heard him curse briefly, quietly and vehemently. "*That* was Skitz?" he asked. "Tony's friend? You're sure?"

"Yes," Helma told him. "The two of them came to . . ."

"I'll be right back," he said and was gone, walking rapidly toward the lobby.

"Uh-oh," Ruth said. "I think our chief wasn't paying attention when he should have been. Distracted by the other buck in the forest. So who's Skitz, besides being a friend of Tony's, and are we speaking of the Tony who confessed to killing QVB?"

"We are," Helma told her. She explained how Skitz had appeared in the library and asked her to inform the police she'd seen Tony on the hill behind the mission.

Ruth whistled. "Bosom buddies, eh? No wonder the police want to talk to him. I predict, with total confidence, that Skitz will not be found anywhere on the premises."

"But he was just here," Helma protested, "in the same room with the chief of police. Why should he leave now?"

"You obviously weren't paying attention," Ruth said with exaggerated patience. "Skitz was *caught* in here so he tried to act cool and then took advantage of the diversion created by Forrest and slipped out." She shook her head. "Nope. He performed that move like a true felon. They won't find a trace of him."

The chief returned, his brow wrinkled, and Ruth said, "You didn't find him, did you?"

"No," he admitted. "I've called some men to check the grounds."

"Not a chance," Ruth said smugly.

"Did he mention to either of you where he was heading next?" Wayne Gallant asked, glancing again toward the spot where Skitz had stood.

"He appeared with Forrest and was only here a few minutes," Helma told him. "He didn't say anything beyond what you heard."

The chief was upset, that was clear to Helma. His jaw tightened when he closed his mouth. He clenched his hands into fists, then flexed them. She watched as he deliberately calmed himself, smoothing his face into professional neutrality, accomplished in a few seconds. A person who didn't pay as close attention as Helma might not even notice. "Can you show me where you thought you saw Tony last night?" he asked Helma.

"Certainly."

Ruth, Helma, and Wayne Gallant walked through the lobby and toward the back door, passing the chapel where Brother Danny, one hand raised, preached to a scattering of men who sat in folding chairs in various poses of interest. Seeing the trio, Brother Danny frowned and faltered mid-gospel, then returned to his text, noticeably speeding up.

"Was it only Tony you noticed last night?" the chief asked as they stepped into the evening air. "Not Skitz or anyone else?"

"Only Tony," Helma said. "Do you believe his confession?"

"We have to take every confession seriously," he told her.

Helma and Ruth stopped at the bottom of the slope where they'd stood the night before and Helma pointed out the area near the blackberry bushes where she'd spotted Tony.

"I didn't see anybody up there," Ruth said. She looked at Helma and shrugged her shoulders. "Just trying to be helpful."

The chief left them and climbed the slope, examining the ground as he went. The fragrant odor of ripe blackberries filled the air and the lowering sun glistened on the fat fruit.

"So what do you think of Forrest?" Ruth asked, watching Wayne Gallant gingerly pull aside the lower branches of a blackberry bush.

"I'm not prepared to discuss him right now."

"So how much preparation does it take?"

"Ruth, we're here to assist in the investigation of a murder."

Ruth blew out her cheeks. "I've done all the assisting I'm capable of. I'm going back inside to add up donations or sort used socks or something. If you guys get stuck and need my opinion, give a shout."

Ruth left and Wayne Gallant returned, brushing off his hands although Helma hadn't seen him touch anything except the blackberry bush. "Did you find any evidence?" she asked.

"There are signs that several people have loitered or sat around those bushes but nothing that could be connected with any specific individual," he answered, still looking up toward the bushes, sounding distant and preoccupied.

"You don't believe Tony's confession, do you?"

Before he could answer, Brother Danny joined them. He still carried his Bible. "I tried to call you earlier," he told Wayne Gallant, "but they said you were out. Did you find a good lawyer for Tony?"

"One was appointed for him," the chief told him.

"Do you think he's good?" Brother Danny persisted. He ran his thumb back and forth along the gold-edged pages of his Bible. "I hope he's good. I can't believe Tony is capable of hurting a living soul."

"He said he was revenging a friend," Wayne Gallant told him.

"Skitz?" Brother Danny asked and Helma saw the look of regret that flashed across his face. He was protective of the men, not to the point of harboring a criminal, Helma was certain, but definitely reluctant to implicate any of them.

The chief saw the regret, too. "Why would Tony revenge Skitz?" He glanced back at the building, as if he expected Skitz to step through the door and explain everything.

"I guess it'll be in your records anyway," Brother Danny said, his southern accent more pronounced. "Skitz and Tony had run off by the time the police showed up, but I'm told that a few days ago Skitz aggressively panhandled Quentin Vernon Boyd downtown. Both men got all hot and the police were called."

"You're saying Quentin Boyd and Skitz argued?" Wayne Gallant asked him. "Vehemently enough that somebody called the police?

Brother Danny clasped his Bible to his chest. "That's the way I understood it."

"Skitz was in the mission a few minutes ago," the chief told Brother Danny. "Have you seen him tonight?"

Brother Danny shook his head. "I'll ask inside. The men'll tell me more than they tell you." He took a step toward the building, then turned back. "But I can't see Tony using a gun. I know weapons are simple to use and too easy to get ahold of, but Tony isn't that kind of sophisticated."

The chief didn't answer and Brother Danny said, "I'll see if I can find Skitz."

"Tony does seem like a simple man," Helma said after Brother Danny left. "Skitz said he's a false confessor, that he confesses to all variety of crimes."

"You spoke to Skitz?" Wayne Gallant asked. He crossed his arms and regarded Helma. "About the murder? When?"

"He stopped by the library today," Helma admitted. Two men stepped out of the mission's back door. One of them broke a cigarette in half and gave it to the other.

"To ask you to help Tony?"

"It's my impression he feels responsible for Tony."

The chief glanced back toward the thick blackberry bushes at the top of the slope. "And maybe Tony's his fall guy."

"That's not fair," Helma protested.

"Maybe not, but it's not unheard of either."

"What has Tony told you about Skitz?" Helma asked.

The chief laughed ruefully. He leaned down and picked a ragged-leafed weed and methodically tore it into shreds as he spoke. "Skitz is a legend in Tony's mind. What he does say doesn't help much in identifying Skitz. No actual name. He can't recall anything unique he's said. You didn't notice any distinguishing marks, did you? Tattoos, scars, distorted limbs?"

"No," Helma told him. "He was wearing a t-shirt that said something about being everywhere you go."

" 'Wherever you go, there you are?' " he asked.

"Yes, do you know it?"

"It's not uncommon."

"Oh. Then it's no help?"

"It's another piece of the puzzle," he said, and Helma could tell he was trying to be kind. He shoved his hands in his pockets and frowned over Helma's head. She heard his keys jangle. She waited.

"Skitz hasn't been positively identified yet," he finally said. "I want to make that clear."

"But you know who he is," Helma guessed.

"When he was at the mission I didn't . . . I wasn't paying close attention. Could you identify him from a photo?"

Helma tried to conjure Skitz's face. So much of him was in his attitude, the way he glowered and slouched and bristled, the menacing stance that made one look away before his features registered. But under any condition, Helma Zukas was an observant woman. "Yes, I believe I could," she told the chief.

"Good." He removed a wallet-sized plastic folder from his shirt pocket and opened it before he gave it to her.

Helma tipped the folder until it caught the fading light. There were two photos, one an older man holding a number in front of his chest, the other one younger, a snapshot taken in what looked like a restaurant. She immediately ruled out the older man but the younger man was familiar. His hair was shorter, the features softer. "His eyes . . ." she said aloud.

"He's been on the run for almost two years," the chief said. "That can harden a man."

That was exactly it. The eyes of the young man in the photo were still direct, still alive. "This is Skitz," she said, touching the photo and handing the folder back to Wayne Gallant. "What did he do?"

"He disappeared before he could be apprehended."

"What was the charge?" she asked again.

He tucked the photos in his pocket before he answered. "He's wanted for questioning in a murder."

Helma gasped. "Murder?" she repeated. "He murdered someone? Who?"

"He's wanted for questioning in Florida," the chief told her. "He's a 'person of interest.' "

"Then you believe Skitz might have killed Quentin Boyd, too?" she asked.

"We'd like to discuss the possibility with him," he said in bland understatement.

"Is he considered armed and dangerous?" Helma asked.

"Definitely dangerous," he told her. "If you see him, use extreme caution."

"What about Tony?" she asked. "Is he wanted for murder, too?"

Wayne Gallant returned his hands to his pockets. "He's from California. His parents haven't spoken to him in five years—and don't intend to now, either. Simple kid easily led astray. They washed their hands of him years ago." He turned and looked out at the bay where the calm water reflected the sunset. "This is a million-dollar view," he said. "It's no surprise this area is going upscale." He nodded toward a battered Victorian house across the street surrounded by scaffolding. It had recently been reroofed and a pile of building rubble sat in the front yard.

"Quentin Boyd was a real estate developer," Helma pointed out. "His death may have been connected to his business and had nothing to do with Tony or Skitz."

"We're checking into it," Wayne Gallant said with maddening professional neutrality.

"Why didn't I hear the shot last night?" Helma tried.

"Listen," the chief said, tipping his head.

Helma listened but all she could hear were the trains switching. "The trains are too loud," she said. "I can't hear . . . oh. I remember hearing the trains while I was working in the office."

He nodded. "They easily would have masked any shots. And the timing fits in with the coroner's report." A maroon car slowed down, the occupants staring out the window and pointing toward the murder scene.

"And the cookies?" she asked. "Was there any significance to the package of Nutter Butter cookies?"

"We do know that according to one of the men, Tony had a package of Nutter Butters when he and Skitz entered the mission last night. We're checking the others," he told her. A third man exited the mission's back door, glanced toward the chief, and went back inside.

"Others? How can you check cookies?"

"They were on sale and purchased at Hugie's."

Helma frowned as the implications of his words became clear. "And people who shop at Hugie's can't take advantage of the sale price unless they have a Hugie's savings card."

It was a recent trend in grocery store shopping, a trend Helma didn't participate in: grocery stores offered special savings to customers who used their cards, and in exchange, their shopping habits were tracked by computer.

"That's right."

"So everyone who bought a package of Nutter Butters would have used his or her card and would be listed in Hugie's computer?"

"That's right," he said again.

"And Hugie's simply supplied you with a list of names of people who bought Nutter Butter cookies?" Helma asked incredulously.

"We *are* the police," he reminded her. Again, the keys in his pocket jangled.

"The library would *never* betray the names of its patrons or their reading tastes," Helma told him. "Not even under police pressure. Or government subpoenas. Never. We'd fight it through every court in the nation."

"These aren't patrons, they're customers and we're talking about cookies, not personal reading preferences." Wayne Gallant spoke more tersely and distractedly than normal, without the teasing light in his eyes that was often evident when he and Helma discussed crime. He acted as if Helma were nothing more than a simple witness.

"Nutter Butters or Baudelaire, privacy is what the public expects from those who serve them."

They stood silently for a few minutes in the early evening light, facing one another. The sun still shone, the air was midwest hot but just for an instant, Helma felt the slanting touch of autumn; a quiver in the air, the way the breeze smelled. A subtle shift of seasons was taking place.

"You weren't fond of Quentin Vernon Boyd," the chief said finally.

"No, I wasn't. Why?"

He gazed out at the bay again. "Someone else noticed and brought it to the attention of the police."

"They did? How?"

"An anonymous letter. They felt you had sufficient motive and opportunity."

Helma took a startled step backward. "What?"

"The letter writer appeared to be familiar with the workings of the library and the library board. Did you have words with Quentin?"

"Once. Not personal, but at the first—and only—board meeting he attended he stated that the library dispensed smut and that children should be barred from using the Internet. I disagreed with him. Can I see the letter? I might recognize the handwriting."

"It was printed on a laser printer. Standard Times-Roman font, one page, nothing unusual about it."

"Besides naming me as a suspect, you mean. *Am* I a suspect?"

"We'll have to question you, that's standard procedure. Carter Houston will probably do it. Don't be concerned about it. You were working here, right?"

Helma nodded. "I lost track of time and stayed beyond the

curfew in the small office where you found us tonight."

"Did anybody see you?"

Helma thought. She couldn't recall seeing another soul. "Not until later when Ruth arrived."

"Well, don't worry about it," he advised again. He folded his hands together and then turned them inside out. Helma braced herself for the crack of his knuckles but there was none. "This Forrest, you've been in contact with him since high school?"

"Only once, at our twentieth high school reunion," Helma explained. "He'd changed the facts of his life and circumstances caught him out."

"He lied?" the chief asked with unnecessary forthrightness. "Made himself wealthier, more successful and wiser than he really was?" He paused and rubbed his chin. "Now he's a changed man and he wants to marry you."

"He can't mean that," Helma said, her voice almost a whisper with wonder. "We hardly know each other. I mean, there was high school. He once said he . . ." She stopped and bit her lip, realizing she was voicing conjecture that was better left unsaid. "I spoke to Lily Boyd this afternoon," Helma told him, returning to the safer subject of murder.

"About her husband's murder?"

Helma shook her head. "She needed a poem for the memorial service. I dropped it off on the way here. She told me she drove Quentin to the mission last night on her way to a Young Readers meeting."

"That's right."

"And she attended her meeting?" Helma asked.

"She did. We checked." He looked up at the darkening sky. "The past couple of weeks have sure been beautiful, haven't they?"

"Beautiful," Helma agreed.

"Wish I had time to do some mountain hiking before the weather changes."

They were talking but not saying anything, marking time, and she suspected that the chief was just as grateful as she was when Brother Danny returned. "Nobody's seen Skitz since you showed up," he said. "He signed in to spend the night but I guess he left because he's nowhere in the building." He stiffly added, "The police you have inside the building will tell you the same thing."

The chief nodded as if the information were no surprise and handed Brother Danny his card. "Give me a call if you see him, will you?" Seeing Brother Danny's reluctance, he added, "I want to ask him a few questions. It's important."

"I'll go back inside now and help Ruth," Helma told the two men.

The chief nodded and for a moment looked as if he were about to say something else besides, "If Skitz contacts you again, call the police immediately."

"I will," she assured him.

🌿 chapter nine 🌿

PRIVACY ISSUES

"**W**hy's everybody so hot to talk to this Skitz guy, anyway?" Ruth asked as Helma drove through downtown Bellehaven. The stores were closed but several people strolled the streets in the warm evening. A group of young people, dressed in black from head to toe despite the heat, sat on the sidewalk on the corner by the post office, smoking cigarettes and drinking from cardboard cartons of chocolate milk.

"He was traveling with Tony, the man who confessed to Quentin Boyd's murder," Helma told her.

"Yeah, so? What's the story? You're holding back, Helma Zukas. I can tell by the way you're avoiding my eyes."

"I *am* driving."

Ruth hissed. "Come on. Is Skitz a murderer or something?"

"He's a 'person of interest' in a Florida murder," Helma conceded.

"Yikes." Ruth turned on her seat. "What kind of murder?"

"The chief didn't say. But he did advise me to consider Skitz a dangerous person."

"Oh, gee, thanks for the advice. And now this murderer's taken a liking to you?"

"I don't believe so. His concern was for his friend," Helma explained. "He thought if I told the police I'd seen Tony it would prove he couldn't have killed Quentin Boyd, despite his confession."

"Is this a gay duo?"

"That wasn't my impression."

"As if you'd know. Sounds like you'd better watch yourself." Ruth leaned out her window and waved to a group of people standing outside a popular bar. "Hey, Rick," she called. They all waved back. Ruth pulled her arm inside. "So in light of Skitz's past, do the cops think he pulled the trigger instead of Tony?"

"I don't know, but they're doubting Tony's confession."

"And Skitz has had prior experience. No wonder he's lying low."

Helma turned her Buick away from downtown toward the slope, the older residential area where Ruth lived. She slowed as a woman and a golden retriever crossed the street a half block in front of them.

"You know I'm not interested in Forrest," she told Ruth.

"Yeah, I know, but let him down easy, okay? The marriage thing was as much a surprise to me as it was to you. The word wasn't mentioned when he called me this afternoon. He's been putting himself right since our reunion and realistic or not, he's been doing it all for you. So don't crush him like an ugly bug, okay?"

"But it's not appropriate for me to encourage him . . ."

"Just be his friend for a couple of days, that's all. He'll be gone by the weekend." She turned to look at Helma, her eyes bright. "How'd the chief of police take Forrest's appearance? Jolt him a little?"

"He was curious," Helma admitted.

"Good." Ruth slouched lower in her seat, pulling her long skirt thigh-high and bracing her bare knees against the dashboard. "Quentin Vernon Boyd was an asshole, you know."

Something in Ruth's voice made Helma turn to look at her. "How well did you know him?"

"Not like *that*, Helma Zukas. Remember my vegetable show? Old QVB called it obscene."

"Vegetables?" Helma asked. "Why?" Ruth's show had consisted of colorful and distorted vegetables, most of them elongated or arranged in curious configurations. Ruth didn't often create representational work so that alone made the show unusual. Mostly her art consisted of bright slashes in colors that were not to be found anywhere in Helma's apartment or closet. Helma hadn't thought Ruth's vegetables made a very interesting show, although during opening night at the gallery the crowd had exhibited an inordinate amount of laughter and uneasy tittering.

"Beats me," Ruth said. "I guess he's tight with the building owner and he threatened Wally with tearing up the gallery's lease if Wally didn't cancel my show. Wally told him to take a hike. And that's all there was to it. He was one of those kinds of assholes who backs down when seriously confronted."

"Not in my experience," Helma told her, picturing again Quentin Vernon Boyd's enraged face at the library board meeting. "Yet he contributed to the community: the children's programs, grants to various charities, the flowers on First Street."

Ruth started to unbuckle her seatbelt, glanced at Helma and left it buckled. "The flowers were Lily's doing. Yeah, so okay he did some good but it got mixed up with what *he* believed were worthy causes. Why didn't he do something about those kids at the mission? He must have known about them. Unless it wasn't high profile enough. Maybe once you grow so powerful you have the ability to make changes for the good, you think you're powerful enough to pass judgment on what's a worthy cause and what isn't."

"Don't we all pass judgment on what constitutes a worthy cause?" Helma pointed out.

"Don't go reasonable on me, okay?" Ruth asked. She turned on Helma's radio, heard the first few notes of the easy-listening station it was tuned to, then switched it off. "Do you know what word foreigners think is the most beautiful in the English language?"

"I understand it's 'cellar door,' " Helma told her. She turned up the wide side street, passing Victorians mixed with colonials, ancient trees, and uniformly well-tended lawns.

"Nope. It's diarrhea," Ruth said.

"Can you attribute that information to a legitimate authority?" Helma asked.

"A legitimate authority?" Ruth repeated. "Is Kelly's Bar legitimate enough for you?"

"No."

"Well, look it up, then," Ruth grumbled. "Besides, 'cellar door' is two words, not one."

Helma stopped the car in Ruth's alley. Lights blazed from every room in Ruth's small house. "Do you have company?" Helma asked.

"Nah, I left the lights on in case we found another body or two and were late again. How many hours do we have left?"

"*I* have forty-four," Helma told her, "but there's no reason for you to do any volunteer work at the mission. It was thoughtful of you to help but it isn't necessary."

"No, I agreed to do it and I intend to. An elephant faithful one hundred percent and all that. If you see this Skitz again, run, okay?" And Ruth slammed the car door. Helma leaned across the seat and pushed down the lock on the passenger door, then waited until she saw Ruth step safely through the front door of her house before she pulled away, carefully avoiding the worsening potholes in Ruth's alley.

At the Bayside Arms, Walter David stood in the parking lot talking to two young men in a black Camaro. The bass of rock percussion boomed rhythmically and Walter David shouted to be heard.

As Helma stepped from her car, she heard him say, "Yeah, several people have applied. I'll let you know." The driver gave a thumbs-up sign and Walter waved them off. The Camaro rumbled to the street and away, thumping music in its wake. Walter waved to Helma and walked to meet her as she crossed the parking lot.

"Don't worry about them," he said before any greeting. "I wouldn't rent Mrs. Whitney's apartment to that crew. Not with all the work I've done here." He made a sweeping gesture to the Bayside Arms, the charge of which he took as seriously as any professional career.

"Who are the several people who've applied?" Helma asked.

Walter David blushed and shrugged. "Well, they *will*. August is just slow but it'll pick up in a week or so."

"Did Sara Hill, the woman who was here this afternoon, decide against it?"

"Not yet, but she's more interested in a ground-floor apartment. She would be perfect."

Helma agreed.

"And the woman who looked at the apartment last night?"

"She said our decks faced west, which was the wrong direction for the best tan. She's looking for a deck with southern exposure." He glanced away from Helma. "And fewer cats."

"I'm confident you'll choose a good neighbor." Helma thought a moment and asked, "Did you know Quentin Vernon Boyd?" Walter was one of the dwindling numbers of life-long Bellehaven residents and more than once he'd known a stray bit of vital information about Bellehaven or its inhabitants.

"Not really. But when I was a kid, he and his wife Lily paid for a few of us to attend a diabetic camp. They even rented a van and drove us to it. The newspaper took pictures and wrote an article. I still have it somewhere. He was a great man. Pretty rotten that somebody at the mission killed him." Walter waved to Mrs. Dibbs from 1B who, despite the late hour, was sweeping the landing in front of her door. "I've got those paint chips to show you," he called to her.

"Mr. Boyd was only found *near* the building," Helma clarified, waving to Mrs. Dibbs. "There's no proof that a mission resident killed him."

"I heard one of the residents confessed."

"The police are still investigating."

"Sounds pretty open and shut to me. Are you helping the police again?" From the open door of Walter's apartment, Moggy, his white Persian cat, meowed, and Walter David stiffened, just as Helma had seen many mothers in the library do when their young children cried out.

"I'm very busy at the library . . ." Helma began but Walter nodded as if she were finished and said, "Well, I'd better get moving. I'll keep you posted about what happens with the apartment."

As Helma climbed the outside stairs to the third floor she heard the sound of Walter David crooning to his cat.

On the doormat in front of Helma's apartment sat a vase of mixed flowers: daisies and carnations, a sprig of baby's breath. She stopped, recalling another, unhappy time when she'd discovered anonymous flowers on her doorstep. But no, she spotted a white card on a plastic trident holder inserted into the bouquet. She opened the card right there, before she even contemplated taking the vase inside her apartment.

"With regret for the past and hope for the future," the card read, and it was signed, "Truly, Forrest." There was also a P.S. at the bottom of the card and it read, "You're as beautiful as I remember."

Helma sighed and reinserted the card in its envelope, then carried the vase of flowers inside and set it on her counter. Here was a complication she hadn't expected and didn't have much experience in resolving. Her mind was so involved with Forrest, anonymous letters, and murder, that when her phone rang, she let it go unanswered, and since Helma Zukas didn't believe in the impersonal features of answering machines and therefore didn't own one, the phone call was missed completely.

During times that required intense thought, Helma frequently gave in to a compulsion to Cut Things Out. It had always been a habit of hers from the time she was a child and began by cutting out portions of pictures from *Life* magazines. She liked the intensity of having one single detail of an illustration excised from its surrounding and lying before her so starkly itself. Coupled with that was the challenge of cutting out pictures so precisely that no edge was discernible.

She now owned three pairs of German scissors in varying

sizes that had been made by a knife company and which cut
clean excisions at the slightest pressure, leaving no raw paper
edges or twisted inner angles. She was very good and sometimes when Helma had several perfectly excised illustrations,
rather than toss them into her trash, she glued several onto
a sheet of paper in configurations and colors she didn't really
understand but which pleased her. She stored these for a
while in the back of her closet of her second bedroom before
she relegated them to the trash, and no one was aware they
existed.

So now, after crossing off hours forty-seven, forty-six, and
forty-five on the chart inside her cupboard door, she sat on
her sofa beneath the beam of her halogen lamp, meticulously
cutting the large cartoonish word BOOM! out of a magazine
advertisement and thinking about Forrest and Skitz and Tony
and Quentin Vernon Boyd.

She was interrupted by her telephone ringing and this time
she answered it.

"*Labas, labas*, Wilhelmina."

"Hello, Aunt Em. Do you need any more help putting your
apartment together?"

"Apartments aren't so interesting," Aunt Em said, her re-
sidual Lithuanian accent turning "interesting" to "interes-
tink." "Everybody's talking about the murder here; you'd
think nobody'd ever been bumped off before."

Aunt Em had only recently moved to Bellehaven from
Michigan, after a "brain incident" that had altered her gentle
outlook on life and returned her to an earlier, secret self that
Helma still hadn't adjusted to.

"It doesn't often happen to people you know," Helma reminded her.

"Maybe not to *them*," Aunt Em said with a sniff. "Your
mother said that police chief always asks you for advice
when somebody gets murdered."

"That's not exactly . . ." Helma began, but Aunt Em went
on, "A man *should* ask a woman, that's one thing your
mother and I can agree on. So here's *my* advice. You tell it
to the policeman. You tell him that Mr. Boyd was snuffed

because of love or money. That's what it always comes down to: love or money."

"Not random acts?" Helma asked.

"Not in a little town like this. Love or money. That's all I have to say. Good night, dear."

As Helma picked up her scissors again, thinking of the endless permutations of love and money, she thought that surely in one form or another, Aunt Em was right.

Shortly after ten o'clock, Helma was startled by a noise. The late news was being broadcast on her television and she couldn't discern the sound's origin, but Boy Cat Zukas rose from his basket and stood like a Halloween cat. His golden eyes blazed toward the wall that Helma had shared with Mrs. Whitney. She clicked the remote and turned off the news, rising quietly to stand in the middle of the room, listening with the same intensity as Boy Cat Zukas. Her kitchen clock ticked, the refrigerator hummed. In the distance a car honked. She glanced at her telephone, deciding that if she heard so much as an unidentified creak she'd phone the police. After standing stone still for a full five minutes, hearing nothing unusual, she finally turned on the television again, muting the sound. Boy Cat Zukas resettled in his basket but every once in a while he'd cast a wary glance toward the wall of the empty apartment next door.

Helma sat straight up in bed. It wasn't another suspicious sound that had awakened her but her sleeping mind playing with a snatch of conversation and turning it into a shocking realization. This wasn't the first time her slumbering brain had made sense of the previous day or of a knotty problem, but seldom was the realization so disturbing. The digital numbers on her bedside clock radio read 3:19. She touched the lighted numbers with her fingertip before flicking on her bedside lamp. Three-nineteen in the morning but this couldn't wait, not even five more minutes.

Helma's bedside telephone was positioned so she could easily dial 911, even half asleep. Now, she quickly tapped out a phone number. As the telephone at the other end rang six, seven, then ten times, Helma pulled a pillow behind her back and arranged it against her headboard, prepared to wait however long it took.

Finally, on the sixteenth ring, Ruth answered. "This had better be good or you're dead."

"What did you mean when you said you'd *agreed* to volunteer at the mission?"

"Oh, it's you," Ruth said around a yawn. "Can't this wait until tomorrow? I'm not up for one of your semantic-splitting conversations."

"It cannot wait. What did you mean?"

"Refresh me. What did I say?"

"As you were getting out of the car tonight you said you'd agreed to serve the same hours as my sentence and then something about an elephant."

" 'An elephant faithful one hundred percent.' Didn't you ever read *Horton Hatches the Egg*?"

"No." Helma pulled her covers to her neck.

"Why am I not surprised?"

"Ruth."

"Okay, okay." Ruth yawned again in Helma's ear. "I didn't mean anything by it. Nada. No big deal. I'm serving time with you. I mean, what are friends for? I have the mission-ary spirit. Ha-ha."

"I've never known you to volunteer before."

"Funny, isn't it, how you can get inspired?"

Helma went silent, the only method she knew to unnerve Ruth. Quarreling Ruth loved, was inspired by even. Silence she couldn't stand.

"I'll hang up," Ruth threatened.

Helma held her tongue.

"Okay already. I surrender. I agreed to hang out down there with you. Safety in numbers etcetera ad nauseum. So big deal. It's good for my soul to give comfort to the downtrodden."

"With whom did you agree?"

"Aw, Helm. Come on."

"Helma," Helma corrected. "Was it my mother?"

Ruth snorted. "Surprisingly not."

Helma held her silence again and Ruth exhaled into the phone. "Last night you were late getting home, remember? Only now I guess it was the night before last, right? Oh God, he's going to kill me. Anyway, the chief had that meeting in Seattle and he tried to call you at home but there wasn't any answer. Picture his concern. Men can be so imaginative."

"The chief of police?" Helma asked stupidly.

"So he phoned me, thinking maybe you were here, even though he knows my house makes you crazy. That's how worried he was about you, Helma. Worried sick. That's all. You can't blame him. So I said sure, I'd go looking for you and being such a good friend and all, I'd even serve time with you."

"Wayne Gallant?" Helma asked.

"Well, spell it out if you need to," Ruth said.

But in her bedroom, Helma stared at nothing, her thoughts burning hot.

"You still there?" Ruth asked. When Helma didn't answer, she said, "Suit yourself. I'm going back to sleep," and hung up.

Helma did not go back to sleep. She spent the rest of the night sitting up in her bed and thinking of all the ways that she and Chief of Police Wayne Gallant disagreed about the right to privacy.

🌿 chapter ten 🌿

UNREST

At 5:30 a.m. Helma turned off her alarm and fell into a fitful doze, certain she wouldn't sleep more than a few minutes, if at all. How could she when her closest friend, no, make that *friends,* were in collusion, doubting Helma's common sense and self-reliance? Wayne Gallant had practically asked Ruth to *baby-sit* Helma. She closed her eyes, drew her knees to her chest and pulled the sheet over her head.

Banging doors and loud voices awakened Helma. Far from it being 6:00 a.m. as she expected, it was nine-thirty and the sun was high in the sky, burning into the new day. She sat up, already alert and listening despite a headache and dry mouth. The sounds came from Mrs. Whitney's empty apartment next door. So it had been rented after all. She'd have to deal with that later, but right now, she was late for work. Sitting on the edge of her bed, she dialed the library, sighing when Dutch came on the line.

"May I speak to Ms. Moon, please?" she asked. She didn't give Dutch her name but his next words left no doubt that he recognized Helma's voice.

"Ms. Moon is in a meeting and the library is currently open and we're extremely busy because we're short-handed. May I take a message?"

"Please connect me to George Melville, then," she said, choosing the next librarian in seniority, beyond herself. She had no intention of leaving a message that Dutch could deliver to Ms. Moon with aggrieved self-importance.

"Of course," he said, and just before he switched her to George, Dutch added in a low voice, "you're late."

"I'll be in by ten-thirty," Helma told George when he came on the line.

"Don't worry. The Moonbeam is too frenzied to notice."

"Has something happened?" Helma heard the soft click of computer keys. George was proud of his ability to "multi-task," but then she herself was making her bed as they spoke.

"Not that I know of," George told her. "She's taking the audit personally, saying it's an affront to librarians and God or somebody like that. You sick?"

"No, just delayed."

"Got it. I'll pass the word along if an emergency reference question rears its ugly head."

"Thank you."

Helma showered and dressed and was preparing a quick breakfast, still hearing voices next door, when she finally took a moment to open the shades on her kitchen window and glance down into the parking lot, intending to make a note of which moving company was so inconsiderate so early in the morning. She only heard men's voices.

But what she saw were two police cars sitting in the parking lot. She recognized the retired couple from 2C who always dressed in matching shirts. They stood beside the covered parking area, wearing plaid, faces raised and eyes shaded even though the sun was behind them. They appeared to be intently watching unfolding events on the third floor.

Helma turned off the tea kettle on her stove and stepped outside onto the landing of her apartment. Fog had already burned off and the day was sunny, without hope of a cloud, but still the slightest haze hung in the air. The *Bellehaven Daily News* lay on her mat and she absently picked it up and tucked it beneath her arm.

The door of apartment 3E stood wide open. Men's voices came from inside, one of which she recognized as Walter David's.

Helma was not one to interfere with police procedure so

she cautiously took a single step inside the empty apartment, which still smelled of Mrs. Whitney's perfumed deodorizers. She was naturally prepared to leave the instant she became an impediment to an investigation. A policeman wearing plastic gloves examined the kitchen sink, another spoke with Walter David, and she glimpsed a third policeman just stepping into a bedroom off the hallway. A shaft of sunlight lay solidly across the green carpet, unhampered by furniture or possessions.

Walter David saw her first. "Did you see anybody?" he asked, stepping away from the policemen. He was distraught, she could tell because he still wore his Seattle Mariners' cap inside the building. He held the apartment key in his hand, twisting it between his fingers.

"When?' Helma asked. Through the sliding glass door onto the balcony she saw Boy Cat Zukas leap across from Helma's balcony to the railing of the vacant apartment. He glanced inside, then began washing himself.

"Last night maybe, or this morning. Somebody spent the night in here. I was planning to show it at ten and I came up to open the windows." The policeman said nothing, only listened intently to Walter and Helma's conversation.

"The trespasser was here when you unlocked the door?" Helma asked.

Walter vigorously shook his head. "Gone, but there was an empty smoked oyster can in the sink and banana peels and a half-eaten package of cookies on the counter."

"Nutter Butters?' Helma asked.

He frowned and the policeman glanced sharply at her. "Oreos," Walter David said. "Most of them had the centers eaten out of them."

"I thought I heard a noise between ten and ten-thirty last night but nothing else disturbed me until I heard you this morning."

"Can you fix the time any closer?" the policeman asked.

"I remember that the newscaster had just finished a story about Seattle having the seventh worst urban sprawl of any city in the nation. You might check with the station as to its air time."

"Will do," he said as he jotted in his notebook.

"Did the intruder damage the apartment?" Helma asked Walter. She glanced around the vacant living room. It was spotless, the trails of the vacuum cleaner still visible on the carpet where the police hadn't walked.

Walter shook his head. "No, luckily. I should have locked the dead bolt. Anybody could have slid a credit card up the jam to open the lock. But they didn't turn on any lights or I would have seen them." He jiggled the key. "I think I would have, anyway."

The doorway darkened and Helma turned to see Wayne Gallant, his bright blue eyes focused on her. "Are you all right?" he asked. He wore suit pants but no jacket, as if he'd come here straight from his desk.

"Of course. Why shouldn't I be?" Even to Helma, the words sounded snappish.

He tipped his head slightly, looking momentarily uncertain, then became all business, ignoring Helma and talking to the three other policemen and Walter. Helma had assessed the situation to her satisfaction and slipped out the door and back to her own apartment, locking the door behind her, the dead bolt, too. Inside, she removed the newspaper from under her arm and set it on the counter. The clever fold the papergirl used came undone and the paper fell open to the front page.

Did you buy Nutter Butters? read the headline beneath *President denies any wrongdoing* just above *Mideast Peace Talks Scheduled.* Helma picked up the paper and skimmed the article. Hugie shoppers were outraged to discover policemen on their doorsteps questioning their snack habits. "We only cooperated with the police," a Hugie spokesperson explained, "to further their criminal investigation." But shoppers weren't buying it, claiming invasion of privacy whether the Nutter Butters were a clue in the murder of a prominent citizen or not. "I'm turning in my card," said one woman who declined to give her name but claimed tearfully that she was the butt of jokes in her diet club. Only a few shoppers were able to supply the police with proof they hadn't dropped their Nutter Butters beside the body of Quentin Vernon Boyd. Allowing herself a moment's satisfaction, Helma hoped Wayne Gallant's newspaper had been delivered on time and that he'd seen her own concerns echoed by the populace of Bellehaven.

When Helma finally left her apartment, the policemen were gone and Mrs. Whitney's door was closed and presumably locked, but Wayne Gallant stood at the bottom of the steps, his elbow resting on the railing, curiously reminding her of a scene in *Gone With the Wind*. She felt his eyes on her as she descended the steps but kept her own focused on the fir tree at the edge of the parking lot. On the bottom step she gave the chief a curt nod, then walked past.

"Helma?" he asked.

"Yes?" she inquired politely, turning only halfway round.

"Did you see Skitz last night after you left the mission?"

"No." She forgot her anger for a moment and gasped, pivoting to face the chief, dropping her blue bag. "Did Skitz break into the apartment?"

He picked up her bag and handed it to her, hefting it first as if weighing it. "It's a possibility. He may still be in Bellehaven even if he didn't spend last night at the mission."

"But how would he have known Mrs. Whitney's apartment was empty?" she asked. When the chief hesitated, she answered for him, "Unless he's been watching me."

The chief nodded. His face was grave. "Can you think of any reason why he'd follow you?"

"No. I've spoken to him twice but that's all."

"Did he threaten you in any way?"

Helma shook her head. "No, I didn't feel threatened, only . . . uncomfortable."

"Was he angry? Unstable?"

"Sullen and manipulative perhaps." She tried to explain, raising her voice over the engine noise of a water delivery truck pulling into the driveway of the Bayside Arms. "There's an undercurrent of rage, and isn't it obvious his life is unstable? Is his friend Tony still being held?"

The chief nodded. "He knows a couple of details about the murder that it would be too coincidental to fabricate."

The curtain of the first-floor apartment opposite them was pulled aside about six inches and Helma lowered her voice, stepping closer to Wayne Gallant. "Then you don't believe Tony murdered Quentin Boyd?"

He didn't directly answer her question. "He might have witnessed Quentin Boyd's death. If that's true, to release him could put him in danger."

"From Skitz?" Helma asked.

Walter David stepped out of his apartment and raised his hand in a half wave to Helma and the chief, then walked toward the stall where he kept his motorcycle. The chief watched Walter, saying, "Possibly."

"Have you found the gun?" Helma asked.

"Not yet."

"Skitz said Tony claimed he ran away from the scene and threw the gun in the bay." The chief didn't answer and Helma went on. "By now you must know what caliber of handgun you're looking for."

"That's true, we do," he said, and Helma tucked away the fact that Quentin Vernon Boyd had been shot with a handgun. She remembered the way he'd looked lying on the ground behind the mission and deduced the weapon hadn't been a high-caliber handgun.

"You're drawing conclusions," he said, smiling at her. "I can see it happening before my eyes. Care to share them with me?"

"I'm sure they're nothing you don't already know," Helma said.

"I see. Well, it might be a good idea if you stayed with a friend until this case is cleared up."

"Perhaps the same friend you asked to keep an eye on me at the mission?" Helma asked.

Maddeningly, he said nothing, only looked at her mildly and Helma wondered if this was a police tactic, comparable to librarian tactics to handle unruly patrons: disarm the angry person by not responding to his or her challenge.

"I'm perfectly capable of serving my own sentence without help from you and Ruth," she told him.

"I believe you," he said, still mild, "but now Ruth is volunteering at the mission and I'm sure she's got herself involved in its operation."

"She intends to do something about the children who come in with their parents for meals," Helma told him.

He nodded, his face saddening. "Those are the tough ones."

But Helma was not to be swayed by any show of softness. In fact, his untroubled manner about the matter with Ruth piqued her enough that she went on, "You could have told me you'd asked Ruth to . . . baby-sit."

His eyebrows raised. "Really?"

Helma shifted her purse from one shoulder to the other. "Maybe not," she conceded, "but I don't appreciate it."

He didn't apologize, didn't explain, only said, "Call me if you sense you're being followed, if you even think you see Skitz, or if anything unusual happens at the mission."

Helma refrained from saying that *everything* that happened at the mission was unusual. They said their good-byes with unaccustomed formality and as Helma climbed into her car, she suddenly remembered Sara Hill. She got out of her car and walked back to the chief, who still stood beside the staircase, facing her direction.

"Excuse me," she said. "It may not be relevant but there was a woman here yesterday looking at Mrs. Whitney's apartment. Her name was Sara Hill and she mentioned seeing a man around the building who seemed . . . rougher than she expected."

"Rougher?" the chief asked.

"I believe he spoke to her," Helma continued, "and may even have masqueraded as a friend of the manager's."

He jotted Sara Hill's name in his notebook and looked up. "You didn't see him?"

"No."

"Thanks." He slipped his notebook back into his pocket. "I'll check it out."

"You're welcome," she told the chief and returned to her car, continuing on her way to the Bellehaven Public Library, driving along the curve of the bay without noting the shimmer of sun on water or the passage of a gleaming white tugboat, and once—despite the crime that had led to her current sentence—driving through a yellow light.

Ms. Moon was sequestered in her office with reams of computer printouts. No whale song or sitar music wafted through her office's open door. She wore half-glasses and punched in numbers on an adding machine that clicked like rain in her green, green office.

"Something's up," George Melville said as Helma passed his desk. "Maybe she'll end up at the mission, serving the homeless at your side."

"Are you suggesting Ms. Moon may have committed a crime?" Helma asked.

"Why else is she hiding in her leafy bower with an adding machine? And the auditors arrive on Monday. Coincidence? Uh-uh, I don't think so. Did you ever think that QVB wanted an audit for a legitimate reason? He had inside information."

The words "inside information" reminded Helma of the anonymous letter naming her a suspect in Quentin Boyd's death. "Do you remember the board meeting where I disagreed with Mr. Boyd?" Helma asked George.

George grinned as if she'd asked an amusing question. "I wasn't there but oh boy did I hear about it. Harley acted like he was terrified he was going to get hit by crossfire." He ducked to illustrate his point.

"Then everyone in the library knew about it?"

George laughed. "Right down to Jack the janitor and half the city, I'll bet." He grinned apologetically. "It was a hot topic around here for a few days. Why? Scared it's going to come back to haunt you?"

"I only wondered who else knew, that's all," Helma told him. Wayne Gallant had said that whoever had written the letter to the police had been familiar with the library's inner workings. According to George, *anyone* in the library and half the people outside it could have written the letter.

Helma was a few minutes into her three-hour stint on the reference desk when she spotted Trudy Jones in the education section. Trudy was a regular and seeing her reminded Helma of an article she'd read a few months earlier in the *Bellehaven Daily News*. She clicked on the Bellehaven organization file on the reference desk computer, quickly typing in "Young Readers," the association meeting Lily Boyd had attended the night her husband was killed. In less than a second, there it was, scrolling past on her screen: the particulars of the Young Readers organization. Trudy was its secretary/treasurer.

Helma blanked the screen and walked to the education shelves. "Are you finding everything all right?" she asked Trudy.

Trudy was tall, maybe even taller than Ruth, but she didn't emphasize it like Ruth did and seemed much smaller. She was slender and wore flat shoes and neutral colors, her brown hair cut in a style close to her head. Trudy was an active community force—and someone noted for voicing her opinion.

"Hello, Helma, I'm doing fine, thanks," she said and returned a book on student motivation to the shelf. "Still a little shaken up over Quentin Boyd's death, though. Lily was at our meeting when it happened, you know."

"That's terrible," Helma sympathized.

Trudy nodded. "The police came to break the news just as she finished giving a report on a creative writing project they're trying in the Seattle schools. It was like all the air went out of her, like she was going to just shrivel away to nothing, or maybe crash and burn like the Hindenberg. Did you ever see that old newsfilm?"

Helma nodded, encouraging Trudy to continue.

"Terrible, but it was better that Lily was with us than home alone. Can you imagine? I believe in giving people every chance but I hope they string up that man from the mission who killed Quentin."

"Was Quentin involved in the Young Readers group?" Helma asked.

"He headed a fund-raiser for us once." She hesitated and ran her fingers along the spines of the top shelf of books. "He liked to run things his own way," she said. "It upset a few people."

"Anyone specifically?" Helma asked.

"Well, me, for one. I was in charge of ticket sales. I assure you it was titular only. Quentin did it all. I don't like to badmouth the dead, but I bet he acted the same on all his committees. Lily was more patient with him than I could ever be. It's hard to figure out what makes a marriage work, isn't it?"

Helma nodded. "Lily told me once she was nervous about speaking before groups."

Trudy laughed. "She has been as long as I've known her. She gets nauseous and turns into jelly, but then she always pulls it together and does a beautiful job. I saw Quentin coaching her once before she gave a speech. He could be tender when he wanted to." She reached for another book. "A complicated man, I guess."

Later, a whispered exchange caught Helma's attention because few people whispered in the library anymore; they simply spoke out loud as if they were in a grocery store. Helma raised her head to see Lily Boyd walking toward her. Two women near the periodical shelves stared, their heads close together and speaking in hushed tones behind upheld magazines.

"Hello, Miss Zukas," Lily Boyd said. She wore a dark blue long-sleeved dress that set off her silver hair and made her appear even tinier. "I'm so sorry to bother you again but I've thought of another poem that would be more appropriate for the . . . to the situation. It came to me in the middle of the night last night. Have you ever had that happen to you?" she asked, then went on without waiting for an answer, "Can you locate the verses that were spoken in that movie a couple of years ago, the wedding and funeral movie?"

"Certainly," Helma told her, knowing immediately that she meant "Funeral Blues," the Auden poem in *Three Weddings and a Funeral*, requested so often since the movie was filmed that the librarians kept a copy at the reference desk.

Helma found the poem and gave it to her to copy. Lily Boyd took it but still stood in front of the desk. She glanced behind her. No one else waited for assistance. "I understand you can identify the man who shot my husband," she said in a low voice.

"Not at all," Helma told her.

"But you gave a statement to the police," she persisted. Then she flushed and touched Helma's hand. "I'm sorry. I know I'm talking about confidential matters. The chief of police is naturally keeping me apprised of the investigation." She shook her head. "I feel such a need to know."

She looked beseechingly at Helma, and Helma thought that not only was Wayne Gallant intruding in her life but he was relating information she'd given him in what she believed was confidence. But then, didn't Lily Boyd have a right to know? Still, if there had been anyone within hearing distance, Helma wouldn't have divulged as much as she did. "My identification may actually help clear the man they've arrested."

Lily nodded. "The chief did intimate that might be the case. If he's not the one, then he should be cleared. I couldn't bear to see the wrong man convicted, not on top of this. I just wish . . ." She smiled sadly at Helma. "This library is a credit to Bellehaven. Even though Quentin might not have been the board member you'd hoped for, he and I were both proud of our association with this institution." She glanced at the poem, then smoothed it flat on the desktop. "It's surprisingly hard to think of your husband's faults after he's dead. In a way, death transfigures a person, doesn't it?"

"We forget the worst," Helma agreed.

Lily Boyd held up the poem. "Thank you again. This means a great deal to me."

*   *   *

"I tried to phone you last night but there was no answer," Forrest told Helma when she answered her phone. "Is your answering machine broken?"

Helma sat at her desk in the workroom, a list of history CD-ROMS in front of her. "Choose only one for the collection," Ms. Moon had written in the top margin. Helma knew Ms. Moon meant the least expensive.

"I'm sorry," Helma told Forrest. "I don't have an answering machine and I didn't get home until late. Are you enjoying your visit?"

"I am. This is a beautiful city." She heard him take a breath; his voice dropped in timbre. "Seeing you—I mean just the two of us—is the only thing that would improve it. I'd like to invite you for a drink tonight after your volunteer work."

"I'm not finished until eight o'clock," Helma warned him.

"I'll meet you wherever you say," he said. His words came in a rush, as if he'd been holding his breath, waiting for her reply. "Just name the place."

Helma remembered Ruth's admonitions and gave in. "Eight-fifteen at the Bay House," she said, naming a quiet restaurant/bar with a view of the bay.

"Got it," Forrest said. "Great. Thank you."

Half of Helma's roast beef sandwich still sat on her plate when she rose from her table at Saul's Deli, and thirty-one minutes still remained of her lunch hour.

"I can wrap it up for you," the waitress offered, "for a little midnight snack," but Helma declined, disliking the way condiments soaked into bread over time.

Dietrich Morgan's insurance office sat in the heart of downtown Bellehaven, on the second floor of a renovated department store that had abandoned downtown for the mall. She already knew he would be in his office, having phoned earlier and discovered he had a lunch date at one o'clock because of an appointment in his office at noon.

His secretary wasn't at the front desk and Dietrich himself stuck his head out of the inner office. He frowned, half recognizing her. "I'll be with you in five minutes," he told her, holding up his hand spread-fingered, and disappeared into his office. Behind him, Helma saw the stuffed head of a prong-horn antelope hanging on the wall, gazing down at Dietrich's desk.

While she waited, Helma sat in the shadow of an overgrown ficus and read an insurance brochure that advised her she was at risk for every calamity known to man or woman and more than likely she wasn't properly prepared.

Dietrich Morgan ushered his appointment, a small man with a stunned expression, through the office and out the door, heartily congratulating the man for making "excellent choices for your family's future."

He closed the door and turned his smile on Helma, greeting her with a warm handshake. "What can I do for you, Mrs. . . . ?"

"Miss," Helma corrected. "Helma Zukas. We met at the mission the night that Quentin Boyd was killed."

He remembered her, extinguishing his heartiness, slowly shaking his head and brushing his hand through his thick gray hair. "Yeah. Bad night. Are you here to talk about that or insurance?"

"Mr. Boyd."

Dietrich sat in the chair opposite her and crossed his ankle over his knee. "I already spoke to the police. Your interest is . . . ?"

"Purely personal," Helma told him. "If you don't care to speak with me about Mr. Boyd, I'll leave immediately."

He clasped his hands over his knee and regarded Helma, his expression growing more guarded. "A straight shooter," he said, sounding as if he were almost paying her a compliment. "Go ahead."

"Can you tell me if Quentin had any enemies?" Helma asked.

"Sure he did. You don't get that rich or wield that much power without making enemies."

"Who were they?"

"I couldn't say exactly. People were always griping about

his pushiness. But then, he got things done so they couldn't gripe too loud." He smiled the way people do when they recalled a difficult person they didn't have to deal with ever again. "He was the most hard-headed person I ever met."

"Was there any other reason to hate him besides his pushiness and hard-headedness?"

"Not that I know of. He had a good reputation in his business deals." He laughed. "But maybe that means he just never got caught."

Helma remembered what Aunt Em had said about love and money. "Did he and his wife have a good relationship?"

"Do you mean did he fool around? Probably not. I would have heard about it if he had. I don't actually know much about his personal life."

"But he didn't approve of the mission?" Helma asked. The phone on the receptionst's desk rang and Dietrich ignored it.

"Quentin lacked patience for people who didn't pay their fair share, at least in his opinion. But he wouldn't have voted against the grant if there was good publicity connected to it." Dietrich grinned. "Whatever Quentin did, he had an ear out for the spin."

Helma glanced at her watch. She had nine minutes before her lunch hour ended. "How long did you know Quentin Boyd?"

He shrugged. "Twenty years, give or take a few."

"And you were good friends?"

"I wouldn't say that. Some golf, a few of the same committees. We were acquaintances. Quentin had a lot of acquaintances, but no good friends that I know of."

Helma picked up her purse and prepared to leave. "His wife Lily said you were Quentin's closest friend."

A look of surprise crossed his face. "Isn't that the damnedest thing?" he asked softly.

Helma left Dietrich Morgan's office and hurried through downtown Bellehaven. As usual, when she was in public, several people nodded or said hello, recognizing her but not recalling *how* they knew her. As she passed the drugstore, a popular spot for panhandlers and the location of Skitz and

Quentin Boyd's quarrel, her eye was caught by the furtive movement of a child slipping behind a woman.

Helma stopped, recognizing the woman and then, as the smaller figure peeked around the woman's body, she saw the leather patch over one eye and recognized Barry, the boy she'd given two scoops of chocolate ice cream to the night before.

"Hi, Miss Zoo," he said.

"Hello, Barry," she said. She then turned to his mother who, even when she stood still, seemed about to bob or tap or slip away, and said, "Why isn't this child in school?"

"He got out early today."

A flush reddened Barry's face and he bit his lower lip. The woman nodded to the cup on the sidewalk in front of her that held a few coins. "Spare any change?"

Barry turned his head away and Helma, who had never given a panhandler a cent in her entire life, slipped a dollar into the woman's hand and said, "We'll expect you at the mission for dinner tonight."

The woman shrugged. "Sure. Why not?"

❧ chapter eleven ❧

INQUISITION

Early in the afternoon as Helma returned a copy
of *Value Line* to the reference stacks, she passed Helen
Orem, a former library board member. Helen taught at the
local college and was a dedicated library user. She stood in
front of the talking book collection, fanning herself with a
back issue of *Alternative Healing*, her dark hair piled on top
of her head, as if she'd pulled it up in a hurry to lift it off
her neck.

"There's a silver lining for you," she said.

"I beg your pardon?" Helma asked, pausing beside her.

"The loss of Quentin Vernon Boyd, Mr. QVB. I heard he
advocated chaining the books to tables with every word or
idea he disapproved of blacked out with indelible ink. He
would have happily set the library back a few hundred
years." She studied Helma's face, then raised her eyebrows
and said, "*You* can't disagree with me. I understand you
made your feelings clear enough at the last board meeting."
Before Helma could respond, Helen Orem glanced over
Helma's shoulder and smiled. "Hello, detective," she said.
"I've been meaning to call you about speaking to my psy-
chology class this fall."

Helma turned to face Detective Carter Houston, whose
small eyes pierced through his glasses at her, on his face the
same determined expression as usual, no matter what the
situation. He wore his dark suit and shiny black shoes and
appeared impervious to the heat. Ruth had declared once, "I

don't think the guy *has* sweat glands." Helma couldn't imagine his small feet clad in sneakers. "Detective Houston," she acknowledged.

He blinked at Helma without smiling and turned briefly to Helen Orem. "I'd be glad to," he said. "Call the office and leave me some optional dates. Fridays are the only days I'm unavailable." He looked back at Helma. "I have some questions I'd like to ask you, Miss Zukas—in private."

Helen Orem glanced curiously between Carter Houston and Helma. "Good luck solving this case," she told him. He nodded without comment.

Even though the library wasn't very busy, it also wasn't very private, so Helma led Detective Houston to the old typing room where coin-operated typewriters had once been available for public use. Now the room was used for storage of reams of computer paper and occasionally for private study. An old oak library table sat in its center with four metal and naugayde chairs around it. At least once a month someone offered to buy the oak table from the library.

Helma chose the chair at the head of the table and sat down, folding her hands in front of her. "How may I help you?" she asked.

Carter sat opposite her and, when he made an extended show of flipping through pages in his notebook, Helma took a more forthright approach. "I understand the police department received an anonymous letter naming me as a suspect in Quentin Vernon Boyd's homicide."

The detective's shoulders bowed as if he were a hunter whose quarry had spotted him first. He clicked his pen twice against the table and turned to a clean page in his notebook, sitting taller. "It was curious, all right, for an unknown person to implicate you."

"Very," Helma agreed.

"You weren't fond of Mr. Boyd?" he asked.

"I didn't know Mr. Boyd personally," Helma said, and seeing his lips purse to a thin line, she added, "but it's completely true I did not agree with his theories of libraries.

Limiting public access to knowledge counters the purpose of libraries—and librarians."

"I see. And where were you when Mr. Boyd was killed?"

"I was at the mission, as I'm sure you already know, working on a database in a small room after hours and I'm unaware of anyone who might have seen me and could attest to that fact, so you only have my word. Although that *is* where my friend Ruth found me shortly before the body was discovered."

"Ruth Winthrop," he said. Not a question, so Helma didn't respond. He glanced down at his perfectly manicured nails and flexed his pale fingers. "And the figure you claim to have seen in the bushes?"

"It wasn't a claim," Helma clarified. "I *did* see a figure, which I took to be Tony, the man who confessed to Mr. Boyd's murder. But I doubt if he would have had time to get rid of the gun so effectively—I understand you've scoured the area—and still return in time to watch the discovery of the body."

He tipped back his head and looked at her from the bottoms of his eyes. "Suppose somebody got rid of it for him so he could conceal himself in the bushes to watch the excitement?"

"Is that what he told you?" Helma asked politely. She caught sight of movement outside the room and spotted Eve peeking in through the glass door, wagging her fingers at Helma.

Carter Houston looked over his shoulder but Eve was gone. He turned back to Helma, scowling. "Where was Daniel Davis at the time?"

"Who?" Helma asked.

"Brother Danny."

"He returned from the store just before the body was found. He was carrying a box of sugar cubes."

"Was he out of breath?"

"No." Helma thought and amended. "Well, perhaps a little because he was concerned about meeting the grant inspection committee on time. He was perspiring."

He leaned forward slightly and looked Helma straight in the eyes. She saw her own pale reflections in his lenses. "Do you own any type of firearm, Miss Zukas?" he asked in a low voice that reminded Helma of one of the urgently sincere police dramas on television.

"No."

"Are you sure?"

"Yes. I can say with certainty that I do not own any type of firearm."

He jotted that fact in his notebook and asked, "Have you seen the man who calls himself Skitz?"

"Not since last night, when the chief was at the mission. No one's told me his given name."

"At the moment, it's police business."

"Why is he called Skitz?"

The smug hunter's look returned to Carter's face. "I thought you would have figured that out by now since you work with words. It's short for 'schizoid,' as in 'schizophrenic.'" On that triumphant note, he rose from his chair, slipped his notebook into his pocket, tucked and smoothed himself and said, "This is a dangerous man and I suggest you use extreme caution. If you do see him call us immediately."

Helma and Detective Carter Houston went their separate ways at the door of the typing room, the detective heading toward the front door, Helma toward the workroom. She hadn't taken two steps when she noticed Ms. Moon, her lips tight, enter the public area through the workroom door.

Before Helma could step out of Ms. Moon's line of vision, a man Helma recognized from the food line at the mission glanced up from the nearest table. He was taking notes from the want ads and he smiled at her. Helma nodded and he said in a polite voice that certainly carried to both Ms. Moon and Carter Houston, "I'll see you at dinner tonight."

A half hour after Carter Houston left the library he phoned Helma.

"Is there another question I can answer for you?" she

asked the detective, keeping her voice as polite as if he were one of their best library patrons.

"Maybe," he said. He paused and Helma waited.

"We could make it pretty discreet," he said, being unusually oblique. "It could even be a woman. Somebody to watch who's in your vicinity, that kind of thing."

"Are you asking me if I want police *protection*?" Helma asked.

"Well, yes."

"Was it the chief of police's suggestion?"

Carter didn't answer.

"No thank you," Helma told him. "The answer is definitely no thank you."

"So big deal," Ruth said. Again she waited for Helma outside the front door of the mission where she'd been gazing out at the bay. She wore a variation of her Major Barbara costume: a mud-colored dress that ended below her calves. Black shoes with thick soles and wide straps added another two inches to her height. "Now I'm here because I *want* to be here. Temporarily, natch. But here I am. If you don't like it, take it up with the man who lured me into this gig in the first place." Ruth lifted her paper bag. "Look what I brought." She pulled out a half-gallon of chocolate milk and three cans of dinosaur-shaped ravioli. "And in keeping with the spirit," she said, pulling two packages of Nutter Butter cookies from the bag like a magician.

"Did you buy them at Hugie's?" Helma asked.

Ruth returned the cookies to her bag and folded over the top. "Nope. I turned in my Hugie's card. My most favorite doggedly dedicated detective showed up on my doorstep this morning."

"Carter Houston? Why?"

"He was brandishing a computer printout that Hugie's had kindly supplied him. It listed every frigging purchase I made at Hugie's during the past two weeks, Nutter Butters included. Some of the stuff I buy, those guys got no right to know, but there it was in living black and white. Luckily, I hadn't taken out my trash so the Nutter Butter wrapper was still there, proving me innocent of murder, at least. Our little buddy went away disappointed."

"He questioned me at the library this afternoon," Helma told her. Two men climbed the steps to the mission's front door, neither of them looking at the women.

"You bought Nutter Butters?" Ruth asked her.

"No, but someone wrote an anonymous letter to the police suggesting I was responsible for Quentin Vernon Boyd's death."

"Who was the piss ant?"

"It was anonymous."

Ruth waved her hand in dismissal. "There's no such thing as anonymous. Who dared finger *you*, library paragon of Bellehaven?"

"Someone who heard the disagreement I had with Mr. Boyd, perhaps."

"Second-hand knowledge, more likely. They're trying to deflect attention from themselves. All we have to do is figure out who wrote it. Ask your chief of police to give it to you. We'll check the handwriting."

"It was a printed letter. Written on a word processing program. A common font, a common printer."

"Oh, these modern days," Ruth grumbled. "Another threatened career: forgery detection. Your cousin Ruby's going to end up a waitress," she said, reminding Helma of Skitz's gloomy predictions for librarianship. Ruth pushed a strand of hair back into her banded ponytail. "Was the reasoning sound?"

"What do you mean?"

"How'd they justify you being the killer? You didn't like him? So what? Neither did a lot of other people. But that's motive." She held up one finger. "You were tucked in the computer closet, nobody saw you. You knew QVB was coming so you snuck out the back staircase, popped him one and ran back inside. There's method." She held up two fingers. "Now means: how'd you get ahold of a gun?" Ruth tapped her chin.

"This is ridiculous, Ruth. We . . ."

Ruth raised her hand, cutting Helma off. "No, I've got it. Here you are in this place loaded with suspect characters. There are probably more illegal guns among these guys than toothbrushes. You found one lying around and did the deed, then you slipped it back into its place, knowing that every mission resident who's ever had an illegal thought would dart off when the police arrived, none the wiser and taking the evidence with him." Ruth smiled with pride. "It works, doesn't it?" She clapped her hands together as if she were slamming closed a set of jail cell doors.

"Maybe you'd like to explain your theory to Carter Houston?" Helma suggested.

For an instant Ruth brightened, then she slumped and rolled her eyes. "God, I'm sorry. Is this how the wrong guy gets sent to the gas chamber? It makes perfect sense but I know you're innocent."

"Thank you," Helma told her.

"You're welcome. So what's in your bag?" she asked, pointing to the large brown paper bag Helma carried.

"One thousand paper napkins."

"A five-year supply, eh?"

A carload of young men careened around the corner and one of them leaned out the window and shouted, "Go back where you came from, you skags."

Ruth calmly raised her hand in a rude gesture and curiously watched them drive away. "Location *is* everything, isn't it?"

"We'd better go inside," Helma suggested.

"Wait. Before we start slinging hash, you know my friend Miki who writes those advice columns for the *Daily Nuisance*? The word in the back shop down there is that QVB's real estate agency had its eye on the mission's property, that he had a deal or was trying to get one going. This is a prime site for over-the-top condos, don't you think?" Ruth swept her arm toward the sparkling bay and distant blue islands. "You position the buildings just right and you'd never even notice the train yards, or maybe QVB had the power to get those moved, too."

Helma Zukas rarely listened to gossip but now she asked in surprise, "Quentin wanted the land? But he was on the inspection committee to grant more funding to the mission, to upgrade the facilities. If he hoped to develop the property, he should have excused himself from the committee. That's conflict of interest."

"That was probably his last thought, too," Ruth said, touching her throat. "Maybe the committee was just jerking Brother Danny around, softening him up for the kill, so to speak. What do you think the chances are that the committee would have approved the grant?"

"I spoke to Dietrich Morgan this afternoon. He said Quentin Boyd might not have approved of the mission but he would have voted *for* the grant if there was a chance for favorable publicity."

"Altruism at its finest," Ruth commented.

Helma remembered Carter Houston's interrogation that afternoon. "Carter Houston asked me where . . ."

"Where Brother Danny was when QVB was killed, I bet."

"Did he ask you?"

Ruth nodded. "What could I say? He came in through the front door just before we heard shouts from outside the back door and dropped his sugar cubes all over the floor."

"No," Helma said, rejecting the idea completely. "He couldn't be involved. The mission is Brother Danny's life."

"Exactly how the police might look at it," Ruth said.

"There's a mother and young son who I believe need assistance," Helma told Brother Danny as he hurried through the kitchen carrying a box of chicken soup.

"Sure," he said, not pausing. "Just point 'em out to me."

Only a week remained in August and the number of families eating dinner at the mission rose. "The food stamps or the subsidies run out, or it's just a long time between paychecks," Brother Danny told them. "When the first of September rolls around we won't see any children for the first week or two."

Brother Danny served mashed potatoes beside Helma, who was again dispensing vegetables. On the other side of Brother Danny, Frank dished out slabs of meat loaf. Ruth had set up a section at the end of the line specifically for children, where she'd arranged her heated dinosaur pasta, chocolate milk, orange carrot curls, and Nutter Butters. Helma saw her ladle dinosaur pasta onto the dish of a woman she'd noticed the first night, who had come through the line talking nonstop to herself. The evening was supposedly three degrees cooler than the previous night but in the dining room that fact wasn't noticeable.

"Have you seen Skitz?" Helma asked Brother Danny as she stirred the pot of corn in front of her.

"Not a hair."

"Me neither," Frank added, leaning forward to see Helma around Brother Danny. "I'll bet you a carton of smokes he blew town. Probably up in Canada by now. A cop was here asking about him, though. Prissy fellow with glasses. Named Tex."

"Tex?" Helma asked. "Could his name have been Carter Houston?"

Frank nodded. "You got it. Skitz offed the guy, not Tony."

"Did the detective say that?" Helma asked.

Frank sniffed. "Didn't have to. Doesn't surprise *me* any."

"Don't jump to conclusions," Brother Danny warned him. He turned back to Helma. "Tony wants you to come visit him in jail."

"He asked for me?"

"Not by name, but by description: the 'library lady.' He asked for you when he was taken in but nobody figured out who he meant. Good to see you're out, Bobby," he told the dark-haired man waiting for potatoes.

"But *why* does he want to see me?" Helma asked. She'd barely spoken to Tony, had only stood face-to-face with him twice.

Brother Danny shrugged. "He won't say but visiting hours are from one to three tomorrow afternoon."

Helma ladled a second spoonful of corn onto the plate of the man in front of her. "I'll be at the library but I'll try to get away for a few minutes. Do the police intend to release him from jail?"

"There's one problem," Brother Danny said as he added extra potatoes to the dish of an oversized young man who ducked his head as if an invisible boxer were aiming punches at him. "Tony confessed to Quentin Boyd's murder."

"But how could—" Helma began.

"I know," Brother Danny interrupted. "I don't believe Tony did it, either."

Helma didn't answer, realizing that Wayne Gallant's doubts about Tony's confessions were still privileged information.

"The police asked me where you were when the murder took place," she told Brother Danny.

He smiled mildly at her. "They questioned me, too. They're just being thorough."

Barry and his mother came through the line. She kept nudging his shoulder to push him forward. "You might like the food at the end of the counter," Helma told Barry, motioning toward Ruth.

He surveyed the food in front of Ruth. "I like those cookies. That guy gave me some the other night."

"Nutter Butters?" Helma asked. "Which man?"

Barry shrugged, tipping his head to look up at her with his good eye. "Kinda fat, with glasses."

"Was his name Tony?"

"I don't remember," he said, wincing as his mother nudged him again.

"Wait," Helma said as he headed for Ruth's table. "Did he give them to you last night or the night before?"

He held up two fingers. "The night before last."

When Barry and his mother had their food, Helma turned to Brother Danny. "That's the mother and son I mentioned."

"Will do," Brother Danny said. He handed Helma his

mashed potato spoon. "You take over here and I'll see to it."

Helma watched him follow Barry and his mother to a table in a corner and sit down with them, his mouth moving, one finger smoothing his lip.

Before she and Ruth returned to entering donation receipts on the computer, Helma phoned Wayne Gallant's office. He wasn't in and although she disliked the foolishness of speaking into a vacuum, she left a message on his voice mail. "This is Helma Zukas. A young boy named Barry claims that a man matching Tony's description gave him Nutter Butter cookies two nights ago. This may be important since the package of cookies found beside Quentin Boyd's body was unopened."

That said, she ended, "Thank you for your time. Goodbye."

❧ chapter twelve ❧

ALTERNATIVE THEORIES

Helma entered the Bay House and found Forrest sitting on the tufted leather seats against the foyer wall waiting for her, his eyes on the door. The Bay House, true to its name, had once been a Victorian house and sat on a high bluff overlooking Washington Bay. It was a restaurant with several small intimate rooms, decorated in dark green and wood with low lights and carpets that muted the sounds of voices and dinnerware to a pleasant drone.

Forrest rose the instant she walked through the door, his smile already in place. "Billie . . . I mean Helma," he said so warmly that Helma felt a curious shiver in her neck, close behind her ears. "I have a table reserved for us in the lounge, is that all right?"

"That's fine."

"Because we could be in the restaurant section, if you'd rather."

"No. The lounge is fine," Helma assured him again.

Their table sat in front of a window facing the bay where the lights from late-returning boats slowly paraded across the view. The sun had set, leaving only a bluish light in a loose band over the humps of the islands. The table was small and Helma pushed her chair back a little so her knees wouldn't touch Forrest's.

Forrest was dressed more casually than the evening before: in gray slacks and a blue polo shirt. He appeared fit, and

Helma had to admit, handsomer than she recalled. His gray hair heightened the blue of his eyes.

"I read about the murder at the mission," Forrest said, his smile dampening to concern. "Do you feel it's safe to volunteer there?"

"I believe it is," Helma told him. "The staff is very aware of the possibilities and take precautions. Every woman who leaves the building alone after dark is escorted to her car." For a moment she considered explaining to Forrest that her work at the mission wasn't *real* volunteer work, not work that *she'd* chosen. But why bring up the long explanation of her traffic misadventure?

"I spent a night in a mission once," he told her. "In Florida. I was down and out briefly and . . . well, it's not a very interesting story but I'm grateful it was there."

Forrest didn't look like the kind of man who'd stay in anything less than a four-star hotel, let alone a mission, yet he mentioned the experience casually, without embarrassment.

"Did you make a donation once your crisis was over?" Helma asked.

"I did and I do—regularly. Some things you don't forget."

"Last night," Helma asked, "when you arrived at the mission, how did you meet the man who brought you to the office where Ruth and I were working?"

Forrest gazed out the window as if he were trying to remember. "I think he was sitting in the lobby. That's right, he was, against the opposite wall. When I asked for you at the front desk, he stood up and offered to show me the way."

"He *knew* where I was?" Helma asked. "Was he hesitant at all?"

Forrest shook his head. "He led me right to you. Why?"

"Someone was looking for him, that's all. Did you see him again?"

"No. That was it."

Their drinks arrived: red wine for Helma, who believed in its health benefits, and Scotch neat for Forrest. He took a fortifying breath and said, "About the reunion . . ."

"Forrest," Helma interrupted. "That's behind us. High school reunions are unnatural events. None of us are the people we were in high school and so often we end up trying to prove we became something we didn't."

"Well, I certainly did." He laughed. "Thank you for saying that." Then he sobered and turned his glass between his hands. "There is one thing I need to clear up. I said I had a wife and daughter, but actually I never married."

"I see. Do you still live in Florida?"

"That part was true but I recently moved to Portland."

"Oregon?"

He shook his head. "Maine. After the reunion, I returned to Florida and started taking computer courses. —I took to computers like a twelve-year-old, can you believe it?"

Helma could. In school, Forrest had always been the brainy one who understood logic and science with such ease it had made him an outsider. He'd once said braininess was an accident, like eye and hair color.

"I landed the job in Portland last spring. Life's moved fast since then. They sent me to Seattle on business and well, here I am."

"Congratulations, Forrest," Helma said, sincerely meaning it.

"Yeah, it's nice to be achieving a little success in life instead of just wishing for it." Forrest turned his glass faster. Helma felt the vibration of his foot tapping against the floor. He swallowed and gazed into her eyes with such intensity that Helma couldn't look away. "Maybe it sounds crazy but I meant it when I said I hoped to marry you, Helma. I know we were only kids in high school but I cared about you then, and I have ever since. Over the years I haven't been able to forget you. The way you always understood yourself. You were never silly or stuck up. Everything about you was just so . . ." He swallowed. "So clear."

No one had ever spoken to Helma Zukas like this before and although it was so unexpected, so obviously based on Forrest's fantasies of her and not what she was *really* like, she felt an unaccustomed flutter beneath her breastbone, a rare blush on her cheeks. She broke away from Forrest's fervent gaze and studied a featureless reflection of light on the surface of her red wine.

"I know this is out of the blue," he went on, "but just tell me you'll think about it, that's all. I know we could be happy together. I plan to buy a house in Portland; we could choose it together." Forrest's hand covered Helma's and she didn't pull away.

"I know about the chief of police," Forrest said and Helma stiffened. Forrest faltered. "I'm sorry. That was crude. I remember from our reunion that you and he were friends but Ruth said it hadn't gone anywhere."

"Ruth said what?" Helma asked, half rising from her chair.

Forrest's face paled. "Has it? *Are* you involved with him? I wouldn't speak to you like this if I thought you were involved in a serious relationship. I apologize."

Helma sat down again and composed herself, straightening her blouse, patting her hair once and folding her hands on the table. She wasn't a person who denied the truth when she heard it even when it was a shock. She took a deep breath, then another one. "Ruth was speaking out of turn, but she may be correct," she said reluctantly.

"Then you'll think about my proposal? I'm not talking about rushing into anything. I could spend some time here and you could visit me in Portland. It's a beautiful city." His hand lightly touched hers again. "There's an ocean there, too."

Helma didn't pull her hand away. She moistened her lips and peered out the window as the last light faded away to the west. It was low tide and she caught sight of a flashlight beam picking out tide pools along the shore. Despite the heat, summer was waning. Time was passing.

"I'll think about it," she finally told Forrest.

As Forrest walked Helma to her car, she smelled the pungent breeze blowing off the bay and wondered briefly if the Atlantic Ocean could possibly smell the same. Before moving to Bellehaven, the largest body of water she'd ever seen had been Lake Michigan.

"Are you okay about driving home alone?" Forrest asked her. "I can follow you in my rental."

"Thank you but I feel perfectly safe."

She'd parked her Buick beneath a street light and as Forrest took her keys and unlocked her door for her, the light silvered his hair. He touched her shoulder. "No matter what you decide, Helma, this night has been . . . perfect. Thank you."

Helma clicked her right blinker as she slowed to turn into the Bayside Arms, her thoughts surprisingly filled with Forrest. She'd known him as a shy child and an awkward teenager. Yet, she didn't actually know this self-assured man. How could she even consider what he asked?

Suddenly, a figure dashed across the parking lot entrance in front of her. She slammed on her brakes, watching in a mix of horror and relief as her left front bumper barely cleared the man's leg.

She expected him to stop or shout at her, even just shake his fist or gesture, but he didn't miss a stride or turn his head, just kept running. Helma briefly closed her eyes, calming herself, until brakes screeched behind her and a car horn blared. Then she carefully completed her turn into the parking lot, feeling the wild beating of her heart.

Her mind was still on the near catastrophe when she reached the third-floor landing and noticed that Walter David had replaced the burned-out bulb above the door of Mrs. Whitney's old apartment. In the light cast by her own outdoor fixture she spotted a piece of blue paper lodged between the doorknob and the doorjamb. Walter David didn't allow soliciting at the Bayside Arms but sometimes a politician or carpet cleaner salesman managed to circumvent him.

She looked over the railing toward the street where the figure had disappeared, then scrutinized the parking lot, especially around the Dumpster. Seeing nothing unusual, she reached for the blue sheet, then pulled back her hand and instead removed a tissue from her purse and used it to dislodge the paper.

With one hand she unlocked the door and stepped into her apartment, holding the blue paper away from her body. The light was on above her stove and she swiftly glanced around her kitchen and living room. She had a well-developed sense about disorder and knew instantly that her apartment was exactly as she'd left it that morning.

Still using the tissue, she set the paper on her counter and now she could see it was a Hugie's grocery ad torn in half, announcing an exclusive gourmet sweet corn sale.

But Helma knew that gourmet sweet corn wasn't the issue here. She gingerly turned over the page and there, scrawled in half-print, half-cursive was a note that read, *That cop better get his butt in gear before you run off with Mr. Silver Hair.*

Helma stared, her breath held. This was absolute proof she was being watched. She read the message again, then twice more. Here was handwriting that perhaps could be identified, perhaps even decipherable fingerprints, but reading the message yet one more time—"That cop had better get his butt in gear . . ."—Helma knew this wasn't a note she'd turn over to the chief of police.

Instead, she removed a paring knife from her knife holder. Holding it with the blade pointed behind her, she opened her door and walked back out onto the landing that stretched across the third floor. The night was quiet. The lights of a few cars passed on the street.

She stood close to the railing and asked in a low voice, hardly more than a whisper, "Skitz?"

There was no answer.

"Skitz?" she asked again in a louder voice. "If this note is from you, I do not appreciate it, do you understand? If you have a topic you'd like to discuss with me, such as your friend Tony or the death of Mr. Boyd, come forward right now. At once. Otherwise, leave me alone."

Movement rustled the tall Photinia hedge near the Dumpster, too much motion to be a dog or cat. "If this is about

Tony's confession . . ." she began, but suddenly, a voice directly beneath Helma asked, "Helma, what's going on?"

She started and looked down. Walter David leaned out from the landing of the second floor, frowning up at her. "Who are you talking to?" he asked.

"I thought I saw someone."

"Where?"

"Near the Dumpster."

Walter David clattered down the first flight of steps and Helma watched him hurry across the parking lot to the Dumpster, gazing in every direction, his body tense. He walked up to the hedge and the nearby bushes, asking, "Anybody there?" He spoke in a deeper voice than usual, low like a growl.

But of course no one emerged. Walter looked up at Helma and in the light from the lamp above the Dumpster, Helma could see he was still frowning. "Nobody here. Want me to call the police?"

"No. It may have been my imagination. Thank you."

When Helma stepped back inside her apartment, Walter David was still gazing up at her landing, still looking perplexed.

Helma was Xing out squares forty-four, forty-three, and forty-two on the chart inside her cupboard door when her phone rang. Her hand slipped, ruining the angled line on forty-two, her mind returning to the man she'd nearly hit, the rustle outside her apartment. She cautiously picked up the receiver.

It was her mother and she was breathless. "Helma, I can't believe it! Why didn't you tell me? What a shock. And a surprise too, wasn't it? What on earth are you going to do, dear? Does *he* know?"

"Mother, what are you talking about?" Helma asked. She closed the cupboard door, concealing the ruined X.

"I was in Hugie's just a few minutes ago to buy a little late night snack. You know how I get the munchies at night.

Nothing fattening, of course. And who do you think I saw in the toiletries aisle buying toothpaste?"

Helma never played guessing games so she remained silent, knowing her mother would tell her whether she responded or not.

"Forrest Stevens! He said he's here in Bellehaven to visit *you*. He was positively glowing. What does it *mean*?"

With the black pen that was still in her hand, Helma drew a thick down-pointing arrow on the notepad beside her telephone. "Exactly that, Mother. He stopped in Bellehaven to say hello."

"But . . ."

"Actually, he called Ruth first."

"Oh. Well, *you're* the one he talked about. I always liked Forrest. His mother used to tat those little lace collars, remember. Nobody tats anymore; it's a lost art, like glass blowing. Why don't you bring him over for dinner?"

"I don't believe he'll be here long enough," Helma told her.

Helma's mother was silent and Helma said, "But it's thoughtful of you to ask, Mother."

"Mm. All right, dear," she conceded with uncharacteristic ease and speed. "Has the chief met Forrest yet?"

"He's very busy investigating Quentin Boyd's death."

"I'm sure. Oh, don't forget that scarf I left at your apartment." Her mother's voice suddenly went calm, dropping an octave. "Do you think you could drop it off tomorrow on your lunch hour?" she asked casually.

"Certainly," Helma agreed with just a touch of wariness.

Before she turned off her kitchen light on her way to bed, Helma parted the curtains and gazed down into the parking lot of the Bayside Arms.

A dark car with only its parking lights on slowly drove along the covered parking area. She dropped the curtains, leaving a slit she could see through and watched the car make a U-turn near the fir tree and creep back along the row of parked cars. As it passed beneath a streetlamp she saw the bar of lights on the car's roof. It was a police patrol car.

Helma watched until the police car smoothly pulled out of the Bayside Arms and continued on down the street out of sight before she stepped away from the window.

The next day, Helma found herself glancing in her rear-view mirror more often than usual, jumping at unexpected sounds and glancing over her shoulder, always conscious of who was approaching her and what was happening on the periphery of her vision.

She noted a hunched figure limping slowly along the side of the street, and when she checked her rearview mirror, she recognized Charlie from the mission. He had a long walk ahead of him. The sun shone on his tonsured head as he leaned down and with both hands gripped his left thigh as though pulling his leg forward.

Helma drove another two blocks and glanced again in her mirror at Charlie's receding figure. "Oh, Faulkner," she said aloud and turned around at the next side street.

Charlie had only made a few more feet of progress when Helma pulled her car in front of him and stopped. He limped to the passenger side and squinted at her through the open window. "Day off?" he asked. He scowled, he slouched; his faded shirt was stained, its pocket torn and roughly mended. The right knee of his once industrial-green pants was worn away to threads. But, as if he couldn't help himself, using the hand with the missing fingertip, he smoothed back the wisps of hair over each temple and ran his hand across his throat and down his chest as if smoothing a shirt front.

"Would you like a ride?" Helma offered.

"Where to?"

"Downtown, or the mission."

He tipped his head, his squint fierce. "You're not going to try and save my soul or drop me off at the hoosegow, are you?"

Taking in Charlie's rumpled clothing and whiskered face, Helma wondered if she'd made a mistake. "If you'd like a ride, please get in the car. Otherwise I'll continue on my way."

"Okay, if it'll make you feel better," Charlie said, opening the door and getting inside. He glanced around her car and over his shoulder into the backseat and then ran his hand over the clear plastic seatcovers. "Bet this gets hot."

"Please fasten your seatbelt," Helma advised him.

"I don't wear seatbelts," he said, crossing his arms. Traffic whizzed past, definitely over the speed limit.

"I don't drive when there are people in my car who aren't wearing seatbelts."

"Were you going to pump me for stuff on the murder?" he asked, not budging.

"No," Helma told him. "I was going to offer you a ride. Now please put on your seatbelt," Helma told him again. A seagull dipped low over the car, checking for food.

"Or what?" Charlie asked. "You'll throw me out?"

"I won't drive."

"And miss the story of my downfall," Charlie asked, his raspy voice taunting, "how a respected family man became a knight of the road?"

"Would it be true?" Helma asked.

"No, but it might make you feel all gooshy inside and give me a buck." He rubbed his thumb and fingers together.

"I don't give money to strangers," Helma said. Then remembering Barry and his mother, she clarified, "Usually."

Charlie's laughter ended in a cough. He opened the door and stepped out, saying, "And I don't wear seatbelts."

As Helma put her car in gear and pulled away, she thought she heard Charlie call after her, but his words were too garbled to understand.

"I'd like to extend my lunch hour by thirty minutes," Helma told Ms. Moon, who sat behind her desk in semi-darkness, the green velvet curtains closed on yet another sunny day in Bellehaven, only her desk lamp shining on a stack of papers and reflecting light upward onto her round face.

"Is it an emergency?" Ms. Moon asked. Three-dimensional

gold earrings in the shape of pyramids glinted in the lamp-light.

"It's a personal matter," Helma told her.

Ms. Moon shifted her papers from one side of her desk to the other with quick, sharp movements. "If it doesn't inter-fere with the work that needs to be done here."

"I don't believe I'm behind in any of my duties," Helma pointed out.

"Maybe not." Ms. Moon dropped her hands on a stack of papers that looked like budget projections: rows of numbers. "I noticed you driving past my house two nights ago. You slowed down."

"I was surprised to see you, that's all," Helma explained. "I hadn't known exactly where you lived."

"Now you do. What else had you so interested?" There was no mistaking Ms. Moon's edgy challenge.

"Now that you mention it, I was curious to note your gro-cery bags."

"What was so curious about them?"

"They were from Hugie's and I wondered why you shopped at Hugie's when their store's located on the opposite side of town."

"They have the best produce," Ms. Moon said curtly. She turned over the papers holding the numbers and said abruptly, "I'd like an accounting of the overdue fines."

"Surely there is one available since we use an automated cash register when fines are paid."

"I'd like an accounting of the amount of money that's *due* in fines right now."

"That would be helpful," Helma agreed, once again recall-ing how in her problem patrons workshop she learned to agree with the agitated patron first, "but wouldn't such an accounting be Dutch's responsibility? He is in charge of cir-culation." In seventeen years at the Bellehaven Public Li-brary, Helma had never ventured into the realm of circulation. That department had first belonged to Mrs. Car-mon, then Dutch, who was so protective that his breathing went harsh when anyone he referred to as an "unauthorized staff member" stepped behind the circulation counter.

"I feel this is more of a professional librarian's responsibility than a clerical responsibility," Ms. Moon said. "And I'd like it completed before the audit begins next week."

"Surely there can't be any concerns about the audit?" Helma asked.

Ms. Moon went still, her hands flat on her desk as if she were about to rise from her chair. Her face pinked. "What are you implying?" she demanded.

"Only that the library has always followed good accounting practices, that's all."

"Oh." Ms. Moon lifted her hands and made motions of dismissal, then returned to her stacks of papers.

George Melville stood by the staff lounge holding a cup of coffee when Helma left Ms. Moon's office. "You ever seen her like this before?" he asked Helma, nodding toward the director's office.

"She seems very tense," Helma agreed.

"Maybe numbers are just too much reality for her world. If they were surrounded by auras or made little tinkling bell sounds she'd be more comfortable. It's tough to assign emotional values to digits."

"But *why* is she upset?" Helma asked. "Has she said?"

"Who knows?" He took a loud sip from his cup. "Maybe it's a guilty conscience. She killed QVB, thinking that if he was dead, there wouldn't be an audit to discover that she's been embezzling vast sums of money to expand her crystal collection."

George spoke in jest, a sardonic expression on his face, but as he finished, his expression faltered and he and Helma stood in silence, avoiding one another's eyes.

"Bad joke," George mumbled and headed toward his cataloging corner.

❦ chapter thirteen ❦

ADVICE AND CONTENT

Helma's mother opened the door of her apartment, already smiling. She wore denim jeans and a purple sweatshirt that said, *Act Your Age!* across the front. "Helma. Come in. We have it all worked out."

Behind her at the table in her tiny kitchen sat Aunt Em and Mrs. Whitney. Plates of sandwich ingredients, a salad, and a platter of baked goods covered the table, along with four untouched place settings. The shallow pot of cacti that usually sat in the table's center had been relegated to the floor behind a life-sized ceramic Scottish terrier.

"I'm in a hurry, Mother," Helma tried, holding out her mother's scarf.

"Nonsense. This won't take long and you can eat while we talk. We've been discussing the situation."

Both Aunt Em and Mrs. Whitney beckoned Helma to the table. They sat in their chairs, but their bodies leaned toward Helma. Aunt Em, eighty-seven, Mrs. Whitney, nearly eighty, their lined faces equally bright, gazed at Helma like women about to spill secrets they were positive she'd love.

"Only for a few minutes," Helma told them. She chose the chair closest to the door and her mother sat down opposite her. There was no way to avoid it. She tucked her purse beneath her chair, braced herself and asked, "What situation have you been discussing?"

"Yours, dear, of course," Aunt Em said. "Now, Forrest is a nice boy. His grandmother and I were good friends, even after his grandfather got in trouble over that land deal. I'm sure he's good enough for you, but Ethel and your mother think . . ."

"Oh, I *do* like that policeman," Mrs. Whitney said, smiling. "He's such a gentleman."

"We've decided you need to take more responsibility," her mother added, passing Helma a plate piled with three different kinds of bread. Helma took the plate but didn't interrupt.

"We're going to help you," Aunt Em said. "We three have gone through more men in our lifetimes than . . ."

"Tsk, tsk, " Mrs. Whitney said, playfully slapping Aunt Em's wrist with her napkin. She looked at Helma. "We have some ideas you can share with your policeman."

"About the murder," Aunt Em finished, taking two slices of roast beef, one each of sliced turkey and ham, and two different slices of cheese from the platter in front of her. "About why that man at the mission killed Mr. Boyd."

The three women gazed across the table at Helma, on their faces a mix of concern and excitement. She was trapped. The best she could hope for was that they hadn't already acted on any of their ideas.

"But the police doubt his confession," Helma told them. "He's a false confessor, someone who habitually confesses to crimes."

If she'd hoped to defuse their interest, she saw immediately that she was wrong. Instead of moving on to other, safer subjects, the three women glanced at each other as if a box of mixed chocolates had been presented to them.

"Then you need new theories," Helma's mother said. She absently took a lettuce leaf off the plate and chewed it. "New motives."

"And suspects," Aunt Em added. "Killers on the loose."

Mrs. Whitney shivered but not in fear, more like someone who'd taken too big a bite of her favorite ice cream.

"Did you know Quentin Boyd?" Helma asked Mrs. Whitney, who, like Walter, had lived her whole life in Bellehaven.

"Not personally. I know Lily. She's a hard worker."

"Maybe," Helma's mother said, her voice dropping to a

dramatic whisper, "maybe Quentin was having an affair and the husband followed him and shot him."

"I like it," Aunt Em said, jotting on a piece of notepaper. "It's open and shut."

"But people say he and his wife were close," Helma told them.

"It always looks that way from the outside," Helma's mother said, and catching Helma's sharp glance, hastily added, "if it's a prominent couple, I mean, like the president."

"Or movie stars," Aunt Em added. "Remember Debbie Reynolds and Eddie Fisher?"

Mrs. Whitney sadly shook her head. "That sweet little thing."

"Well, if *I'd* been Lily and my husband had an affair, *I'd* have shot him," Aunt Em said.

Both Mrs. Whitney and Helma's mother nodded in agreement. "For sweet revenge," Aunt Em whispered. "Think about it."

Helma looked at the faces of the three women as they flashed back over their lives and saw little hard lights come into their eyes as they considered revenge. "It may have been an attempted robbery and the robber was frightened away," she offered.

"A robber from the mission, like we said," Aunt Em told her.

"The man who runs the mission, Brother Danny, he spoke to our Concerned Seniors group," Mrs. Whitney said. "He told us they're always struggling to make ends meet down there."

"Maybe Brother Danny tried to pick up a little extra cash," Aunt Em suggested. Her sandwich was too big for her mouth and she set her palm on it and compacted the bread and fillings.

"Emily," Helma's mother admonished. "He's a religious man."

"Hmmph," Aunt Em sniffed.

Helma escaped after eating only half a sandwich. They'd

barely made a dent in the spread of food even after Mrs. Whitney packed a plastic container with four kinds of cookies for her to take back to the library.

"Don't forget this," Aunt Em said at the door, tucking the list of motives and suspects into Helma's pocket. "And you call your policeman right away." She winked at Helma while both Mrs. Whitney and Helma's mother nodded and smiled.

Ruth sat on a wooden bench in the foyer of the police station. "What took you so long?" She rose from the bench, dressed in her more usual fashion: purple pants and a gauzy shirt. Open-toed sandals showed blood-red nails. "I'm prepared to visit the condemned man, if you are."

"I believe Tony only asked to see me, and he's not a condemned man," Helma told her.

"Not yet anyway. Just joking. I thought you could use a little entertainment to and from the jail, sort of negate the depressing effects of prison. You and Tony can have the visiting room all to yourselves. I'll wait with the free."

"Was this your own idea or did someone request that you accompany me?" Helma asked warily.

"The chief does not know I'm here, I swear." She held up her hand oathlike. "Besides I want to be the first to hear the juicy stuff: who did it and where's the gun?"

As they waited to speak to the officer at the desk, Helma told Ruth about the note she'd found on her door after her drink with Forrest. Ruth pressed her lips together, thinking. A man slipped in front of them in line and Ruth didn't even notice. " 'That cop better get off his butt before you run off with Mr. Silver Hair,' " she repeated. "It's obvious that Mr. Silver Hair is Forrest. I didn't do it but it was a good observation. Super Cop definitely needs to get off his butt. Whoever left it on your door has figured you out enough to believe that you'd be too embarrassed to show it to the police, am I right?"

"I don't intend to give it to the police," Helma agreed, "but I did save it."

Ruth finally noticed the man in front of them and tapped

his shoulder. "No cuts. Didn't you learn that in second grade?" She jerked her thumb behind her, standing three inches taller. The man opened his mouth, then stepped behind them without a word. Ruth turned back to Helma. "You were with Forrest so rule him out. How'd it go anyway?"

"We had a pleasant drink."

"Aha! So he proposed all hot and heavy, eh? Did you turn him down flat out or did you say you'd think about it?" She made motions with her hands as if she were drawing the words from Helma.

"The latter."

Ruth nodded sagely although Helma could see she was bursting to pry out the details of Forrest's proposal, but all she did was ask, "So who do *you* think left the note?"

"Possibly Skitz. I suspect he's been watching me and he may be obsessed with the idea that I can help free Tony."

"So he comments on your love life?" Ruth asked. A breeze from somewhere stirred the air and Ruth lifted her gauzy shirt, trying to catch it. "Are you sure Tony's the reason? I mean, I know criminals are supposed to stick together and all that, but it sounds a little too good to be true."

"No one's proven that Tony is a criminal," Helma pointed out.

"Tell QVB that," Ruth said. "But what about the company Tony keeps? Skitz is wanted for murder."

"He's a person of interest," Helma clarified.

"Same difference." A tall policewoman passed and Ruth straightened her spine and shoulders to make herself taller than the policewoman. Helma recalled sixth grade when Ruth had suddenly shot up taller than every classmate and the teacher, and how she'd slouched in humiliation.

"I know what's going on," Ruth continued. "Skitz is scared you saw more than you did when QVB was killed. He's watching to see if you're going to tell the police."

"I have information implicating him in Quentin Boyd's death?" Helma tried to bring up the memory of Tony in the blackberry bushes the night Quentin Boyd was murdered. If

Skitz had been lurking anywhere nearby, she hadn't seen him. She was sure of it.

"Why not? That's why he has to keep his eye on you all the time, in case you slip away and squeal."

"But there was an anonymous letter implicating *me*," Helma reminded her.

"Written on a computer. I mean, how hard is it to get ahold of a computer these days? He probably carries a laptop in his garbage bag."

"There are computers at the mission," Helma conceded. "But if Skitz is still in town, he hasn't let me see him."

Ruth glanced at Helma's face and said, "What if . . ." She stopped.

"What?" Helma asked.

"Skitz wanted you to clear Tony, right? So maybe he's letting you know he's watching and waiting for you to do it. He's holding you to your promise."

"I didn't promise," Helma said.

"Maybe *you* don't think you did, but to the unbalanced mind of a murderer . . ."

Helma rubbed her arms, considering Ruth's theory and remembering how Skitz had broken the pencil in two at the reference desk, how he'd looked at Dutch.

"That's too creepy," Ruth said. "Tell your cop, embarrassing note or not."

Helma didn't answer and as they reached the police station's front desk, Ruth said, "Forgive the guy, okay? He was just looking out for your welfare."

Helma left Ruth in the front office explaining to the officer on duty how she'd once nearly been shot to death by Detective Carter Houston.

"I'll bring Tony out," the officer escorting Helma said, showing her into a room with a table in its center.

Helma sat in a plastic chair and waited. The room was bare: institutional-green walls, without windows, the only decoration a calendar hanging beside the door that was still open to July instead of August. The room wasn't locked but it still felt confining. She swallowed against the same discomfort she felt at boarding an elevator. She was changing the calendar to the proper month when the officer returned with Tony shuffling beside him as if he were wearing leg irons, which he wasn't, but he was handcuffed. "Are those necessary?" Helma asked the officer.

"Yup."

Tony sat down at the table, grinning at Helma. "Hi, there," he said in his childish man's voice. He wore a single piece jumpsuit and his glasses had been repaired. His hair was trimmed short. He looked proud, Helma thought, like a man who'd accomplished a cherished goal.

"Hello, Tony," she said, sitting across from him. "Did you wish to talk to me?"

He nodded. "Skitz told me to."

"Has he been here?"

Tony vigorously shook his head. "No, no, no. Before. He said to talk to you if I got in trouble."

"I saw you sitting in the bushes after that man was killed. What did you see?"

"I did it." He raised his cuffed wrists together, making a gun shape with his hands which he politely aimed away from Helma. "Pow," he softly said, then smiled. "Somebody had to."

"Why?" Helma asked.

"Because. Just because. Is my picture on TV?"

"No, it isn't. Did you see who shot Mr. Boyd?"

"I did. Pow." Tony sat up tall. He nodded eagerly as she asked each question, leaning forward for the next one.

"Where's the gun?"

"I threw it in the water, down by the boats."

"Tony," Helma explained. "You didn't have time to go to the bay and come back before the police came."

Tony nodded slyly. "I made time."

"Does Skitz have the gun?"

Tony squirmed on his seat. His handcuffs rattled. "Skitz says you shouldn't carry a gun unless you mean it. He says never carry a gun when you steal something or it'll go against you."

"That's good advice," Helma agreed. "Did you know the dead man?"

"He called Skitz a bum who should go to jail."

"Did he hurt Skitz?" Helma asked.

Tony's voice rose. "He was going to, he sure was."

"Then did Skitz shoot him?"

"I did."

"Where do you think Skitz is right now?"

"Free as a bird." He made flying motions with his hands.

Helma sat back and looked at the small man. His story had become gospel in his mind. He spoke with perfect sincerity and conviction, yet with a simplicity that made it a lie. Only facts without details. "Tell me about your family, Tony," Helma said.

Tony's face puckered. "No," he said and closed his mouth tight. And that was the end of their conversation. No matter what else Helma asked, however she framed it, he refused to answer.

A policeman appeared in the open doorway and Helma told Tony, "I left some chocolate and books for you. The police will give them to you." She'd stopped by a drug store that sold comic books and watched a young boy of about twelve browse through the comics and then she bought one of each that he'd perused. "Tell the police to call me or Brother Danny if you need anything else," she said as he was taken from the room, and even then he didn't answer.

"So did they usher him in in chains?" Ruth asked, rising from her chair in the lobby where she'd been filing her nails.

"Handcuffs," Helma told her, "but the door wasn't even locked."

"Dangerous murderer," Ruth scoffed. "So why'd he want to see you?"

"There wasn't any reason that I could discover. Skitz had advised him to ask for me."

"Foresightful. In a jam? Call the chief of police's girlfriend." Ruth paused and nudged Helma, whispering, "Speaking of. Lookee there."

Where the hallway to the offices met the lobby, Wayne Gallant stood talking to Lily Boyd, obviously saying goodbye. The small woman's eyes were red and as she turned away from the chief toward the brighter lobby, she pulled a large pair of sunglasses from her purse and slipped them on.

"Ask her about QVB wanting to develop the mission's property. Go ahead."

"I don't think this is the time, Ruth," Helma said. She smiled and nodded as Lily Boyd caught sight of her and gave a small wave of her hand and then paused, waiting for Helma to join her. Behind Lily, the chief nodded to Helma and then turned back to his office.

Ruth followed close behind and when Helma introduced them, Ruth leaned down to shake Lily's hand. There was over a foot's difference in height between the two women. "I'm sorry about your husband," Ruth said. "Is it true that his real estate firm had plans to develop the mission's property?"

Helma was aghast. She waited for Lily Boyd to tense up, to say something scathing to Ruth, but instead she gazed up at Ruth for a moment and then laughed. "I don't think you're a reporter but you should be."

"Nah, I have the guts, but not the perseverance. But is it true? If you don't mind my asking, I mean."

They left through the police station's glass doors with Lily Boyd walking between them. "The police have asked me the same thing," she said. "It's no secret that the mission sits on very valuable property. Every real estate developer in town would like to develop it, but Brother Danny bought it free and clear years ago. Quentin was interested in it, yes. In fact, I think he suggested to Brother Danny that the mission relocate, that the sale of that property would build him a fabulous facility, but Brother Danny said the mission had to be where the homeless men were." She tipped her head. "But then, when you think about it, the homeless men are there because the mission is there."

"Was Brother Danny upset by the offer?" Helma asked.

"I doubt it. I'm sure the mission's had other offers." She shook her head and glanced at her watch. "Bellehaven's changing before our eyes. I must go now. Will you be coming to the service tomorrow?"

"The library will be sending a representative," Helma told her.

"I don't attend funerals," Ruth said. "But have a good . . . I hope it goes well."

Lily Boyd smiled and walked away. Helma saw her touch a finger to the corner of her eye.

By the time Helma returned to the library, she'd been gone not just one hour but one hour and forty-six minutes. While she returned her purse to her desk drawer, Harley Woodworth looked over the shelves between their cubicles and said gloomily, "Ms. Moon was looking for you."

"Thank you," Helma told him and hurried to the public area. She was sixteen minutes late for her stint on the reference desk, and was shocked to find Ms. May Apple Moon, library director, sitting in her place in the public area, her early agitation replaced by such serenity that Helma felt certain the audit had been canceled. Ms. Moon was making intricate folds in a sheet of red tissue paper. She smiled at Helma.

"I'm sorry I'm late," Helma told her, stepping behind the reference desk with the intent of taking Ms. Moon's place.

Ms. Moon gave an airy wave of her hand. "It's part of the resonance."

"I beg your pardon?"

"The welling of negative forces. What *you* might call misfortune or bad luck. It gathers and flows, spreading across our lives. We have to conserve our strength and wait until it ebbs, as surely it will. Life's forces will not be denied." Ms. Moon made swaying motions with her hands and body that made Helma think of seaweed beneath the surface of the ocean.

"I've heard some people say life is a pendulum," Helma said, trying to be helpful.

"That's why I'm not at all surprised that you're late," Ms. Moon went on in a soothing voice as if she hadn't heard Helma. "It's part of the rising tide. But if we maintain our personal rhythms, the negative energy will swirl around our feet and slip past us, back into the universe, barely wetting the ankles of our energies."

A woman holding a periodical request approached the desk and Ms. Moon languidly reached for it. "Marty will be your page today," she told the woman, smiling. "He'll bring this magazine to your table."

Ms. Moon made no move to rise from the reference desk chair so Helma could take her rightful place. So instead Helma took the opportunity to straighten the desk collection, the books on the low shelves behind the reference desk that the librarians used most often to answer questions from the public: specialized dictionaries and directories, reference books most likely to be mutilated. She looked up once to catch Dutch staring at Ms. Moon, on his face an expression that looked like genuine concern. Another time, a lean man in black shorts and t-shirt slouched past the reference desk and Helma rose to her feet, watching him until he turned and she clearly saw he wasn't Skitz.

She was nearly to the bottom shelf of the second tier of shelves when she heard Ms. Moon gaily say, "I've been expecting you."

Helma turned to see Detective Carter Houston standing at attention in front of the reference desk. The slight gathering of eyebrows and the merest pursing of his lips indicated puzzlement. "You have?" he asked. He flipped open his notebook and glanced at it as if it might hold printed instructions.

"Yes, it's the tide. Did you wish to speak to Miss Zukas?" She waved her hand over her shoulder toward Helma.

Carter Houston nodded a curt acknowledgement to Helma, then told Ms. Moon, "Actually, if you have the time I'd like to ask you a few questions."

"I don't suppose 'if' is really an operative word here,"

Ms. Moon said. She gracefully rose and led the way toward the workroom, her clothing swaying, her stride untroubled.

Not two minutes later, George Melville, Harley Woodworth, and Eve appeared at the reference desk, all three with expectant faces. When Helma didn't say anything, Eve nudged George. "What's going on?" George asked.

"Her door's *closed*," Eve said breathlessly.

"Do you think the detective's come to arrest her?" Harley asked. His eyes were bright at the gloomy prospect.

"I don't have any more information than you do," Helma told them. "He probably has questions regarding Quentin Boyd's death, perhaps about the library board."

"Or the audit," Eve suggested.

"They haven't started the audit yet," Harley reminded Eve. "That's *next* week. I wish we could hear what was going on."

"We'll just have to wait until the shoes start dropping," George said.

"When I was a little girl," Eve said, touching a finger to her cheek like Shirley Temple, "we used to put an empty glass against the wall of my parents' bedroom so we could hear them."

Harley gazed at Eve in admiration. "Did it work?"

"Kind of."

"The Moonbeam's office shares a wall with the staff lounge," George pointed out.

"That's eavesdropping," Helma reminded them. "Akin to wiretapping."

But the three librarians exchanged eager glances and George said, "Come along, children." Harley mused, "Would a cup work as good as a glass?"

With so few patrons requesting reference service, Helma was able to make two private phone calls. First, she called Dietrich Morgan's insurance office. "More questions about Quentin?" he asked. "Just for personal reasons?"

"Yes, that's correct," Helma told him. "Did he ever mention purchasing the mission property?"

"To develop, you mean?"

Helma felt a surge of excitement but she kept her voice calm. "Yes."

"Nope. Never did. *I* thought about it, though. Some first-rate condos with basement parking, maybe an exercise room. Can you picture it? Worth a fortune."

"Did you discuss the idea with Mr. Boyd?"

"No. As I said, we really weren't friends. He would have thought I was trying to hit on him for a loan. If he did have anything in the works, he wouldn't have mentioned it anyway, not until the i's were dotted and the t's crossed on the contract. Those deals have to be done fast and hush-hush or somebody jumps in ahead of you."

Helma thanked him and hung up. She'd dialed the chief of police's number to ask him if he'd talked to Barry about the Nutter Butters when she decided against it and hung up. It was moot anyway when every sign indicated Tony would soon be released.

While Helma waited for the reference phone to ring, she logged onto the Internet herself and typed in the word "Skitz." The resultant message suggested that she check her spelling and try again. When she tried Brother Danny's name, Daniel Davis, she turned up hundreds of irrelevant hits, seventy-eight in Mississippi alone; the positive responses were as useless as none. "Quentin Vernon Boyd" brought up a local advertisement for his real estate company. She tried "Promise Mission for Homeless Men" and permutations of words for urban development and renewal in Bellehaven, all with unsatisfactory results.

Then she phoned Ruth who was usually in her bedroom-turned-studio this time of day.

"Mm-hmm?" Ruth answered.

"This is Helma. Do you know Brother Danny's background?"

"He's from Mississippi or Alabama, I think. But I can find out."

"How?" Helma asked cautiously. Ruth's methods were rarely discreet.

"I'll ask Miki down at the paper. She's got her finger on

the pulse of the county," Ruth intoned, reciting the newspaper's motto.

"I already checked the index for previous news stories when I began working at the mission," Helma told her. "There wasn't anything substantial about him."

"Not in print anyway," Ruth said. "That doesn't mean they don't *know* the juicy stuff."

"I'm not interested in hearing gossip," Helma warned her.

"No, ma'am," Ruth said enthusiastically. "Just the facts. Hey, did you hear it's supposed to rain this weekend?"

"That would be a relief," Helma told her, imagining the palette of grays that better suited the deep greens of Bellehaven than glaring sunshine and frivolous colors.

Ms. Moon and Carter Houston were still in Ms. Moon's office when it was time for Helma to leave the library. George, Harley, and Eve had given up their eavesdropping scheme and each returned to their respective desks. "She turned on her whale music," Harley complained.

"We could only hear mumbling," Eve told Helma. "My parents were lots louder."

Even the warm afternoon was a relief after the stifling library, and Helma stood at the library's rear entrance, savoring it for a moment before she walked to her car, thinking of the forty-one hours she had yet to serve at the mission, and about Lily Boyd's assertion that her husband had offered to buy the mission. Even if Quentin Boyd *had* wanted to develop the land the mission occupied, even if Brother Danny *had* felt his mission was threatened, perhaps even that the grant would be denied, was he capable of resorting to violence? Skitz was another issue. Just thinking of him, Helma glanced over her shoulder and around the parking lot; she couldn't help herself.

Helma unlocked the driver's door of her Buick and opened it.

And stopped. There on the front passenger seat lay a folded copy of yesterday's *Seattle Post-Intelligencer*. Helma didn't subscribe to the *P-I*, nor had she been carrying a copy of it in her car.

She glanced at the lock buttons on the doors. They were all in the down position and her own door had definitely been locked: she'd felt the tumbler disengage when she turned the key.

Four other cars were parked in the library staff parking lot but there was no sign of anyone lurking at its perimeters or on the street. Cars passed at normal speed without drivers glancing her way. Two girls raced past on bicycles. No one suspicious or sinister appearing peered from any corner or doorway.

The proper steps were to relock her car immediately, return to the library, and call the police. She should definitely not touch or disturb this evidence in any way.

The newspaper was folded in half and it was thicker than appropriate. An object lay inside the fold. Helma swung the door halfway closed, then stopped. What could it hurt if she barely lifted a corner of the newspaper? If she used a pencil from her dashboard to do it so she wouldn't disturb the evidence? One small peek?

So that's exactly what she did. Being careful not to disturb the car seat by sitting on it, she leaned across, gripping the back of the seat for balance, and with the eraser end of the pencil, keeping her face averted in case it was explosive, she gingerly turned back the edge of the newspaper.

Inside her car, which she knew had been locked, inside the folded newspaper, lay a steely blue handgun.

chapter fourteen

GUNS AND WOES

The police only had to walk across the street and through Bellehaven Public Library's parklike lawn to reach the library's parking lot, but they came in cars, two with their lights gyrating and a plain blue sedan a few minutes later. Carter Houston merely stepped out of the library where he'd been interviewing Ms. Moon, his notebook still open in his hand. The officers surrounded Helma's car, inspecting the ground, dusting her car door for fingerprints, temporarily leaving the gun where it lay on her car seat.

A motorcycle policeman drove into the lot and parked his bike at an angle behind Ms. Moon's car. Before he removed his helmet, Helma noticed his brushy moustache, his abrupt and soldierly dismount, the blue shirt buttoned tightly across his midriff, and recognized Officer 087, the policeman who'd ticketed her for turning on a red light, who'd wrongfully accused her of "sailing through the intersection," thus setting into motion the events that led to her sentence to the mission.

Officer 087 marched toward Carter and Helma, shoulders back, helmet tucked beneath his arm. Helma saw from the way his moustache quivered, the instant he recognized her. He pivoted smartly on his shiny black boots and approached two policemen on the other side of her car instead.

"Can you ascertain what type of gun it is?" Helma asked Carter Houston who stood beside the open door of her Buick with one of the policemen she recognized as Sidney Lehman. He touched his cap to her. The newspaper was flipped open,

the gun exposed: it was a deep steely blue, not more than
six or seven inches long, with a black checkered hand grip.

"We'll inspect it at the station," Carter told her. "If you
could step back now, please."

"It appears to be small caliber," Helma said, remaining
where she stood. "Perhaps a twenty-two automatic?"

Carter opened his mouth to respond but they were both
distracted by a flurry of colorful movement near the library's
loading dock. Ms. Moon approached the group surrounding
Helma's Buick, on her face a gentle smile.

"As I said earlier, this is to be expected," she said mildly.
"What new brush with lawlessness is this, Miss Zukas?" She
drew out the words, "Miss Zukas" the way she did when she
was exasperated but her face remained benign, unperturbed.
She folded her hands together at her waist, reminding Helma
of the nuns at St. Alphonse long ago.

"I discovered a gun on the front seat of my car," Helma
told her.

"Naturally," said Ms. Moon. Her voice chimed with laughter. "Is that all? No body in the trunk?"

"We haven't looked yet," Carter Houston told her.

"You have my permission to check," Helma said, handing
him her keys. She glanced at her watch. She should already
be at the mission. "Excuse me, but I have an appointment.
Please lock my car when you're finished."

Carter held up his hand, Helma's keys looped around his
thumb. "Wait. I have more questions to ask you."

"I'll be at the mission until eight o'clock and at home
afterward," she told him. "There will be adequate time then."

"And tomorrow," Ms. Moon added, hand hovering above
the detective's sleeve, "Miss Zukas will be here once again,
a magnetic force for further dissonance."

"I *will* be here at the library tomorrow," Helma assured
Carter Houston, who, for a disconcerting moment, looked
almost sympathetic.

"One of the men will drive you to the mission," Carter
said, waving his hand toward Sidney Lehman and officer
087. It may have been coincidental but at that very moment

officer 087 ducked his head like a student fearing he was about to be called on in class.

"No, thank you," Helma told him. "It's a pleasant evening and I prefer to walk."

That taken care of, Helma left the library on foot. She'd already changed into her sensible shoes in the library restroom before she left the building and now she strode purposefully the eight blocks that led past junk shops that were evolving into antique shops, once dirty-windowed cafes that now served lattes and free-range-egg breakfasts, crumbling apartment buildings that had been replaced by two high-rise condominiums. But those most recent changes still existed among the area's coarser history: vacant buildings, an X-rated video store, weedy lots, true junk stores, and the mission. Cars passed steadily, a skateboarder careened around her, shouting, "Coming through!"

The discovery of the handgun added a sinister undercurrent to the perfectly normal day, heightening Helma's awareness of her surroundings. She tried to imagine a criminal who'd break into her car, leave a gun neatly inside a newspaper, and then *relock* her car. Why? To prevent anyone from stealing the gun before she found it? It had been a deliberate and carefully plotted act, performed by a person with an organized mind.

Helma didn't falter, but a block from the mission her step slowed perceptibly when she spotted a group of six men standing on the corner a half block ahead of her. The group was comprised of all of the elements Helma preferred to avoid in her life: they smoked, talked loud, one reeled against another. Swarthy, bearded, in colorless t-shirts and jeans. One was bare chested.

They spotted her about the same time and their conversation ceased as they watched her approach. Helma didn't recognize any of them as men she'd served dinner to in the mission.

She wasn't about to cross the street to avoid them when she was so close to her destination. She remembered what Ruth had said about pretending to carry a ray gun in her pocket when she walked in dangerous places. And how Frank on the kitchen line had said you could tell when a man carried a weapon by the way he walked. Helma supposed that applied to a woman, too.

She slipped her right hand into the pocket of her skirt, envisioning a weapon resting there. Perhaps a handgun like the one on her car seat, with its checkered hand grip and blue steel. Cold, she imagined. If she'd actually touched the gun after she flipped back the edge of the newspaper, it would have been achingly cold. Its presence was a message—to her. From Skitz? That he held her responsible for Tony's imprisonment?

Helma blinked. She was past the group of men and only a few feet from the front door of the mission. She glanced behind her at the men who'd returned to their loud talking and smoking as if she'd passed by them cloaked in invisibility.

As she reached the steps of the mission, she turned at the sound of a motorcycle. A motorcycle policeman did a U-turn in front of the building, touched the visor of his helmet, and slowly drove toward downtown. He wore a brush moustache.

The lobby was empty except for the man at the desk who nodded distractedly, a book open in front of him. Helma never interrupted a person who was reading unless it was an emergency and she silently passed him and hurried to the dining room where Ruth stood in Helma's place on the line, dishing out both vegetables and crinkle-cut french fries. "Where the hell have you been?" she asked Helma, pointing a slotted spoon at her. "Jump in here, would you? Frank went on a binge and is drying out in a dark hole somewhere."

Portnoy stood at the stove, stirring soup. "Busy night," he told Helma. Perspiration glistened on his forehead. "Don't forget the gravy."

"On french fries?" Helma asked.

"Sure. Haven't you heard of New York fries?"

Ruth snorted. "What is this, regional America night?"

"Call it that if you want to," Portnoy told her, looking

wounded. "A big donation of gravy came in this afternoon. Use it or lose it."

Helma donned the clean apron she'd brought from home and took over dispensing the french fries. "Gravy?" she asked the next man in line.

"You've gotta be kidding," he said, drawing back his plate.

"I'm late," Helma told Ruth, "because there was an unexpected development at the library."

"Yeah? Like what? A book misplaced on the shelf?"

Helma waited until there was a lull in the line before she answered. "More like a gun misplaced in my car."

Ruth dropped her serving spoon into the vat of peas. "No shit? *The* gun? How did it get in your car?"

"I don't know the answer to either question," Helma said.

"What else could it be but the gun that did in QVB? I'll bet Carter Houston wet his pants when he saw it."

"If it is the murder weapon, why would anyone leave it in my car?" Helma asked.

"To put the blame on you, why else? I'm surprised Carter didn't put you in chains and deliver you to the cell next to Tony. How about a little more?" she gently asked the last man in line before the public was admitted. Each night he waited until last to be served, approaching the counter hesitantly, saying thank you too many times. He was small, shy, in his late fifties or early sixties, and avoided meeting anyone's eyes.

When the shy man had gone through the line and found a table by himself at the back of the dining room, Helma said, "I don't believe the police suspect me of being involved but they're aware that someone out there *wants* me to be implicated."

Ruth raised her eyebrows and pulled the peas off the counter to be reheated. "It's the elusive Mr. Skitz, isn't it? He's trying to shift the blame from Tony onto you. Pretty clumsy about it, though."

"But Tony will probably be released soon," Helma reminded her.

"Skitz doesn't know that. But be honest, deep down you suspect Skitz tucked it in your car, don't you?"

"It's only a guess at this time."

"That's what this whole thing is about: you make guesses and then you make more guesses to figure out if your first guesses were correct. Skitz shot QVB; he didn't expect Tony to confess so now he's trying to clear Tony and direct the police toward you so he and Tony can blow town. Does that make sense?"

Portnoy set a new pan of french fries in front of Helma, shaking his big head back and forth the whole time. "No, it doesn't make sense," he said. "I bet you a ten-spot that Skitz has already left town. He did what he could for Tony and now he doesn't feel guilty about deserting him so that's what he's done: scrammed."

"You mean Skitz has a conscience that only goes so far?" Ruth asked Portnoy.

Portnoy pinched his thumb and forefinger together until they were a quarter inch apart. "At most. I know these guys."

"I hope you're right and he's history," Ruth told him, "or my friend here could be in trouble." She turned to Helma. "*If* Portnoy's wrong . . ." She began, shrugging apologetically toward Portnoy.

"I'm not," he said, turning on his heels.

"Okay," Ruth continued, looking after Portnoy. "Just for the sake of fantasy, we'll pretend it's the unreal world and you're wrong. Maybe," she continued to Helma, "maybe the gun was Skitz's farewell gift to you. If he's spent five minutes in your company, he knows you'd go straight to the police with it."

"What do you mean?" Helma asked her.

"Figure it out. He *wants* you to give the gun to the police. Skitz's fingerprints are on it because he killed QVB. But what does he care; he's already murdered some poor shmuck in Florida. So he disappears from town, still a 'person of interest,' but he no longer feels guilty about getting Tony busted, because now Tony will go free. Tell the cops about the note on your door," she implored. "Okay? I've only caught a glimpse of this guy and he's definitely trouble. Trust me, I'm more familiar with his type than you are. You know why people call him Skitz?"

"Carter Houston said it's short for schizophrenic."

"Yeah, and you think he religiously takes his meds when he's out there sleeping in doorways?"

"You ready for the next group?" Portnoy interrupted, pointing to the line waiting outside the double doors.

"Yes," Helma told him, rearranging the serving spoons. Apprehension was heightened when the public entered the dining room: the unknown personalities, the lack of a group "sense" that existed among the residents. Everyone grew a little more watchful.

"Oh," Ruth said in a low voice. "Miki at the paper told me she tried to do a human interest story on Brother Danny a few years ago but she couldn't find any info."

"What do you mean?" Helma asked.

"There's no record of his family in the Mississippi town he says he came from, no record at the college he claims he attended. No church affiliation and no previous job record."

"But . . ." Helma began as the first diners, the men she'd walked past on the street, filed in through the door.

Ruth nodded. "They killed the story because they didn't want to endanger the mission. Remarkable discretion for our daily rag, don't you think? Anyway, it's all hush hush so he's either got a past or," Ruth made a face, "he's one of those angels that are all the rage right now, come down from on high to touch our troubled little lives. So make of it what you will."

Ruth and Helma grew too busy to talk. Helma served food mechanically, surprised by the number of people who agreed to gravy on their french fries and thinking about Brother Danny, whose past was perhaps a lie and also about Forrest, who'd lied about both his career and family. And a shocking thought crossed her mind: So what? If the past had truly been left behind, if good had somehow come of it, did it actually matter?

Charlie came through the line, silent for a change. "Thanks

for this morning," he mumbled as Helma dished french fries onto his plate and then left the line before Helma could respond.

"You're welcome to take a napkin," she said to a big man with home-made eagle tattoos up and down his arms, motioning to the stack of white napkins she'd brought. He grunted, then took three and stuffed them in his pocket. She heard Ruth say to a young mother, "Hi, Irene. I brought that extra ribbon I was telling you about."

"Hi, Miss Zoo."

Barry stood before Helma, minus his leather eye patch. The skin around his eye was paler but the eye itself appeared perfectly normal, the same brown as the other, focused, tracking together.

"What is this, some kind of miraculous recovery?" Ruth asked him.

Barry touched his eye. "No, it was just so, you know, people would feel bad."

"And drop more money in your tin cup," Ruth said, offering him a spoonful of peas, which he declined. "Pretty good scam. Wish I'd thought of it."

"Where's your mother?" Helma asked.

"Upstairs talking to Brother Danny. We're staying at a house." He surveyed the food on the counter. "Is there any ice cream?"

"Strawberry," Helma told him. "Would you like to eat dinner?"

He shook his head. "I already ate, but there wasn't any dessert."

"A true hardship case," Ruth muttered while Helma dished up two scoops of strawberry ice cream.

After dinner was served, a bleary-eyed Frank wandered into the kitchen as they were putting away condiments. Barry sat at a table by himself, methodically spooning up his ice cream.

"The cops are here again," Frank said, leaning heavily against the counter, "asking questions." He was rumpled and pale, bent over as if he were in pain.

"About a gun?" Helma asked.

"And the store, too," Frank told her. He rubbed his jaws as if they hurt.

"What store?"

"The gun store over there." He waved vaguely to the north. "Pistol Packers or something like that. It was broke into this morning."

"*That's* where your gun came from," Ruth told Helma. "Somebody stole it from the gun store. Cute."

"It's not my gun," Helma reminded her.

"Well, *somebody* wanted you to have it. It could be a diversion to throw the track off the real gun."

"Guns and Nutter Butters," Frank grumbled.

Barry stood at the counter holding his empty bowl. "The police asked *me* about the Nutter Butters," he said, straightening his thin shoulders and raising his voice. "I told them that little fat man gave me some and they showed me his picture."

"Way to go, kid." Frank started to nod his head, then winced. "You might have saved Tony from the gas chamber."

"We don't have a gas chamber in Washington State," Helma pointed out.

Ruth made noose and hanging motions.

Frank shrugged. "Dead is dead," he said.

Wayne Gallant entered the dining room, his face grim. Frank touched his forehead and scuttled out of the room, his back hunched and head lowered as if he were trying to shrink away. Wayne Gallant didn't seem to notice Frank or his departure. His attention was focused on Helma but she clearly detected police business in his eyes, not personal regard.

"Better go find your mom," Ruth told Barry.

"Okay," Barry said. He waved to Ruth and Helma. "See you again."

"I hope not," Ruth said softly.

Wayne Gallant stopped on the other side of the counter and nodded curtly to Ruth and Helma.

"Was the gun in my car the gun that killed Quentin Boyd?" Helma asked him.

"We're checking it," he told her. "Carter said you'd locked your doors when you left your car this morning."

"That's right. I always do."

"I figured that. Whoever left you the gun used a slim jim to unlock the passenger door. On an older car like yours it would be a snap."

"I used to have a slim jim," Ruth said. She grinned and shrugged.

"If this particular gun *isn't* connected to the death of Quentin Boyd, could it be connected to the break-in at Pistol Packers gun store?" Helma asked.

The chief crossed his arms. Helma could see his notebook in his shirt pocket but he didn't remove it. "Possibly," he said. "That happened early this morning, about four-thirty. The police arrived within ten minutes of the alarm going off."

Ruth licked chocolate pudding off her finger. "I thought guns had serial numbers like cars so you could trace them."

"The serial number on the gun in Helma's car had been removed."

"Curiouser and curiouser," Ruth commented.

"Have you seen Skitz again?" the chief asked Helma.

"No, I haven't," Helma said with certainty. She hadn't. There was the note she'd found on her door but she definitely couldn't say where that had come from. And the movement in the hedge could have been a German shepherd or a large opossum. "Do you have any more information about him?"

The chief frowned and shook his head. "No one's seen him since the night after the murder."

"But you believe he's still in town," Helma said.

He shrugged. "There's no evidence that he's here. He could have left town the night your friend arrived; that's the last time he was seen."

Helma ignored Ruth's pointed stare.

"Did you find any fingerprints in Mrs. Whitney's old apartment?" Helma asked. Portnoy returned from the back storeroom. He picked up a jumble of spoons, and began sorting them, bowl nestled within bowl, edging closer to Helma, Ruth, and the chief.

"None," the chief told her. "None on the door of your car, either. And the gun was wiped clean."

"Obviously a man with experience in the felonious arts," Ruth commented.

"What was stolen from the gun shop?" Helma asked.

The chief massaged his forehead. "The owner hasn't discovered anything missing yet. So either the alarms scared him off or . . ."

"It would take a pretty stupid burglar not to know a gun store would have alarms," Ruth offered.

"Or?" Helma encouraged Wayne Gallant.

"Or he had another motive besides robbery." He shook his head in frustration and brushed his hair off his forehead with his palm. He looked at Helma and she began folding reusable dishcloths, feeling his eyes on her for an uncomfortably long time. "I'm on my way to the office," he said. "I'll talk to you soon. Call me if . . . well, if you think of anything."

Helma and Ruth watched him leave. He paused outside the dining room door, glancing in the direction Frank had gone before continuing up the stairs.

Ruth softly crooned a song off-key: "I'm sorry, so sorry. Please accept my a-pol-o-gy."

Helma ignored her.

"Phone call for you," Portnoy said to Helma from the other end of the kitchen counter. He held the receiver of the wall phone that only accepted incoming calls. "He said it's important."

Helma took the receiver. It was Forrest Stevens. She rubbed her temples, banishing Wayne Gallant from her thoughts and bringing Forrest's face into focus. "I've got something for you," Forrest told her.

"Forrest, it'll be late by the time I get home. Tomorrow would be better."

"No, this doesn't have anything to do with my trying to win your heart. It's an envelope that was left for me at the motel's front desk and inside it is another envelope with your name on it and the words, 'Life and Death.' Sounds urgent to me."

"Do you know who left it?"

"No. The clerk said it appeared at the desk sometime during the day. Can I bring it over to your apartment?"

Helma glanced at the clock above Portnoy's head. It was nearly eight o'clock. "If you wouldn't mind, you could come by the mission. I left my car at the library parking lot. Could you give Ruth and me a ride?"

"Sure. See you in a few minutes."

"I drove," Ruth who'd been openly listening to every word, told Helma. "Thanks anyway."

"Then you could have given me a ride."

"You should have said something."

"I did. My car had a gun in it. I left it at the library," Helma reminded her. "The police were examining it."

"Yeah," Ruth said, grinning, "but I guess it didn't register."

Ruth had already left and Brother Danny sat in the lobby with Helma while she waited for Forrest. The lobby was empty, the front doors blocked open and a breeze barely reached Helma, carrying a mixture of odors from the bay and the train yards. "Thank you for helping Barry and his mother," Helma told Brother Danny.

"Sure. Donna at the women's shelter will do her best. The mother . . ." He shrugged. "If we can get Barry settled in school, that'll help."

"Have you always been interested in the homeless?" Helma asked him.

Brother Danny pulled up his socks. He wore white tennis shoes and black socks. A hole in the knee of his jeans was perfectly patched, nearly invisible. "Not always," he said.

"What drew you to the field?" Helma tried again.

"Saw a need, I suppose." He smiled at her, touching his upper lip, then asked, "Is that your ride?"

Helma rose and Brother Danny with her. A dark car had

pulled up in front of the main doors. "Thanks," Brother Danny told her as he opened the door for her. "We'll see you tomorrow night?"

"For thirty-eight more hours," Helma assured him as she stepped outside.

But it wasn't Forrest behind the wheel of the dark car; it was Wayne Gallant. He stepped out of the car, casually dressed as if his work day were finished, and smiling. "Hi. Can I give you a ride? Maybe we could talk for a few minutes?"

"I'm . . ." Helma began. Strangely, her mind went blank and she stood gazing dumbly at Wayne Gallant.

At that very moment, Forrest pulled up in his dark rental car and parked behind the chief's car. "I . . ." Helma began again. Forrest opened the driver's side and walked around to the other side of the car. "Hello, chief, Helma," he said as he opened the passenger door. "Beautiful evening."

Wayne Gallant stood beside his car. "It is," he said, and said it again. "It is. I'll talk to you tomorrow," and he got back into his car before Helma could say another word. She remained on the steps, watching him drive away until Forrest said, "Ready?"

Forrest turned his car around in the mission parking lot. "We could stop for a drink so you could read the note," he suggested.

"Thank you," Helma told him, "but I'd better go home now. It's been a long day."

Forrest nodded. "When I went out for breakfast this morning, the people at the next table were talking about the murder." He bit his lip. "Your name came up."

Helma didn't care to hear gossip so she asked instead, "You brought the message with you?"

He reached into his pocket and removed a white letter-sized envelope. "This is it. I guess it's too thin to be a letter bomb. I can pull over at the park so you can read it."

It *was* thin, no more than a single sheet of paper. Suddenly Helma was tired, bone tired, desperate for a long night's sleep, a respite from death, mysterious appearances and disappearances, and fruitless conjecture. She slipped the envelope into her purse.

"I'll read it later," she told Forrest. "But why would anyone give a message for me to *you*?"

"I thought it was weird, too, but life out here *is* a little different."

The idea of driving her car home from the library seemed impossible. Helma had experienced these episodes before, when the only demand on her life was to sleep; it was as if a black curtain had dropped over her head, closing off her senses. "Can you just take me home?" Helma asked Forrest. "I'll take the bus to work tomorrow."

"Sure."

Forrest walked Helma to her apartment door and there gave her a hug, which she accepted, even leaned into a little. Her legs felt heavy, her arms so weak it was a struggle to turn the key in her lock. Once inside, she locked the door and headed to her bedroom, stopped by Boy Cat Zukas's insistent meow from her balcony. He glared in through the glass door, his eyes like phosphorous. Helma opened the door for him and he gave her a single glance of dismissal as he padded to his wicker basket.

"You're welcome," she told him.

Her purse was still in her hand and as she dropped it on her bureau the envelope Forrest had given her fell out. *Life and Death*, the neatly written words on the envelope read, just as Forrest had said. The contents were a matter of life and death? She yawned and sat on the edge of her bed as she slit the envelope with the nail file she kept on her night table. Whatever was inside, it didn't even thicken the envelope.

She held the gaping envelope to the light, careful not to touch the contents. Inside was a pink slip of paper approximately four by six inches. It was flimsy, like a carbon copy. She shook the envelope and the paper fluttered onto her bureau top beneath the glare of her lamp.

It was the copy of a receipt from Pistol Packers, the gun shop that had been broken into, for the sale of one Llama .22 automatic pistol. It had been purchased six months ago and the buyer was Quentin Vernon Boyd.

❧ chapter fifteen ❧

SLEEP DELAYED

There was no answer at Wayne Gallant's home phone so Helma called his office, even though it was nearly nine o'clock in the evening.

"Yeah, he's here," the officer on the desk said when Helma gave him her name. "Just a sec."

It seemed to take an unusually long time for Wayne Gallant to answer his extension. Helma stood beside her telephone in the kitchen, wearing her yellow dishwashing gloves, the receipt from Pistol Packers flat on the counter, and beside it the envelope with the words "Life and Death," and beside that, the note she'd found tucked against her door when she'd returned from her drink with Forrest: "That cop better get off his butt before you run off with Mr. Silver Hair." The note was scrawled in a rough print, the envelope addressed in careful cursive. She couldn't tell at all if the same person had written them both. Someone with more expertise than she had would have to examine them. But she didn't intend to hand over the scrawled note to the police unless it became unavoidable, and she couldn't think of a single reason why it should.

An unknown person was giving her answers, dealing them out to her clue by clue, allowing time between each one to form assumptions. It seemed too calculated for Skitz, at least from what little she'd seen of the sullen man. But then how could she know? In his earlier life, Skitz might have been a scientist or doctor, even an accountant. But she doubted it.

Plus, he was wanted in connection with a murder, perhaps by now, even two. She touched the receipt with the tip of her gloved finger. If this receipt was for the .22 that had killed Quentin Boyd, then Mr. Boyd had bought the gun himself only six months ago.

Finally, the chief came on the line. "Yes?" he asked. Hesitantly, Helma thought.

"An item has been delivered to me that I think you should see."

"What is it?"

"A receipt for a twenty-two-caliber Llama automatic pistol. It's from Pistol Packers and it was sold to Quentin Vernon Boyd."

She felt his breathing quicken against her ear but he said just as calmly, "I'll come get it."

"No," Helma told him, glancing around her apartment. She hadn't put away her breakfast dishes and her paper cutouts were scattered across her coffee table. Boy Cat Zukas had made a muddle of his bed. "I'll bring it to your office. I'm wearing gloves and I haven't touched it."

He agreed and Helma hung up. She slid the receipt back into the envelope and stood in the center of her apartment, tipping her head and listening for sounds from the empty apartment next door. She remembered George, Harley, and Eve and pulled a glass from her cupboard, then stood next to the wall that separated the two apartments. Feeling slightly silly, she placed the mouth of the glass against the wall and put her ear to the bottom end.

She heard a low hum: electricity or refrigerator motors, maybe even from her own apartment, but nothing that sounded suspicious, nothing at all.

So Helma set the glass in her sink to wash later and left her apartment, the gun receipt in her purse, tucked securely between her plastic pack of tissues and her checkbook.

And it wasn't until she set foot on the first step of her apartment staircase that she realized her car wasn't in the Bayside Arms parking lot; it was still at the library.

"Oh, Faulkner," she said aloud, taking a step backward

onto the landing. Back to her apartment where she first considered calling Ruth but instead called a taxi. "I'll be waiting outside on my landing," Helma told the dispatcher, "so please hurry."

"Got it," the dispatcher assured her.

The evening wasn't as warm as the night Quentin Boyd was killed but still she needed only a light sweater. She stood by the railing, glancing now and then toward the hedge where she'd seen movement the night before. Nothing unusual caught her eye. No rustle of leaves or shadowy figures. It was still light enough to discern most shapes but still, after checking to be sure no one was nearby to hear her, Helma asked in a soft voice, "Skitz, are you there?"

There was no response, no answering shudder in the shrubbery, only a faint prickle at the back of Helma's neck and along her arms that indicated as loud as spoken words that the evening might not be as benign as it appeared.

When a red light flashed before her eyes, Helma realized she was holding her breath. She exhaled and returned to her apartment to watch from her window until the yellow taxi arrived.

Wayne Gallant stood in the lobby talking to the policeman at the front desk when Helma entered the station. He wore a gray sweatshirt over his white shirt. On the front of it in gold FBI-style letters it read, *Good Cop*. He greeted her with a professional eagerness he couldn't conceal, glancing quickly over her body as if the gun receipt should be in plain sight, perhaps pinned to her sweater.

"Come on back," he told her, stepping aside so she could walk in front of him to his office. "It's a quiet night," he said distractedly, making pleasantries yet clearly not expecting an answer.

In his office, impersonally decorated except for the photographs of his two children, he motioned her toward the table opposite his desk. A square of heavy paper lay in the center of the table and Helma removed the envelope from her purse and set it on the paper.

The chief nodded and read the words on the outside of the envelope aloud: "Life and Death." He drew on a pair of clear plastic gloves. Helma watched as he fit them over each finger, thinking that for some reason, she hadn't imagined plastic gloves being available in such a large size. He removed the pink carbon from the envelope and unfolded it, gazing at it for a long time before he said, "February."

Helma nodded. "So Quentin bought the gun six months ago. Could he have been killed with his own gun?"

"The lab's testing the gun we found in your car and the bullet we recovered from his body. But yes, the gun in your car was a twenty-two-caliber Llama automatic."

"Will you be able to tell if the receipt and the gun match?"

"Hopefully. I phoned Lily Boyd and caught her on her cell phone. She'll stop by in a few minutes."

"Tomorrow's her husband's funeral."

He nodded as he gingerly flattened the receipt on the heavy paper. "I remember after my father died, my mother saying that the worst time is after the funeral when everybody's gone and people expect you to get on with your life. Closed chapter."

Helma thought of her own mother, who'd never made any such comment after Helma's father died. Of course, at the time Helma had flown back to Bellehaven from Michigan and it was only a few days later that her mother discovered her father had lied about the insurance. That deflected the more introspective aspects of grieving for a good long time.

"By the way, your car's here in the parking lot. I had one of the men drive it over from the library."

"Thank you. Did you speak to Sara Hill about the man she saw at my apartment building?"

"I did. She couldn't positively identify him as Skitz, though." He drummed his fingers on the table.

"Your days going okay?" the chief asked. "Everything smooth at the mission?"

"Yes," Helma told him.

He nodded. "Mm-hmm."

Wayne Gallant pretended to study the receipt and Helma

pretended to read the brochure that sat on the table: "Know Your Police," filled with colorful graphics and smiling people in uniforms. Once the chief looked up at her and cleared his throat and Helma glanced at him, waiting.

"Interesting," was all he said, bending back to the receipt.

His phone rang and he picked it up, saying, "Gallant here." Then after a pause, "I'll be right out." He hung up and said to Helma, "Lily Boyd's arrived."

Helma sat in one of the chairs facing his desk. She turned the brochure end over end in her hands and waited until he and Lily returned.

Lily Boyd wasn't wearing black but a dark purple dress that had a somber air and black pumps. A black sweater hung over her shoulders. Her expression was slightly dazed, as if the lights in the chief's office were too bright. She held out her hand to Helma and said, "I'm so sorry that you're being drawn into this."

"If it helps to solve your husband's death, it's perfectly all right," Helma told her.

Wayne Gallant motioned Lily toward the table. "Here's the receipt," he said. He pulled a book from his shelves, checked its index, and opened to a page of handguns. "Are you familiar with this gun?"

She squinted at the receipt, then removed a pair of half glasses from her purse and put them on. She took her time, reading every word. Then she did the same to the description beneath the illustration in the chief's book, touching her finger to the depiction of the handgun. "I don't know very much about guns but Quentin had several, mostly for hunting. He went to Colorado every year to hunt elk with his brother, not that he ever shot any animal that I heard of. A twenty-two isn't big enough to kill an elk, though, is it?"

"No," the chief told her. "This is a small handgun, mostly used for self protection."

Lily nodded. "I think Quentin had two handguns. He didn't often carry them, as far as I know. But on the night he died, he may have." She blushed and glanced apologetically at Helma as if her next words might offend Helma. "He didn't really trust the men who stayed at the mission. But if he had it in his pocket when I dropped him off, I don't know."

"Have you noticed if any of his guns are missing?" Wayne Gallant asked.

"I haven't thought to look and I'm not sure I'd know, anyway. He kept them in his study—in locked cases, of course. Please, you're welcome to inspect them. In fact, I'd rather someone else did. And could I arrange through the police to have them removed from the house?"

"We could do that," the chief agreed.

"Thank you. If this gun," she pointed to the receipt, "isn't there, does that mean that Quentin was killed with his own gun?"

"Possibly."

"Oh." She raised a hand to her mouth. "But you don't mean . . . suicide, do you?"

"No," Wayne Gallant assured her, "he was shot from behind. If we can tie together this receipt, the bullet, and the gun we found today, we'll have more to go on."

"You found a gun today?" she asked.

The chief hesitated and Helma answered, "It was on the front seat of my car."

Lily Boyd turned to Helma and Helma saw the dark suspicion in her eyes before Lily forced her face into neutrality. "Your car?" she asked. "How did it get inside your car?"

"My car was locked," Helma told her, "so someone unlocked my car, left the gun, then relocked the car doors."

Lily stepped closer to Helma, removing her glasses as if that would help clear up her confusion. "To plant a gun in your car? Does someone suspect you killed Quentin?"

"Or somebody's trying to deflect attention from himself to Helma," the chief said.

Lily frowned. "*Are* you a logical suspect?" she asked Helma.

"If you consider the facts alone," Helma admitted. "I suppose I could be."

"Not a sane soul on earth would believe that," Lily Boyd

said. She snapped her glasses closed. "No one. Whoever did this is playing a very bad joke."

"But with potential clues from your husband's death," Helma reminded her.

Lily shuddered. "Have you talked to the owner of the gun store?" she asked Wayne Gallant.

"Not since this receipt came to light."

"That's why the gun store was robbed, to find this receipt." She sat in the chair next to Helma's, slumping into a tiny dejected figure, her feet two inches off the floor. "It had to be someone who knew that Quentin had bought the gun at Pistol Packers. Another hunter maybe? But why? How did this person know the gun had killed Quentin unless he killed Quentin himself?" She sighed. "It's so confusing, isn't it?" She stared at her hands for a few minutes and then asked the chief, "What about the man who confessed?"

"He may know a few details about the crime but he didn't kill your husband. We'll release him within the next forty-eight hours."

Lily sighed and rose from her chair. "As soon as we can find the . . . real felon, we'll all sleep easier." She patted Helma's arm. "Don't you worry. The Bellehaven police are among the best in the nation. Quentin told me so many times."

The chief walked Lily and Helma to their cars, telling them both he'd be in his office a few more hours if they had any ideas or concerns they wanted to share with him that night.

Lily drove off first and Wayne Gallant stood with Helma beside her Buick. She was parked directly beneath a street light and it cast a greenish hue across their faces, sucking away colors. A flock of Caspian terns flew overhead, squawking their eerie parrot's cry. "Late for them," the chief commented, looking up. "Are you having a good visit with your friend Forrest?"

"I haven't had much time to spend with him."

Wayne Gallant didn't look particularly sympathetic. "Can

you think of any reason why he was given the receipt to give to you?"

"None at all," Helma said. "Could it possibly be Skitz? Trying to clear Tony? He might have written the letter implicating me on a computer at the mission. They have several second-hand computers the residents use to update their skills."

He shook his head. "'It's more likely that Skitz has left town. We do have contacts in places where he's likely to show up and nobody's seen him. Let's say he had a shred of conscience about his friend Tony, so he made a couple of moves to pull the light off him, even onto himself. And now he's gone. This isn't a stable person we're discussing, Helma."

"Why haven't you released Tony?"

"He's free to go."

"Does he know that?"

The chief shrugged. "Technically, yes. We'll give him another day and then we'll turn him over to Brother Danny. Tony will need help to get his life going again."

"He may be waiting for Skitz."

"We'll keep an eye on Tony after he's released, in case Skitz comes back. When does your friend Forrest leave Bellehaven?"

"On Sunday," Helma told him and he nodded as if the information were of little interest.

Helma's earlier desire for sleep was gone. She sat on her sofa beneath the beam of her halogen lamp, turning the pages of a *National Geographic* magazine, studying each photograph and searching for a segment that was suitably dark, dreary, and complicated. Her smallest pair of German scissors sat on her coffee table, the pair that was best suited to cut out an intricate and attention-consuming illustration. Boy Cat Zukas lay curled in his wicker basket beside the door to her balcony. He appeared to be asleep but every time she turned a page, he opened one eye and glared at her.

It was late so when her doorbell suddenly jangled she

gasped and dropped the *National Geographic*. Boy Cat Zukas hissed.

"Oh Faulkner," she whispered, and retrieved the magazine and set it on the coffee table beside her scissors.

Her first thought was Skitz, then Wayne Gallant, then Forrest Stevens, but when she peered through the peephole in her door, she saw Ruth.

"I've got this great idea," Ruth said when Helma opened the door. "Wait until you hear it." Ruth strode inside, bringing with her an odor of alcohol and cigarettes. Ruth didn't smoke but she'd obviously been with people who did. She was dressed in a bright dress that looked vaguely Hawaiian and in one hand she carried a small brown grocery sack that held a rectangular item.

"Does it have anything to do with Quentin Boyd's death?" Helma asked.

"No, but I'll get to that. This is about those kids who come to the mission for meals. I hate it but I'm ready to concede they have a right to be there, so I'm going to orchestrate a show to pay for stuff for kids: some kid food, dishes, a couple of booster seats and a high chair, maybe some of that pint-sized kid furniture. What do you think?"

"I think that's a very generous idea," Helma said, both cautiously and with admiration. Ruth often had "great" ideas; it was the follow-through where she lagged.

"I've already talked to Wally," Ruth continued in a rush, her enthusiasm filling Helma's apartment. "He'll donate the gallery space, and I've lined up four other artists to donate a couple of works apiece. I know I can hook a few more." Ruth leaned down and swept Boy Cat Zukas out of his basket. "What do you think, kitty kitty?" she asked. Helma could hear Boy Cat Zukas purring before Ruth kissed him between the eyes and dropped him like a lump into his basket. Then she turned to Helma. "I did this scientific experiment I want to show you."

"Regarding the children at the mission?" Helma asked.

"Of course not. The subject is murder, ma'am." Ruth pulled a box from the grocery bag like a magician. "Ta-ta.

Sugar cubes. Remember the night QVB bought the farm and Brother Danny came running in all hot and bothered? And then we hear shouts of peril and shock from the rear of the building. What does Brother Danny do?"

"He . . ." Helma began.

"Exactly right," Ruth said. She held the box of sugar cubes at waist height. "He drops them." Ruth released the box and it fell to the kitchen's tile floor, crunching one corner. "So what do you think of that?" Ruth asked, bowing as if she expected applause.

"That it might be wiser to buy granulated sugar," Helma said.

"Big funny. Now, what's important here is that sugar cubes didn't go flying all over the floor like they did at the mission."

Helma examined the dented box, remembering the white cubes scattering across the office floor, crunching and crumbling. Who had cleaned them up, she wondered. "Drop it again," she told Ruth. "Maybe it has to hit just right."

They spent the next fifteen minutes dropping the box of sugar cubes from knee high to Ruth standing on one of Helma's dining room chairs and holding the box as high as the ceiling. The cubes crumbled; the box grew lumpy; granules of sugar seeped out the cardboard corners onto the floor, but the box did not break.

Finally, Ruth picked up the misshapen box and dropped it in Helma's trash. "Now what are we to make of this curious fact?" she asked.

"Brother Danny's box of sugar cubes was already open," Helma said, "although he claimed he'd just bought them."

"Exactly."

"He may have opened the box on the way into the building to save time," Helma suggested.

"Could be," Ruth said, tapping her chin. "Or, he never went out to buy sugar cubes at all. He might have been busy assuring that the biggest obstruction to the mission getting the grant was out of the picture—permanently."

Helma removed a broom from her closet and began sweeping up loose sugar granules. "It's a giant leap from sugar cubes to murder."

"Tell me the thought hasn't crossed your mind," Ruth challenged her.

"Not seriously," Helma admitted.

"It makes perfect sense to me. Discuss it with the chief in shining armor." She made Groucho Marx eyebrows and when Helma didn't answer, said, "If Skitz is still around, I've got an idea how to flush him out, too."

"How?"

Ruth took a banana from the bowl on Helma's counter and dropped into the rocking chair. "We'll get Tony released and I bet Skitz will show up, pronto. Look at all the work he's done to take the heat off Tony."

"But the police already plan to release Tony," Helma told her. She emptied the dustpan into her trash basket, hearing the sugar sift like sand to the bottom of the bag, then sat on the sofa opposite Ruth. "They don't consider him a suspect."

"Like I said before, how's Skitz supposed to know that? He's been hiding in the bushes somewhere all this time."

"If it is Skitz who's been leaving me the notes and clues, as much as he knows about my private life, he'd know Tony was free to go," Helma said. "Besides, the police now think Skitz has left town."

"Do you?" Ruth asked around a mouthful of banana.

"I don't know. It's possible. Wayne Gallant believes that if Tony witnessed Quentin Boyd's murder, he'd be in danger from the real killer if he were released, and what if the real killer is Skitz?"

"We could keep an eye on Tony," Ruth suggested nonchalantly. "He could stay with you or me."

"I don't think so, Ruth. But Wayne Gallant said he'd release him to Brother Danny in a day."

"That's stupid," Ruth said, halting the chair's rocking motion. "Delivering Tony to Brother Danny could be like delivering the lamb to the wolf. When'd you talk to the chief?"

"An hour ago." She told Ruth about the receipt for the handgun.

Ruth whistled and dropped her banana peel on the coffee table. Helma moved it onto a coaster. "Has anybody investigated Forrest?" Ruth asked. "I mean, I love the guy but this all started happening when he showed up."

"Forrest couldn't have anything to do with Quentin Boyd's murder. That would be impossible."

"Yeah, probably." Ruth ran her hands through her bushy hair. "You and Forrest have your heart-to-heart yet?"

Helma shook her head.

"Hey, murder's a piece of cake compared to that," Ruth said.

❧ *chapter sixteen* ❧

TRUE CONFESSIONS

Helma's dreams were a strange soup of guns, misshapen sugar cubes, vats of mashed potatoes and peas, and Forrest Stevens in his high school guise discussing mortgages and two-car garages. Once she woke to the sound of stealthy movement and sat up in bed, gasping. The low glow of her nightlight caught the gleam of cat's eyes in her bedroom doorway. Boy Cat Zukas was not allowed beyond his basket in the living room but there he sat in her doorway like ancient statuary. He gazed at Helma for a few moments, then yawned and padded back down the hallway toward the living room.

Curiously, Helma then fell into a deep sleep that lasted until her alarm sounded. If she experienced dreams, good or bad, she couldn't recall a single one.

During breakfast, eaten while facing Washington Bay where banks of fog evaporated beneath the rising sun, Helma made two lists, one titled "Library," and the other "QVB." Her QVB list was the longer of the two.

George Melville wore a gray suit and blue striped tie and his beard was neatly trimmed. In response to Helma's appraising glance, he shrugged and said, "I drew the short end of the stick. You're gazing at the library's official representative to QVB's funeral."

"I thought Ms. Moon would attend."

George tugged at the hems of his suit jacket, smoothing

181

the creases across the waistline. "So we all hoped. But she phoned me last night to ask if I'd be the patsy."

Eve, who was passing by carrying her morning coffee in a Pizzeria cup, warned, "Don't make faces at the casket."

"Evie," George admonished, clicking his tongue.

"Where *is* Ms. Moon?" Helma asked. The lights were off in the director's office.

"She said she had personal business this morning, whatever that means. Oh," George said, raising a finger, "the auditor's stopping by this afternoon to take a look around the building. He's the advance scout, I guess, coming to decide what kind of an assault team to bring in here bright and early Monday morning."

"Does Ms. Moon know?" Helma asked.

"She's the one who told me last night," George said.

At her desk, Helma looked up Quentin Boyd's real estate office in the phone book and then dialed the number. The funeral began in twenty minutes and she expected the office to be closed but the phone was answered, "Boyd Realty. This is Pamela."

Helma didn't lie. She was always very careful not to lie, but she made her voice familiar and authoritative. "Hello, Pamela. We're forming some plans here and I have a few questions about the stability of some of your company's projects now that Mr. Boyd is gone."

"Who's calling please?" Pamela asked.

Helma paused as if Pamela should have recognized her voice. "This is Wilhelmina Zukas at BPL. Should I speak to someone else?"

"No, I can answer any question to do with the business," Pamela said, her own voice growing stronger with authority.

"My question is about the Bayview Street project."

"The Bayview Street project?"

"Yes, on the land where the Promise Mission stands. I understand there have been negotiations to acquire that property."

"Not that I'm aware of. Since the city's business district is expanding into that area now, it's prime property, but the

mission is very established there." Her voice dropped.
"That's where Quentin died, you know."

"That's what I understand. So he wasn't trying to acquire
that property?"

"No, *I* would have known, I assure you." She spoke as if
there were implications Helma should understand. "What
company did you say you were with again?"

"BPL. Thank you. It sounded like an excellent investment," and Helma hung up, puzzled. Quentin Boyd *might*
have kept his plans to himself, only telling his wife and
Brother Danny. The Promise Mission was owned by Brother
Danny but for Quentin to be negotiating for property which
was essentially viewed as belonging to an institution would
be a touchy transaction.

Next she dialed the mission and asked for Brother Danny.

"He went up to the border to pick up a turn-back," the
receptionist told her. The Canadian border was only twenty
miles from Bellehaven and it was common for the indigent
to be turned back when they tried to cross the border, usually
by walking through. Promise was the closest mission.

"Thank you. I'll call again later. By the way, has Skitz
been seen at the mission in the past twenty-four hours?"

"Nope. How come everybody's asking for Skitz?"

"Who else has?" Helma asked.

But suddenly the receptionist became cagey.

"That's private business. I haven't seen him and that's all
I've got to say. Anything else?"

"No. Thank you."

The auditor was a woman, young, beautiful, and early.
Since Ms. Moon was gone and Helma had the most seniority,
Dutch referred her to Helma, ushering her into the workroom
himself with a near smile on his face, two rarities on his
account.

"I'm Delia Bonner," she said, offering Helma a perfectly
manicured hand. "I'm only here to find the best place to set
up our equipment, if you don't mind." Delia's blond hair
curled delicately around her ears and brushed her slender

neck. Her eyes were blue, the bright Baltic blue of Helma's relatives. Her pale peach suit was sleek and modest, yet somehow accentuating her body. Dutch couldn't take his eyes off her.

"To set up a command post?" he asked.

"Very similar," Delia said, smiling, and Dutch's shoulders straightened to square angles. He pulled in his stomach and appeared ready to salute.

"Thank you, Dutch," Helma said before Dutch could offer any military fealty.

Dutch grunted, pivoted, and left the workroom.

"Is Zukas Lithuanian?" Delia asked.

"Yes," Helma told her. "How did you know?"

"My maiden name is Kaunas." Her smile widened. "*Labas*." Hello.

"*Labas*," Helma answered.

"You guys should have a secret handshake, too," Eve said as she passed Helma's cubicle.

In the cubicle next to Helma's, Harley Woodworth rose from his chair and peered over the bookcases that separated his territory from Helma's. "Can I help?" he asked Delia, his long face widened by a smile.

"I'll be fine, thank you," Delia told him.

"You could be undercover," Harley said. He flushed and stammered. "I mean looking like that. Really good, I mean, like you didn't know math. A lot of blondes don't."

There was no way to rescue Harley and he sank back into his cubicle, disappearing in a cacophony of sniffs, coughs, and throat clearings.

"I'll show you around," Helma told Delia.

"Librarians probably hear that, too," she said as she followed Helma out of the workroom. "That, 'Gee, you don't look like an accountant' kind of statement."

"Sometimes," Helma, who'd often heard the corresponding phrase when she first graduated from library school, told her.

Most every inch of the library was in use and since the old typing room didn't have the correct computer connections, Delia decided to set up her own equipment in the staff lounge. "I'll be back tomorrow and on Monday we'll begin," she said as she measured a corner of the room with a carpenter's yellow tape measure. "We'll try to be as unobtrusive as possible."

"How long will the audit take?" Helma asked.

"A week to two weeks. It depends."

Helma thought of Ms. Moon's curious behavior and now her unexplained absence and wondered just what "It depends" might entail.

Delia left just before lunch and after she was gone, Helma tried to reach Brother Danny again but this time she was told he was driving four residents to a job painting a fence.

"Are you working through your lunch hour?" Eve asked as she picked up a stack of books and a small cardboard box that Helma knew hid Snickers bars, for her stint on the reference desk.

"I'm making up an hour I missed yesterday," Helma told her.

Eve nodded. "Ms. Moon said you've been 'preoccupied,' but then I think *she* has." Eve glanced at the clock. "Yikes. I'd better get out there."

Helma went back to her project in the quiet workroom. On her computer she perused the overdues list she was preparing for Ms. Moon. The majority of patrons owed less than five dollars, but then there were the "stars," people who owed in excess of fifty dollars. Ruth was in that category, barred from checking out any library materials, a fact that didn't seem to bother her or embarrass her enough to make amends.

"Excuse me, Helma."

Helma looked up from her computer to find Forrest standing beside her desk, smiling. He wore khaki shorts and a short-sleeved shirt, with spotless white tennis shoes. "The girl at the desk said I could come back. I'm going on a whale-watching cruise in an hour. Can you take the afternoon off and come with me? My treat."

Helma looked with longing from Forrest to the sunny day outside. Only once had she seen one of the pods of Orca whales that frequented the waters around the islands. The memory was vivid: those impossibly huge gleaming black and white bodies rising out of the water. "I wish I could," she told Forrest, "but I have too much work to do here. I'm sorry."

"I'm sorry, too, but I thought I'd ask. If we're lucky, I'll take a few pictures for you. Any more word on the gun receipt?"

"How did you know what was in the envelope?" Helma asked.

"The chief of police and I had breakfast together this morning. He wanted to ask me a few questions."

"About the receipt?" Helma asked.

"Mostly." Forrest regarded her thoughtfully. "I couldn't help him much. He's concerned about your welfare, I think. Would you like to have dinner with me tomorrow night?"

"I have to work at the mission but yes, if you don't mind a late dinner, I'd enjoy it very much."

Forrest leaned over and lightly touched her cheek. "Thanks. I'll call you tonight when I get back and we'll set a time and place."

Helma watched Forrest leave the workroom. He walked with light steps, a man unburdened, on vacation. She half rose from her chair, imagining the sun on water and majestic Orca whales. Her hand moved her computer mouse to the EXIT command. Then she hesitated and sat down again, turning her eyes dutifully to her computer screen. There was so much to do.

At one o'clock George Melville returned from Quentin Boyd's funeral, without his suit jacket and with his tie undone. His eyes were bright and his cheeks flushed and when he stopped beside Helma's cubicle, she caught a whiff of alcohol. "Great food," he told her. "Classy event."

"The funeral?" Helma asked.

"First class from A to Z," he said. "You'd expect a spread like that to take months to put together. There was even a . . . Whoops, I'll tell you later." He nodded his head across the workroom where Ms. Moon had just entered through the rear door, her face set, lips tight, eyes red but steely. She marched directly to Helma and George, dressed in an unusually subdued green suit.

"There will be a staff meeting immediately," she said tersely and marched just as resolutely to her office.

"Be there or be square," George murmured. "I think we're going to be enlightened as to what's been going on." He leaned into Harley Woodworth's cubicle. "Come on, little buddy. Stow your doldrums. It's show time."

As the librarians entered the staff lounge, there was no talk of shifting seating to improve the group dynamic. Ms. Moon stood at one side of the round table and the others automatically aligned themselves as far from her as possible, creating a definite hierarchy: Helma; George; Harley; Roger Barnhard, the children's librarian; and Eve. Roberta, the history and genealogy librarian, wouldn't be back from her Williamsburg vacation until September fourth.

"I've called this meeting to clear the air," Ms. Moon began. She swallowed, her eyes grew misty, and she clasped her hands together at her waist, rocking on her feet before she spoke. The lounge was silent; no rustle of papers or shifting on chairs, no exchange of glances. The coffee pot burped and Ms. Moon's hands tightened.

Helma felt the librarians around her—all except George, who sat forward eagerly—grow as uncomfortable as she felt. A very personal admission was coming, a confession of some sort, Helma could sense it. She glanced around the staff lounge contemplating ways to forestall it, her eyes settling on the door. Leaving was her only option and that was unthinkable.

Ms. Moon took a deep breath. "I've abused my position as your director and I have no alternative, no recourse, but to admit it to you, my peers." She glanced soulfully into each librarian's eyes and before Ms. Moon reached her, Helma looked down at her hands. "To ask for your forgiveness."

Ms. Moon took a second breath and picked up an encyclopedia ad from the table and fanned herself for a few moments, then set it down again. Her voice dropped. "I've bought books using the library discount," she confessed.

George let out his breath in a whoosh and sat back in his chair. "What's wrong with that?" he asked in obvious and cranky disappointment. "It's one of our few perks around here."

Helma raised her head and saw Ms. Moon's face tighten. George had disrupted the crescendo of her confession.

"I have interests that foster expensive books and to develop an adequate collection I bought . . ." She swallowed. "Several thousand dollars worth on the library discount."

Roger Barnhard whistled between his teeth. Eve's eyes widened. Her lips formed a silent "Wow."

"I buy medical books sometimes," Harley offered in sympathy. "They're really expensive, too."

"Must be some collection," George commented.

"Is this why you've been upset about the audit?" Helma asked.

Ms. Moon nodded. "I knew I would be exposed," she whispered. "I wasn't aware of how much I'd purchased until I added it up." She dabbed at her eyes. "It was a terrible shock."

"It's okay," Eve said. She pushed a plate of chocolate chip cookies toward Ms. Moon. "The auditor probably won't do anything to you." She looked at George. "Will she?"

"Might raise their eyebrows a little," George said. "Give them something to talk about at the head office. But so what?"

"Does this mean . . . Do you—can you—all forgive me?" Ms. Moon asked. She gazed at them hopefully, her eyes widening.

"You got it," George said. "Why not?"

"Sure," Eve told her.

Both Harley and Roger nodded.

"Helma?" Ms. Moon asked.

"I don't believe it's my place to forgive," Helma told her. "There's no crime here that I can perceive."

"That's because your judgment is blinded by too many

murders," George suggested. "*All* other crimes look insignificant by comparison."

The first hint of Ms. Moon's beatific smile returned. "Thank you," she said, her voice dulcet with gratitude. "Thank you." And she sat down as if she were melting into her chair. "You may all return to your duties now."

"To whistle while we work," George said quietly. As they left the lounge, he pulled off his tie and told Helma, "That was small potatoes. I thought we were in for something juicy."

So had Helma. She asked George, "Which lines of the Auden poem were read at Quentin Boyd's funeral?"

"None. No poems. We barely had time to consign him to the earth before we began the festivities."

"No stanzas from Auden's 'Funeral Blues'? Are you sure?"

"Positive. We heard the usual Bible stuff, then some old guy who reminisced about what a good kid QVB was before he grew up to be an ass. But no poetry."

"That's odd. Lily Boyd expressly asked for the poem so it could be used at her husband's funeral."

"Well, it wasn't. Great food, though."

"That man who came to see you this afternoon was so cute, Helma," Eve said as she passed Helma and George. "He looked like Richard Gere." She winked and stepped into her own cubicle, shaking her hand as if it were hot.

This time when Helma phoned Brother Danny, he was in. "What can I do for you, Helma?" he asked. "Do you need a night off?"

"Not yet. I have two questions to ask you. Did Quentin Boyd try to convince you to move the mission so he could develop the mission's current property?"

"No, he never approached me with that idea."

"You're sure? Not even obliquely? He didn't offer to build a new shelter for you if you'd sell him the mission?"

Brother Danny laughed. "No. I'd definitely remember *that*.

He may have coveted this property but he never voiced it. That would have been a very touchy issue."

"Thank you," Helma told him. "I'll see you tonight."

"Wait, I thought you said you had two questions."

Ms. Moon walked past Helma's cubicle, humming, and Helma covered her ear. "That's right. It's about the sugar cubes you brought to the mission the night Quentin Boyd was murdered. Had you just purchased the box?"

"That's right. I drove over to Hugie's. I was in a hurry and it was the closest grocery store."

"But you dropped the box when we heard the shouts and the sugar cubes scattered all over the floor, as if the box were already opened."

Brother Danny was silent for several seconds. Helma heard him sigh. "Well, you caught me." His southern accent was more pronounced. "It's a bad habit, I know. I grew up dirt poor, like people say, and candy, real candy, was way out of my reach. I used to sneak those little cubes from the teacher's desk. She liked her tea. They're still a treat for me, a kind of comfort food that reminds me of being a kid when life was simple. I don't mean better, just simpler."

"So you'd opened the box to suck on a sugar cube because you were nervous about the grant committee meeting?" Helma asked.

"That's right." He laughed. "Don't spread it around, okay? Anything else I can help you with?"

"No, that's all." She thanked him again and hung up.

Around Helma the library pulsed as it processed information while she sat at her desk and twirled the phone cord around her finger, thinking. Then she removed the Belle-haven phone book from her shelf and opened it on her desk. She ran her finger down the columns of "Jones" entries; there was a page and a half of Joneses.

She was interrupted by a phone call from Ruth. "Can I put you down as a supporter of my benefit show?" she asked. "All it means is that your name will be on a list at the gallery. No donations required."

"Of course," Helma told her. "And I'll be happy to donate."

"I was hoping you'd say that. See you at the mission tonight for another fun-filled evening."

"I may be a few minutes late," Helma told her. "There's something I need to check."

"Uh-oh," Ruth said. "You sound serious. Does it have anything to do with dead men?"

"Possibly. It's too soon to tell."

"Well, fill me in later. If you don't show up at the mission within a reasonable time, I'll call your favorite cop."

Helma returned her phone book to its allotted space and clicked through her computer until she found the Young Readers' association and Trudy Jones's phone number.

"Mom's in the kitchen," the young voice told Helma.

"Please call her to the telephone," Helma said.

"Why?"

"Call your mother to the telephone at once," Helma advised.

"I hate you."

"That's immaterial. I'd like to speak to your mother."

"Mom!" the child screamed in Helma's ear.

After she identified herself, Helma asked Trudy, "Did you have refreshments at your last Young Readers meeting?"

Trudy laughed. "We always do. The richer, the sweeter, the better."

"Do you recall who brought them?"

"Mmm. Not really. Usually three members share: one brings beverages and the other two edibles. I can look it up if you want."

"Please."

There was a rustle of papers and a child's plaintive cry for two cookies, not one, before Trudy returned to the phone. "Here we are. I haven't had time to type up my notes. Donna Gordon brought beverages. Tracy McKnight and Lily Boyd brought food."

"Do you recall what Lily brought?" Helma asked.

"I don't. Is it important? Oh wait. I do remember. She didn't bring anything. She was so flustered because of her talk that she forgot."

"Did she mention what she'd intended to bring?"

"Not that I heard."

In light of Ms. Moon's renewed good mood, Helma left the library fifteen minutes early and drove to Lily Boyd's house, parking along the street in front. Helma expected to find several cars but only the silver BMW sat in the driveway. She rang the doorbell, pressing twice on the pearly button in the bronze frog's belly, prepared for no one to answer.

But again, the dog yapped at the back of the house. Lily Boyd's voice was audible through the screened windows as she hushed it and then she opened the door.

"Why Helma, how nice. Won't you come in?" Lily wore shorts and a t-shirt, casual for the drama of the day. She saw Helma take in her clothes and said, "I'm just cleaning up. Excuse the way I'm dressed."

"I expected you to have company."

"No, I preferred to be alone. It's been a long and emotional day. There was no family to speak of, except Quentin's sister and we never got along. She's much younger. What can I do for you?" She motioned inside. "Would you like a cup of tea?"

"No thank you," Helma told her. "I need to be at the mission in a few minutes."

"Then let's sit down out here," Lily said, leading her to a set of three wicker chairs on the front porch. "We can't have many more days like this."

"You mentioned that your husband wanted to develop the land the mission occupies," Helma said. She set her purse on the floor beside her chair and crossed her legs at her ankles.

Lily nodded. "But it was still very hush-hush, I believe. You can imagine what a touchy issue it would have been."

"That's exactly what Brother Danny said."

"Of course he'd say that. Despite his generous heart, he's no political innocent. If word were to get out . . ." A yellow cat raced across the lawn and disappeared into the hedge.

"Do you have any idea why someone took great pains to

let *me* know your husband had bought that gun?" Helma asked Lily.

"Perhaps the killer himself has a guilty conscience and admired your sense of justice and perseverance. Criminals frequently *want* to be caught, I've read."

"But that would mean the killer *knows* me," Helma said. "The gun had no fingerprints, no serial number, no way to connect it with the killer, only to your husband."

Lily shook her head and picked a piece of lint from her t-shirt. "I don't understand it either; it's very confusing but I have faith the police will find the answer—and the man who killed my husband."

"The killer could have attacked your husband, perhaps for money," Helma mused. "Quentin tried to protect himself by pulling his gun from his pocket. Then the killer wrested it away from him and shot him."

"It's very difficult for me to imagine Quentin pulling a gun."

"And then there were the Nutter Butter cookies," Helma said.

"Didn't your policeman tell you?" Lily asked. "Quentin bought them for refreshments at the inspection committee's meeting. The killer may have been trying to take them from Quentin. All for cookies." She rubbed her temples and said, "I'm sorry. This kind of talk . . ."

"No, *I'm* sorry," Helma told her. "I'll leave now. Thank you." She'd already taken two steps away from the front door when she turned and asked, "Did Quentin keep the bullets to the gun in the glove compartment?"

Lily Boyd hesitated. "I really wouldn't know," she said.

"Good-bye now," Helma said, giving Lily Boyd a small wave.

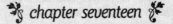

🎝 chapter seventeen 🎝

FATAL DISCUSSIONS

Helma had just parked her car in the mission parking lot when Brother Danny walked into the lot, a car key in his hand.

"Hello, Helma," he said. "It's a little cooler tonight."

"Slightly," Helma agreed. "Even that's a relief. Are you on your way to pick up residents?" She motioned to the key in his hand. "Should we set aside some food?"

"I'm off to the Fireside Bakery to pick up a donation of baked goods. Should be back in an hour." He took a step past her, then stopped. "About your phone call this afternoon. Can I ask where you heard that Quentin Boyd wanted to develop the mission's property?"

"It was a rumor, that's all. I was curious."

He nodded. "Me too. This mission's too important to me to abandon for mere money."

"Even for a more modern building?" Helma asked.

He rubbed his upper lip, studying her. Then he relaxed and grinned. "You're a curious woman, Miss Zukas. And a thorough woman if that database you're developing is an indication. Would I be out of line here to think you've been asking around about me and maybe the answers don't add up?"

"I'm having trouble finding *any* answers," Helma told him. "Even your name . . ."

The yellow cat that lived in the car with the broken window cautiously slunk from beneath the car and curled around

194

Brother Danny's legs. He absently picked it up and began rubbing its ears. Helma could hear its rumbling purr.

Brother Danny laughed. "I know. It's a simple story, not even that interesting. Once on my way down I helped somebody, not in any spectacular way, I thought. But when I was at rock bottom, this person died—I'd forgotten him by then—and he left me money, provided I pull myself together. It was one of those bolt-of-lightning moments that change your life." With his finger, he made a zig-zag lightning motion in the air between them. "I became a new man and have never looked back."

"You reinvented yourself," Helma said.

"I found myself," Brother Danny corrected.

Helma walked into an emergency at the mission. Chaos reigned in the kitchen where a new cook who'd just taken up residence at the mission had disagreed with Portnoy over which size pot to use to steam a donation of fresh green beans.

"The war escalated into parental issues," Ruth explained as she swept up shards of crockery.

The green beans—and all other food items—still sat undisturbed on the counters, but pots, dishes, and cooking utensils were strewn across the kitchen. Frank languidly picked up utensils one at a time, gazing calmly at the destruction.

"Is Portnoy here?" Helma asked.

Ruth nodded toward the back door that led to the service entrance. "He's out back smoking a cigarette and licking his wounds." She raised her hand. "Mental wounds only, but there were some whoppers that cut to the core."

"You tossed in a couple of good ones yourself," Frank told Ruth as he inspected a spoon with its bowl bent backward.

Ruth ducked her head modestly. "I tried to get into the spirit of the event."

It was ten minutes until dinner when lines of hungry and expectant men would begin snaking into the dining room. The green beans were cleaned and waiting in a colander. "I have to call Wayne Gallant," Helma told Ruth.

"Don't you dare leave me with this mess," Ruth said, waving her broom around the disheveled kitchen, "not with a horde of ravenous, unstable people out there."

The phone in the kitchen only took incoming calls. Outgoing calls, usually emergency requests for assistance, only went as far as the front desk.

"But . . ." Helma began.

"Is anybody dead?" Ruth demanded.

"Not recently."

"Then save it until after dinner. No way is Portnoy or his cohort coming back in time. We've been drafted to get this meal out tonight, start to finish. Well, we've had a little help. Look out there. Irony in motion." She pointed to the table that usually held desserts. On it sat three trays of canapés, crackers with sculpted toppings, vegetables with cream-colored fillings, smoked salmon on beds of radicchio. Another tray held pastel petit fours, glazed fruits, and squares of cake in fluted paper. It was all very elegant, a mirage arranged on the formica and metal table.

"Who donated those?" Helma asked.

"Leftovers from QVB's funeral," Ruth told her. "Must have been some party. I just hope they're not poisoned."

Helma hesitated and then grabbed the colander of beans. This was her sentence and this was what she was supposed to be doing under penalty of law. She'd call the chief when dinner had ended.

It was an unusually busy evening. When the second wave, the public, entered the dining area, they ran out of chairs and diners sat on the floor, their backs against the walls, or they stood balancing their plates on one hand and eating with the other. When a mother with two preteen children entered, Helma beckoned them into the kitchen where, even though there weren't any chairs, they could stand at the counters and be out of the press of men.

Quentin Boyd's funeral leftovers were the first to go. Some men bypassed the dinner line and filled their plates directly from the canape trays. The fresh beans ran out and

Helma found cans of green beans in the back storage area. The spaghetti and meatballs were consumed and they were reduced to serving spaghetti with tomato sauce. No one complained about the food.

However, tempers were short. When two men began arguing over who was holding up the line, Helma said in her silver-dime voice, "You are here on these premises to eat. You will be civil." She ignored two men who glared at one another from opposite sides of the room, but when one taunted the other with kissing motions, she made an elaborate show of reaching for the telephone and both men turned their attention to their plates.

In the rush and heat of the meal, Helma forgot about calling Wayne Gallant, even forgot the reason she'd so urgently wanted to talk to him. All she could do was work as quickly as she could to stay ahead of the diners. She felt her clothes clinging to her body; her hair sticking to the back of her neck. True to Ruth's prediction, neither Portnoy nor the new cook returned to the kitchen.

Finally, everyone was fed and the food cleared away and the dining room back in order. Ruth sat on the table in the center of the kitchen and pressed a towel beneath her shirt, blotting her skin. "Thank God that little bit of hell is over. How'd you talk me into this anyway?"

"I hardly . . ."

"Just kidding," Ruth said. "If I had big bucks I'd install air-conditioning in this place. That's why Brother Danny should have requested a grant. The hell with roof repairs."

Helma glanced at her watch and saw she only had ten minutes before her shift ended and she could go home. "I have to phone Wayne Gallant," she said as she removed her apron.

"So you claimed earlier." Ruth sat up and wrapped the towel around her neck. "You got a lead on QVB's murder or are you going to let the poor guy know he's forgiven?"

"I need to discuss an idea with him, that's all."

Ruth waved her hand. "Go ahead. I'll meet you upstairs."

Helma went upstairs but the steel door leading to the offices was locked. The only other phone was at the desk in the main lobby where several men lounged, looking half asleep or worse. There was a pay phone on the corner across the street but she supposed a few more minutes wouldn't matter; she could phone Wayne Gallant from home.

Ruth joined her in the lobby and together they walked out the front door. "That was like being squeezed through the proverbial wringer," Ruth said. "Right now I wish I smoked."

Helma didn't wish she smoked, but she knew what Ruth meant. Her head buzzed and her shoulders ached. She thought with longing of the chair on her deck overlooking the bay. To sit there with a cup of tea and watch the fading sky . . .

Ruth paused to watch two men coming up the steps. One staggered and the other one, tall and lanky with dark hair, grabbed the first man's elbow, saying, "You okay?"

"Bart?" Ruth asked in a soft voice.

The tall man turned and looked at Ruth, recognition flickering in his eyes, and then he looked away without a word or a change in expression, continuing to help his friend up the steps. Ruth watched him, her expression sorrowful. Then she raised her face to the clear blue sky and said, "The line is damn thin sometimes, isn't it?"

Helma thought of the mother and children who'd eaten in the kitchen that night, who'd looked like any mother and children she'd seen shopping in the grocery store or downtown. "Frighteningly so. Can I give you a ride home?"

"I think I need to walk tonight," Ruth said distractedly, gazing behind her toward the front desk where the two men were signing in. "Thanks, though."

Helma nodded and walked to the fenced parking lot where she'd left her car. The lot was full; it would be a busy night at the mission, with extra beds set up in the chapel and maybe even the dining room. A brown dog barked in one of the pens. "Hush," she told it and it did. Then, remembering how the facilitator in her problem patrons workshop had stressed rewarding proper behavior, she added, "Good dog."

The dog tipped its head and dropped to its belly, issuing a few perfunctory growls.

Helma first checked the front and rear seats of her Buick before she unlocked the door. Both were empty. Heat rushed out of the door when she opened it and she gingerly touched the plastic seat covers; she'd have to let them cool down for a few moments. She turned at the sound of gravel crunching behind her, expecting to see Brother Danny carrying baked goods.

"Hello, Helma."

It was Lily Boyd. She wore the same shorts and t-shirt she'd worn earlier that day. On her face was a look of concern. "May I talk to you for a moment?"

"Of course," Helma told her. She stood in the open door of her car, waiting. In the train yards, a whistle blew and she heard the faint beep of the warning at the crossing guards.

Lily waited until the whistle died down. "We can sit in my car," she said, pointing to her silver BMW parked between a van and pickup on the opposite side of the lot. "It's air-conditioned."

"It's cooler now than it was earlier, and definitely cooler than inside. I'm fine."

"I'm very warm," Lily said. She slipped her hand in her pocket. "I'd rather we spoke in my car."

Helma peered around the parking lot. Every space was taken. The blue van Brother Danny had taken to pick up the baked goods sat in its slot. No one would be pulling in. It was curfew so no one would be leaving, either.

"Do I have a choice?" Helma asked. The bulge in Lily's pocket didn't appear large enough to be a weapon but Helma knew guns came in unusually small sizes.

"Not really," Lily said pleasantly and waved graciously toward her car.

Helma led the way to Lily's BMW, feeling the older woman following close behind her. Lily opened the driver's door with her free hand and stood beside it until Helma opened her door and climbed into the passenger side. Then Lily slid into the driver's seat and turned on the engine and

the air-conditioner. Cool air blew against Helma's legs. The
car's interior smelled of leather and Lily's perfume, a deli-
cate floral.

The car was pulled forward into its space, its nose nearly
touching the chain-link fence. Helma's Buick sat on the other
side of the lot. She could see its right rear fender in the
passenger-side mirror of Lily's car.

"I'm curious as to how the investigation is going," Lily
said, turning in her seat to face Helma. She pulled one leg
beneath her like a child.

"It's Wayne Gallant or Carter Houston you need to talk
to, not me," Helma told her.

"I believe the police investigation is taking a slightly different tack than yours," Lily said.

"I'm not conducting an investigation," Helma told her.

"Then perhaps you've already reached your conclusions,"
Lily said, still pleasant, gracious as if she might offer Helma
a cup of tea or pass a silver dish of pastel mints.

"There's nothing unusual about people speculating after
such a crime."

Lily smiled at her, fondly Helma thought. "I have a feeling
you're not the type of person who idly speculates. I'm curious why you asked me about the bullets to the handgun.
Why did you think they'd be in the glove compartment?"

Helma hesitated, then decided to say the things she hadn't
yet had a chance to tell Wayne Gallant. "I believe the gun I
found in my car will prove to be your husband's gun and
also the murder weapon. Whoever put it there, and sent me
the receipt, also knows who killed your husband."

Lily ran her hands around the steering wheel. "And that
is?"

Helma was silent.

"You think I did, don't you?" she asked, not looking at
Helma but straight out the window at the chain-link fence.
"You actually believe I could shoot my own husband."

"If you did, I suspect it would have been in a moment of
passion, when you lost control and the deed was done before
you had time to think about it."

When Lily remained silent, only running her hands round

and round the steering wheel and gazing out the windshield, Helma went on, keeping her voice quiet and even, remembering how her mother had claimed that prominent marriages always appeared close-knit from the outside. "I think it would have happened after years of unhappiness, of silently enduring another person who was overbearing and controlling, of always having to give way and concede to his desires before your own." Helma took a breath. "Perhaps even being forced to give up worthy projects for which you'd laid the foundation." Lily was listening, her eyes distant, and Helma added, "Like the library board."

Lily nodded, just slightly, and repeated in a soft voice, "The library board."

"Everyone on the staff hoped you'd be appointed," Helma told her. "We knew you were sensitive to the needs of the reading public."

Lily nodded again and Helma asked, "Why didn't he want you to serve on the library board?"

"He wanted it more," she said simply. "Anything, any position he could have that would improve his 'profile.' He wanted to be visible. He had aspirations. Mine were secondary to his."

"But this time you didn't give up so easily," Helma guessed.

"Oh no, I did," Lily said, "just like that." She snapped her fingers. "But I didn't want to. He knew that and he humiliated me. He said to forget it, that my only skill was in laying the groundwork for him, that I lacked the intelligence to follow through and I should stick to what I knew best." She glanced out at a bicyclist coasting down the steep street. "That I couldn't even prepare a simple talk without suffering stage fright."

"So you drove him here to the mission and you shot him when he got out of the car, believing the blame would fall on someone here. *You* bought the Nutter Butters for the Young Readers group," Helma guessed. "The package fell out of the car when you shot Quentin. Maybe one of the men picked it up, perhaps the man whose scream we heard when he found the body, and in his shock he dropped the package beside Quentin."

Lily didn't answer for more than a minute. Helma didn't move; she barely breathed. "So many of these men have no lives," Lily said softly. "They're used to running. The evidence and the suspects would be scattered immediately. I knew the chance of any one of them being arrested or charged was very slim."

"You wrote the letter implicating me," Helma said.

"Quentin told me how you'd stood up to him at the board meeting. I knew it was a public quarrel. Everyone knew."

"So you thought the police had two leads to follow," Helma said. "And you'd be free to finally follow your own pleasures, to serve on the committees you wanted to—or didn't want to."

"Finally," Lily whispered. "There's so much I can do now. So much good."

"It's too late," Helma told her.

Lily looked at her, and Helma felt a shiver along her arms at the cool calculation in Lily's eyes.

"You have to tell the police what you've done," Helma told her. "Explain how it happened, the years of unhappiness. There may be mitigating circumstances."

"But they wouldn't turn me loose to continue my life, would they?" Lily asked, her voice touched with sarcasm.

"No," Helma conceded, "they wouldn't."

Lily straightened in her seat and drew her seat belt across her lap. "Please leave your belt unbuckled," she said.

"If you intend to drive us somewhere," Helma told her, "I never ride in a car without my seat belt buckled."

"This time you will," Lily said and when Helma reached for her belt anyway, Lily leaned over and pulled a handgun from beneath her seat, smaller than the one found in Helma's car. So it hadn't been in her pocket after all.

"I'm sorry," Lily told Helma. She sounded genuine, as if the matter were out of her hands, an accident with no one to blame.

It was then that Helma noticed the covering over the

passenger-side air bag was loose. "The air bag will prove to be defective and I won't be wearing my seatbelt. Is that what you're planning? A fatal accident? People who know me would never believe I'd ride in a car without buckling my seatbelt."

"I'll tell the police you didn't think it was necessary since we were only going a few blocks. You trusted my driving."

"Don't do this," Helma tried. "Talk to the police. There are no good deeds or community projects you can do that are worth one life, let alone two."

"It's the freedom," Lily said. "The freedom. I can't give that up now."

Helma slid her hand to her side and Lily raised her gun. "Keep your hands where I can see them, please," she requested politely.

Helma folded her hands on her lap. Lily handled the gun awkwardly but that only made her more unpredictable. A click sounded and all the car doors locked as Lily shifted into reverse. The seat belt warning alarm chimed and Helma glanced at Lily, but the older woman ignored the sound and finally the alarm stopped.

The air-conditioner hummed, the car backed without a sound, and Helma felt the sad slow pounding of her heart. Only a few blocks, Lily had said. Did that mean she was driving down toward the bay, toward the concrete bridge abutments near the train switching area? Lily had a seatbelt and an air bag to protect her. Helma had nothing. She was a "loose marble," as Ruth would say. She thought furiously but the gun in Lily's hand blocked each avenue of escape. Lily drove slowly, using her free hand while keeping the gun pointed at Helma.

The car rolled sedately to the parking lot entrance and just as Helma had decided to chance being shot, to unlock her door and try to roll out of it before Lily could pull the trigger of her gun, two things happened. A crash jolted the car and the rear window exploded into the back seat. Chunks of glass clattered against the windows and thudded on the leather upholstery. Helma felt two pieces land in her hair. A brick tumbled onto the seat beside her.

At the same moment Ruth stepped in front of Lily's car in the manner she always treated traffic: with casual disdain.

"No!" Helma cried and leaned across the seat, jerking the wheel to the right.

The car veered into the metal post of the chain-link fence and Helma slammed into the dashboard. At the same instant, Lily's air bag deployed, a flash of blooming white; hardly time for Lily to cry out before she slumped on the seat.

Time stopped. Helma tried to sort out the shattered rear window, the brick, Ruth standing white-faced beside Lily's car, her aching shoulder. And Lily hunched so still in the driver's seat.

"You okay?" a man's voice asked through Helma's open door. Hands pulled her from the car and held her upright, roughly shaking her. It took her a moment to recognize Skitz's face since his normally resentful expression was replaced by true concern and maybe even pleasure at the excitement.

"I think so," Helma gasped, still in Skitz's arms. He squeezed her shoulders and let her go.

"It's Lily Boyd," Ruth said.

"She's got a gun," Skitz warned her.

"Geez," Ruth said, looking through the window at Lily's slumped body. "Is she dead? You know what they say about short people and air bags."

Skitz reached across the seat and touched Lily's throat. "Nah, she'll probably wish she was, though."

"What's going on?" Ruth asked. "Why's she got a gun? Oh," she said, blinking. "Is *she* the one?"

Skitz looked around as if he was sniffing the air. He stood light on his feet, alert, every movement tense and hurried. "Did you get the details?" he asked Helma. He reached inside and with the back of his hand, knocked the gun away from Lily's still form.

"The important ones," Helma told him as she rubbed her shoulder. "She shot her husband. Tony saw it and told you, is that right? I'm guessing you followed her, saw her get rid of the gun, and then retrieved it. And then you broke into the gun store to link the gun back to Lily and Quentin. That was excellent deductive reasoning."

"Thank you. Now get Tony out of jail."

Helma didn't have the heart to tell him Tony had been free to leave for two days. "He'll be free tomorrow, I'm sure. But you'll need to explain the details to the police."

Skitz shook his head. He glanced at the mission's back door, behind him, at the brown dog growling in its pen. "You do it. I can't."

"Why not?" Helma asked.

Finally, he met Helma's eyes. His face was dead serious, his eyes old and resigned. "I did something. Not here. They're looking for me."

"Maybe this . . ."

He shook his head. "No. There wouldn't be any way out of it because I did what they claim I did. So that's that." In the distance, a siren was joined by a second siren. "I gotta go."

"Wait." Helma touched his wrist. "Have you been watching me? Was that you in the apartment next to mine? The notes about the chief of police?"

"Gotta go," he said and walked out of the parking lot and up the street, keeping close to the bushes.

"Wait," Helma tried again but he didn't pause.

Ruth looked after Skitz as he slipped behind a row of shrubbery and disappeared. "You know those lone cowboy movies where the mysterious stranger rides out of the prairie and helps the solitary woman save the ranch and then disappears into the sagebrush? This is kind of the lone criminal."

"Why did you come back?" Helma asked her.

"I decided I wanted a ride after all."

Lily Boyd moaned as the first police car pulled across the parking lot entrance.

Helma and Forrest sat across from one another at the Bay House restaurant. The sun hadn't set yet and shades were drawn far enough to keep the bright light out of their eyes.

Having finished dinner, they lingered over coffee and tea.

Forrest smiled at Helma and said, "So what you're diplomatically telling me is that you like me but there's no chance, right?"

"I like you very, very much, Forrest," Helma told him honestly, "and I'm proud that we're friends. I hope we always will be."

He touched her hand and she didn't move it away. "If you ever need anything at all," he told her, "you know . . ."

"I know," Helma said, "and I hope you understand the feeling is mutual."

In the car, as they left the restaurant and drove the road that skirted the switching yards, Forrest asked, "You're in love with the chief of police, aren't you?"

They were passing a line of empty freight cars being switched from one engine to another. Box cars clanked and bumped, loud even inside the car. Suddenly Helma spotted a lanky figure pulling a shorter, heavier figure in through the open door of a box car. The shorter figure wore glasses.

"Wait," she told Forrest. "Turn around."

"Why?"

"Please."

He pulled into the next turnout and swung his rental car around. "Just drive along this line of train cars, please," she asked.

They did. The train moved slowly to the south and most of the box cars were empty, their doors rolled open so she could see straight through them to another row of cars on the next track.

"Could we do it again?" she asked Forrest.

"Sure. Why?"

"I thought I saw a friend."

He gave her a sharp glance but obligingly turned around and they drove the length of the cars again.

She had no doubt she'd seen Skitz and Tony but now there wasn't a trace of them. No men sitting in the open doorways, no dark figures visible inside the boxcars. Nothing.

"All right. We can go now," Helma told Forrest.

❧ *chapter eighteen* ❧

ART CAPTURED

It was the night of Ruth's art show to benefit the children who ate dinner at the mission. When Helma arrived, there was a crush of people in the gallery and it was impossible to see any of the work by the twelve artists Ruth had recruited. She spotted Ruth's tall figure at the rear of the gallery, dressed in blood-red and black, a black turban covering her hair, and began to slowly make her way toward her.

She passed George Melville who winked and said, "Helma, I never knew."

"I beg your pardon?" she asked but two college-age students dressed in black had stepped between them.

Brother Danny waved and gave her a thumbs-up sign. She smiled and nodded.

"We got the grant," he told Helma. "I won't have to walk up Bayview Street on my hands after all."

"Congratulations," Helma was able to say before the crowd separated them.

"Congratulations to you, too," he called back.

She spotted Portnoy and Frank standing in front of the refreshment table. She'd never seen Portnoy dressed in anything but white aprons, and in regular clothes with his pale hair slicked back, he *did* look like a chef critically surveying a competitor's offering.

"It's supposed to rain tomorrow," someone to Helma's left said.

"It can't come soon enough," another voice answered. "This has been ridiculous."

Through the crowds, Helma glimpsed a bright watercolor and a small weaving of a reclining figure. Both sported red "sold" dots.

Delia, the beautiful auditor, slipped away from three men and raised a glass of wine to Helma. "*Labas.*"

"*Labas.* I understand you're nearly finished with the audit."

"It's taken less time than I expected. The library's financial records are in very good order."

"And Ms. Moon's book purchases?" Helma asked.

"Unusual, but not a crime," she told Helma as one of the men lightly touched her arm. "Beautiful work, by the way," Delia told Helma as she turned to the waiting man.

"I haven't seen it all yet, but I'm sure Ruth put together a very good show," Helma told her, surprised when Delia laughed and shook her finger at her.

Finally, she reached Ruth, who grimaced and said, "Don't start on me. I'm not about to apologize."

"What are you talking about?" Helma asked her.

"Oh," Ruth said, her eyes widening. "You haven't seen them? Well, obviously you haven't. Come on. I guess it's fitting that I be the one to show you." Ruth pushed her way across the gallery with Helma in her wake. She stopped and stepped aside.

Helma gasped. She raised her hands to her cheeks. For a moment she couldn't breathe. She glanced away in embarrassment and then was drawn to look again.

Hanging on the wall in front of her were three of her own arrangements of cut paper illustrations. The last time she'd seen them they'd been in the back of the closet in her second bedroom. Here they now hung, behind glass, in metal frames, looking alien, certainly not her own aimless cutting and gluing.

"Lookee here, would you?" Ruth said gleefully, pointing to the cards beside each frame. To each, which listed the artist as W.C. Zukas and named the works as "Untitled I, II, and III," was affixed a red dot. "Sold like hot cakes."

"Where . . . how did you get them?" Helma asked.

Ruth shrugged. "I took them out of your closet. You always think you're doing that stuff in secret."

"But when?"

"While you were at work. You gave me a key a zillion years ago, remember? One of those 'just in case' things."

Helma remembered. Ruth would have given Helma a key, too, if she'd bothered to ever lock her door.

"This is an invasion of my privacy," Helma began. "I . . ."

"Oh Helma, dear. I didn't know you were an artist." It was Aunt Em on the arm of Helma's mother. She beamed. Rouge and lipstick brightened her wrinkled face. "Ruth told us to come because she had a surprise for us."

"I *am* surprised," Helma's mother said. "I hope this doesn't mean that you'll take up the artist's lifestyle." She carefully avoided looking at Ruth.

"This is all a mistake, Mother," Helma began.

"Oh, I hope not," Aunt Em cut in. "Will you make one for me? I'll hang it in the living room."

"Well," Helma tried. Her mother nudged Aunt Em and looked meaningfully over Helma's shoulder.

"Oh my," Aunt Em said, "Oh yes. Well, we'll be on our way, dear. You speak to your fans now." And the two women bumped shoulders and winked and left Helma frowning after them.

She turned to find Wayne Gallant behind her, smiling. "Congratulations," he said. He looked at her appraisingly, bemused. "I thought I knew you. But these . . ." He waved his hand at her collages.

Ruth leaned between them, her black turban brushing the chief's nose. "Helma's full of surprises."

"I realize that." He took Helma's hand and said in a voice that was lost to everyone in the crowded room except Helma, "How's your shoulder?"

"Fine," Helma told him. Then under his probing gaze, she modified, "Actually, it aches but it's much improved."

"Good." Still holding her hand he glanced above her

head and asked, "And your friend, Forrest? Did he return to Maine?"

"He did."

Wayne Gallant nodded. "Will you be visiting Maine any time soon? It's a beautiful state."

"I have no plans to visit the East Coast," Helma assured him.

He smiled. "That's good news. Then you'll be here to meet . . ."

Roger Darrow, one of the city council members, jostled the chief's shoulders. "Whoops, sorry, Wayne. Racquetball tomorrow?"

"Six a.m. sharp."

Roger Darrow made an okay sign with his fingers and moved on.

"You wanted me to meet someone?" Helma asked.

"Yeah. My children will be here for a month. It's time they met you, got to know you."

For a moment, Helma couldn't answer. She'd seen photos of the chief's two children: a boy and girl, young teenagers. She knew they visited him for long weekends and during vacation but she hadn't met them. "To get to know me?" she repeated so softly the chief bent closer to hear her.

"I'd like them to care for you the way I do. I mean, not the same way, but to like you, do you know what I mean?"

"I do," Helma said, although she didn't hear herself speak the words, only felt her lips move.

But Wayne Gallant seemed to have heard her. He squeezed her hand and said, "I've been thinking. I shouldn't have asked Ruth to volunteer with you. I'm glad I did but now I wish we'd discussed it first. Will you forgive me?"

Helma looked into his eyes. He smiled at her. Whatever she'd been about to say, the words she did say were, "Of course."

CHECK OUT MISS ZUKAS

Librarian and Sleuth Extraordinaire

by
JO DERESKE

MISS ZUKAS AND THE LIBRARY MURDERS

77030-X/$5.99 US/$7.99 Can

A dead body stashed in the fiction stacks is most improper.

MISS ZUKAS AND THE ISLAND MURDERS

77031-8/$5.99 US/$7.99 Can

A class reunion brings back old friends, old enemies...
and a new murder.

MISS ZUKAS AND THE STROKE OF DEATH

77033-4/$5.99 US/$7.99 Can

OUT OF CIRCULATION

78244-8/$5.99 US/$7.99 Can

FINAL NOTICE

78245-6/$5.99 US/$7.99 Can

MISS ZUKAS IN DEATH'S SHADOW

80472-7/$5.99 US/$7.99 Can

Buy these books at your local bookstore or use this coupon for ordering:

Mail to: Avon Books/HarperCollins Publishers, P.O. Box 588, Scranton, PA 18512   H
Please send me the book(s) I have checked above.
☐ My check or money order—no cash or CODs please—for $_____ is enclosed (please
add $1.50 per order to cover postage and handling—Canadian residents add 7% GST). U.S.
and Canada residents make checks payable to HarperCollins Publishers Inc.
☐ Charge my VISA/MC Acct#_____Exp Date_____
Minimum credit card order is two books or $7.50 (please add postage and handling
charge of $1.50 per order—Canadian residents add 7% GST). For faster service, call
1-800-331-3761. Prices and numbers are subject to change without notice. Please allow six to
eight weeks for delivery.

Name_____
Address_____
City_____State/Zip_____
Telephone No._____   ZUK 0999

Murder Is on the Menu
at the Hillside Manor Inn
Bed-and-Breakfast Mysteries by
MARY DAHEIM
featuring Judith McMonigle

BANTAM OF THE OPERA

76934-4/ $6.50 US/ $8.99 Can

JUST DESSERTS 76295-1/ $6.50 US/ $8.50 Can

FOWL PREY 76296-X/ $6.50 US/ $8.50 Can

HOLY TERRORS 76297-8/ $6.50 US/ $8.50 Can

DUNE TO DEATH 76933-6/ $6.50 US/ $8.50 Can

A FIT OF TEMPERA 77490-9/ $5.99 US/ $7.99 Can

MAJOR VICES 77491-7/ $5.99 US/ $7.99 Can

MURDER, MY SUITE 77877-7/ $5.99 US/ $7.99 Can

AUNTIE MAYHEM 77878-5/ $6.50 US/ $8.50 Can

NUTTY AS A FRUITCAKE

77879-3/ $5.99 US/ $7.99 Can

SEPTEMBER MOURN

78518-8/ $5.99 US/ $7.99 Can

WED AND BURIED 78520-X/ $5.99 US/ $7.99 Can

SNOW PLACE TO DIE

78521-8/ $5.99 US/ $7.99 Can

LEGS BENEDICT 80078-0/ $6.50 US/ $8.50 Can

Buy these books at your local bookstore or use this coupon for ordering:

Mail to: Avon Books/HarperCollins Publishers, P.O. Box 588, Scranton, PA 18512
Please send me the book(s) I have checked above.
❑ My check or money order—no cash or CODs please—for $_____is enclosed (ple
add $1.50 per order to cover postage and handling—Canadian residents add 7% GST). L
and Canada residents make checks payable to HarperCollins Publishers Inc.
❑ Charge my VISA/MC Acct#_____Exp Date_____
Minimum credit card order is two books or $7.50 (please add postage and handl
charge of $1.50 per order—Canadian residents add 7% GST). For faster service,
1-800-331-3761. Prices and numbers are subject to change without notice. Please allow si
eight weeks for delivery.

Name_____
Address_____
City_____State/Zip_____
Telephone No._____   DAH 09